Frank came to suddenly. A bank of machines stood nearby the bed. A single IV dripped from a tree to his right. He hadn't expected a hospital room. A cell, yes. An interrogation room. A torture chamber.

Presently a young man in a white coat came in. "You seem to be doing fine," he said pleasantly. "You're in perfect health physically. Spiritually, not so good though."

"Yeah? What's wrong in that department?"

"No Innerverse."

"I see. What's that?"

"A guide to right behavior. Nothing more."

"And I don't have it."

"*Didn't* have it. We corrected that.

Other AvoNova Books by
John DeChancie

MAGICNET

InnerVerse

JOHN DeCHANCIE

AVON BOOKS • NEW YORK

INNERVERSE is an original publication of Avon Books. This work has never before appeared in book form. This work is a novel. Any similarity to actual persons or events is purely coincidental.

AVON BOOKS
A division of
The Hearst Corporation
1350 Avenue of the Americas
New York, New York 10019

Copyright © 1996 by John DeChancie
Cover art by Thomas Canty
Published by arrangement with the author
Library of Congress Catalog Card Number: 95-96105
ISBN: 0-380-78108-5

First AvoNova Printing: July 1996

AVONOVA TRADEMARK REG. U.S. PAT. OFF. AND IN OTHER COUNTRIES, MARCA REGISTRADA. HECHO EN U.S.A.

Printed in the U.S.A.

RA 10 9 8 7 6 5 4 3 2 1

To Margaret Leman

≫ Prologue ≪

Frank Sutter hoped that he would not have to kill the woman, but he feared he would have no choice.

He wondered if the reason for his reluctance was that she was not only a female, but also a young and attractive one. All right, then: was it her age, or her beauty? As to beauty, he could not see her face; but he didn't have to. Attractive women are usually attractive even at a distance. So: age or beauty?

He took his eyes from his electronic field glasses and looked at the terrorist encampment below. The Imperial Army called these units "Special Task Shock Brigades." Meaning: terrorists.

His eyes were good. Yes, he liked her even distance. He could tell.

Yes, what bothered him was *both* her age and her physical characteristics.

But she would probably not survive the initial attack, which would come from the flitters. Well, okay. As long as he didn't have to do the job himself in the mop-up.

He ducked back behind the rock, turned, and leaned back and let the hot Texas sun roast him. He looked at his watch. Thirty seconds.

Letting the digits tick off he cocked his ears. No, they were a little late. Well, hard to time a raid to the second when you're based as far away as Austin.

He touched a pressure-sensitive strip on the inner surface of the rim of his helmet, just over the right ear.

"Blue Leader to all Blue Devils, stand by."

"Standing by, Blue Leader." He heard Jane Borman's voice in his ear.

Another woman, also attractive, and as highly skilled and specialized a soldier as the woman below. Though on opposing sides, they were both special forces personnel. He wondered if any of the males on the other side would regret having to kill Jane. Probably. They were mostly Latinos, and Latino men were supposed to be traditional-minded. But he didn't really know. An ultraconservative and revivalist Roman Catholic Church ruled the central and southern Americas—always had, at least by proxy, and, from the looks of the present political situation, always would. On the other hand, soldiers were soldiers everywhere. If they had to kill, they most likely would kill.

As he himself would.

A realization came over Sutter at that moment—a feeling he got now and then—a sense of wonder over the myriad wrenching changes that had come over the world since he was born in the last year of the twentieth century. Who then could have foreseen that the Rome would again rule half of Europe? Or that the Russians would once more revive Tsarist claims in Alaska and Northern Canada. Or that the Mayan Emperor of Mexico—indeed, the very notion of such a critter would have astonished his parents—would at the Pope's instigation be reasserting ancient Spanish and Indian (the Emperor played up the latter angle greatly) territorial rights in Colorado, Texas, much of the Southwest, and coastal California, except for The Republic of Los Angeles.

His parents, both very liberal-minded, would have been appalled that sub-Saharan Africa had sunk back into colonialism of the worst sort. But it had. And they weren't around to be bothered by it.

If his parents would have been shocked, his grandparents would have been stunned by a geopolical reality in which the only true world power, of the sort known in the last century, was Great China. That in itself wouldn't have shocked his parents, but that China itself was again ruled by Mongolian conquerors would have stunned them. (True, the Mongolians were Japanese pawns, but that would have not ameliorated the strangeness.)

But the strangest reality by far was the fate of the eastern United States. "The Republic," as it was simply known, ruled by unknown and unseen powers, bulked as the biggest political enigma of this century.

All of the above was to say nothing of what his parents would have thought about the current capital of the United States (what was left of it) being Peoria, Illinois. They had been typical New Class Easterners. To them the great flat mass of Middle America was the land of Babbitts and boobs. And worse.

These thoughts crept through his mind on tiptoe, neither disturbing him or breaking his concentration. He was battle-ready and poised for action. He picked up his wire-stocked automatic carbine and checked it over.

The flitters were late. Really late. He was not worried, though. He could not allow himself to be worried. All would go according to plan.

Suddenly, there were shouts in the camp below, accompanied by the sound of running feet and the frantic starting of machinery. A truck began to move, then a land rover. There was a truck-mounted anti-aircraft unit off to one side, in the juniper tree. Sutter looked over the rock and saw its crew running toward it.

The terrorists had been warned. By remote lookouts, probably. The result of bungling by the leader of the raiding flitters, maybe, or by his navigator. But maybe not. Signals from Chinese navigation satellites were sometimes blotted out by sunspots. A design flaw. The satellites were more sophisticated but not as dependable as the old American and European ones they had replaced. So, because of a tiny blackhead on the sun's hot skin, the flitters may have strayed from their flight plan, which had been laid out to take advantage of weak spots in the Imperial air defense network.

In any event, the Imperial terrorists had some warning. The attack would not be a complete surprise. Which meant that the mopping-up would be all more difficult and dangerous.

But that came with the job description.

The AA-battery crew had reached the truck when the flitters arrived, whooshing in from the northwest like a swarm of angry hornets. A series of explosions began and continued for at least five minutes. Dust rose in one cloud from the rocky canyon like a dun-colored mushroom, followed by plumes of black smoke. The flitters' rapid-fire gun pods rattled and spat, answered only by futile single shots and the occasional short burst of automatic fire. The AA-unit got off a mere dozen rounds before abruptly ceasing operations. The truck rose into the air on a cushion of flame, flipped and landed upside down in the dry wash that cut through the camp. Smokes and fumes spread. The stench of high-explosive and burning rubber obliterated the sweet smell of piñon campfires.

Sutter ducked his head, anticipating the coup de grace— a rain of fragmentation bombs that wracked the canyon with a hailstorm of spent-uranium pellets, scourging the ground and reducing to mincemeat anything that lived there—anything unprotected, that is; but in and around a desert bivouac in west Texas there isn't much cover but a few Joshua trees and the odd sinuous tributary of a wadi.

Then, too late to ward off disaster, came the roaring of answering fire in the form of surface-to-air missiles. Hand-held and launched, they began to exact their toll. A flitter burst into flame directly over Sutter's head.

Chugging and throwing off impellor blades, the sleek black craft pitched to the right and went down, crashing into the canyon. A tremendous explosion sent up gouts of earth and debris. Sutter flattened himself on the ground.

Another explosion, farther away, marked the crash of a second flitter.

But that was all. At the end of several more strafing runs and after a few more anti-personnel cannisters had blossomed death, no more missiles left the flats.

"Red Leader to Blue Leader."

"Blue Leader here, over," he answered.

"Proceed with Phase Two, Blue Leader. Over."

"Blue Leader to Red Leader. Roger, over, and out."

Phase Two of Operation Pacos began. The tough part. Hard as it was to believe that there could be anything left alive down there, there always was. Sutter had been on many Special Forces operations. Most of them had involved close air support, but all the ordnance in the world would not do the dirty job of killing what needed to be killed, up close, hand to hand.

"Blue Leader to all Blue Devils. Move in! Now!"

It was simply a job of killing, and a necessary one. This was a terrorist advance camp. A staging area for operations specializing in devastating raids on civilian targets. A platform for terrorism. An encampment of monsters who had massacred whole towns, lopping the heads off six-year-old children. Who had raped, tortured, and murdered indiscriminately.

The purpose of these enormities—as is the purpose of most warfare waged over territory—had been to create terror in the hearts and minds of the inhabitants in areas under dispute. Terrorized people pack up and leave. It's easier to dicker over unpopulated territory. No locals to raise a fuss if one side cedes a section of living space to the other.

Sure, it was easy to demonize the enemy. Especially when the enemy had done some demonic things. On the other hand, Sutter knew that bombs and missiles of the Combined Air Forces of the United Central States of America had killed thousands of civilians in the Holy Mayan Empire of Mexico. However, Sutter regarded those as regrettable but unavoidable casualties. Like all soldiers in all wars, his moral calculus was skewed to one side. Hadn't the Emperor started this whole thing? Didn't national boundaries count for anything? Were they arbitrary lines to be disregarded on the flimsiest of pretexts? As for Emperor Quetzal II's so-called historical claims to land lost in wars long ago, they were absurd in the extreme.

Had there been similar atrocities committed against Imperial subjects in disputed border areas? Yes, no doubt about it, but not officially sanctioned ones, and certainly on a lesser scale.

This was a simple job of killing the killers. That gave a moral cast to what was a filthy business. These were highly trained men and women down there. None of them could be suffered to live.

Why not take prisoners?

The simple fact was that the UCSA could not afford to house and feed any more prisoners of war. Also, these special brigade sorts could easily escape to attack again. Wiping them out for good was the only answer. They could not be allowed to continue to ply their deadly trade.

And of course there was the issue of retribution. Punishment.

Sutter moved carefully but lost no time coming down through the rocks to the flat sands of the canyon. He hid behind a stack of crates for a moment to get his bearings and scout. He saw no movement but rising smoke. Straightening up, he began a sweep of the area bounded by two outcroppings of talus.

Out of the corner of his eye he saw his comrades on similar patrols. The idea was to keep the squads spread out, converging only when resistance was encountered. You don't want a neat, military line of men mowed down by a hidden machine-gun emplacement.

A single shot sounded, answered by automatic fire. He looked across the canyon and saw a body fall.

He encountered his first body. It was nearly cut in two, hit by large rounds, possibly from a flitter's rapid-fire 15-millimeter guns. It was a man, around twenty-two years old. He looked young to Sutter. Too young.

Sutter moved on, eyes sweeping back and forth. He

caught movement to the left. He went to one knee and took aim.

It was a terrorist commando, staggering, his left arm reduced to a bloody stump fountaining blood. His face didn't match the circumstances. He was smiling, and the smile was incongruously sheepish, as though some elaborate practical joke had been played on him. The smile unnerved Sutter a bit. The man, who wore captain's bars on his shoulders, walked straight up to Sutter as though coming to greet him. At the last moment, though, he stopped short.

"*Jesús y María,*" he said simply, without inflection. "*Jesús y María.*"

Sutter shot him through the chest. One round. The man fell backwards and was still. His expression hadn't changed.

Sutter walked on, passing a burning land rover and dozens of flattened tents, their plastic cloth ripped to tatters. Camping gear lay everywhere, along with clothing, mess kits, and personal effects.

More bodies, these more or less intact. Two men, one woman; nearby lay a stack of three men who had fallen on top of one another. Nobody was moving. But Sutter kept his eyes on them as he passed. He had been fooled on at least one occasion by a "body" that had come suddenly to life. He would not make that mistake again. He'd been lucky; usually you only get to make it once.

He moved on. The fumes were beginning to get to him, but this was not the time to be putting on a respirator mask, so he veered off to the right, away from a trailing stream of oily smoke.

A disembodied head, lying on the ground, began shooting at him.

That's what it seemed at first. A single round whizzed by his ear and he dove. When he chanced a look up he understood—the person shooting at him was in a hole in the ground, a narrow slit trench. A latrine. This someone had probably survived by taking cover in it.

With one smooth movement he plucked a concussion grenade from one part of his belt, touched it to the code bar on another part to activate it, and lobbed it in the direction of the latrine.

The grenade hit, bounced, and rolled into the far end of the hole from where the sniper crouched. A short three seconds later the explosives went off, raising a gout of liquid muck. The head disappeared.

Sutter waited a good thirty seconds before he risked getting to his knees. No head appeared.

Warily, he approached the latrine, the barrel of his gun describing an arc before him. He looked in.

It was the girl, sure enough. She was flat on her back in the muck, out cold. Her weapon had somehow fetched itself up against the near side of the trench, its barrel sticking up a bit above the rim.

Sutter raised the rifle and aimed at her head, but something stopped him. At his feet lay a twisted length of metal, the trim off some vehicle it looked like, one end of it curled to form a perfect hook. He picked it up and put the end in the hole, looping the hook through the belt of the girl's khaki fatigue trousers. In one forceful movement he yanked her up out of the hole like a gaffed fish. In the process she lost one shoe and the trousers ended up down around her knees. She wore no underwear. He stared at her neat triangular tuft of pubic hair and felt a spasm of desire.

Still staring, he was aware of the approach of one of his comrades—Sergeant Borman.

"What are you going to do with her, Lieutenant?" She chuckled. "As if I didn't know."

He shot her a dark look. "You don't know anything, Sergeant. I'm taking this one prisoner."

"Yes, sir. Sir, our orders are to—"

"I know what the orders are. I gave them to you. Take her to the pick-up point. I don't want her harmed in any way. Is that clear?"

"Clear, sir."

The girl had come to. Her eyes focused. She looked up, and a look of fear came over her face. She made an effort to sit up, groaning, but couldn't quite make it, but she did see the condition of her pants and reached a hand down to tug them up.

Sutter watched her. She seemed afraid, but there was still a glint of defiance in her dark eyes. He wondered who she was, what her name was. He wondered also if it was a name as pretty as her face.

A pretty face. Is that what it all boiled down to? If her head weren't a pretty one, would he have blown it off without a thought? He felt guilt for something, but he didn't quite grasp what it was.

"On your feet," he told the girl. She seemed to understand and picked herself up and hitched up her pants.

"Move her out, Sergeant."

"Yes, sir, but you'll be shorthanded while I'm doing it."

He looked at his watch. "The flitters have landed by now. Drop her off and report back."

"Anything you say, Lieutenant Sutter."

Sutter walked away. He hadn't got more than ten paces when he heard Borman's rifle fire three bursts. He whirled and ran back to see the girl back in the latrine again, this time face down in the filth and excrement, the back of her fatigue shirt blooming red stains.

"She made a move for her weapon, sir," Borman explained.

"Goddamit, Sergeant, I told you—!"

"Sir, she was going for the gun," Borman shouted.

Sutter looked into the trench. True, the gun was within reach. But so was her shoe.

"The shoe," he said.

"Sir, it looked like she was making a move for the gun. I'm sorry."

He looked at the girl's body and spreading red stains. He had made an instant decision to spare her. But just as quickly it had been revoked.

"You could have handled it better, Sergeant," was all he could say.

"Rogers saw it, sir. Rogers, tell the lieutenant."

"Looked like she was going for it, sir."

"Yeah," Sutter said.

"Sorry, sir," Borman said again.

"Carry on, Sergeant."

"Yes, sir."

Sutter turned away from the slit trench and didn't look into it again.

"Come in, Frank. Let's make this informal. Sit down."

"Thank you, Colonel Lehman."

Lehman was a man of solid features: sharp eyes, hawkish nose, square jaw. He had sparse gray hair and bluegray eyes. His manner of speaking was forceful and direct, though tempered with an underlying charm and mildness. He was about fifty years old. The war had kept him on active duty.

"Did you have a good R&R?"

"Yes, sir, very good. Got in some fishing up in Michigan."

"Great. What do you go out for? Pike, bass?"

"I like trout, sir."

"Trout's good," Lehman said, nodding. "I always have trouble with the bones, though."

"You have to know how to prepare trout."

"Never was much of a fish cutter myself. Nearly slice a finger off every time I try. Usually give my catch to someone who knows what he's doing."

"I'll cut for you next time, sir, if you like."

"I would like that, Frank. Next time." Lehman reached over and touched a computer terminal. "I have something here—"

"Sergeant Borman?"

"You're psychic. Has it been on your mind?"

"Yes, sir. Thought she'd be filing something. I don't know why."

"Guess to protect herself."

"I hadn't given a thought to reporting her."

"She must have thought you had," Lehman said. "If she's lying, she was being insubordinate."

"I doubt it. She was just trigger-happy."

"Something else here. Your psych debriefing. Says all your indicators are down. Nothing worrisome. Not really . . . what's the word here . . . 'endogenous depression.' Says it's not that. What about it, Frank? Is this right? Do you feel as depressed as the shrinks make you out to be?"

"Haven't been feeling one hundred percent. If I have to be honest."

"I'd like you to be honest with me. Have a line on what could be wrong? Or is it just the weather?"

"Hard to say, sir."

"Your job?"

"Maybe. That girl . . . she was a girl. Too young. She n't have to die. Not like that."

ers you."

oked out the window. It was a soft spring day eoria, Illinois.

"She was a combatant," Lehman said after a silence.

"Probably."

"You're not convinced."

"No chance she could have been a camp follower."

"She was shooting at you, Frank."

"Yes, sir. She was, at that. Doesn't make me feel any better, sir, for some reason."

"No, why should it? She was a kid. Who do you blame, Frank?"

"Blame, sir?"

"Yes, who's responsible for things like that, for kids getting killed? Is it us? The way we're conducting this war, the fact that we're waging war at all? Is it the brass? Who is it?"

"Sir, I don't think it's our fault."

"You don't. Okay. Then it's old Quetzal's fault? Is he an evil nasty man who wants to kill kids?"

"Probably not. He probably doesn't think of himself as anything but Defender of the Faith, or whatever it is he's fighting for."

"Well, he's Catholic, but he's got some weird Toltec slant on it."

"Toltec? Were they Mayans, sir?"

"Related. Strange, the hybrid religions that have been cropping up lately south of the border and in the Caribbean, mixture of everything."

"I don't know much about religion, sir."

"I'm no expert. And I'm not so sure that religion is the issue. Territory is. The oldest human conflict."

"Kind of depressing. The way it goes on and on."

"What do we do, Frank? How do we stop it? Give up Texas, along with New Mexico, which we've already lost?"

"No, sir. Not that. We have a right to Texas."

"So does old Quetzal, so he says."

Sutter's eyes narrowed. "I think you're try me out on something, sir. On what? Do you thin turned pacifist?"

"Don't get defensive, Frank. I'm trying to find out what's bothering you."

"Nothing's bothering me, sir." Sutter stiffened a little in his chair.

"Don't take it like that, Frank. Do you think you're the only one with doubts? This has been a dirty war. Not that there are many clean ones. But what choice do we really have? We've negotiated till we're blue in the face. His Imperial Majesty won't budge. What's his is his. What's ours is a bargaining chip. So the war goes on."

"Yes, sir. But I don't have to like it, sir."

"No, you don't. Nothing in the regulations says you have to like it. You don't have to like mass slaughter. But we have to do it. Would you prefer that we retaliate against Imperial subjects? Better, if we have to commit outrages, that it be against combatants, and combatants guilty of the worst offenses in this regard. Or ... how about we nuke Mexico City?"

"We couldn't, sir. It would never get through Congress."

"Who says it has to go through Congress? The President is still the commander in chief in this country, for all the changes. But you're right. Such an action would be politically insupportable. But if it were the only way to stop depredations against our citizens, Congress would support it. Thankfully, it isn't the only way. So, we go after the Lightning Shock Brigades, wherever we can find them. Their training bases, their operations centers, their supply storage areas, their forward bases. Sometimes in these operations, there are unavoidable civilian casualties. The only other alternative is to let them keep operating with impunity. Would you want another El Paso Massacre?"

"It's not that, sir, or the civilian casualties."

"It's not the civilian casualties?"

"It's more than that. The persistence of the need for violence. It never seems to end. No matter what new scheme or treaty or international convention they come up with, the carnage still goes on, all over the world."

"The twenty-first century has been rough so far, I'll grant you. But I'll lay odds that we're behind the twentieth in body count, year for year. Why, the first World War—"

"Doesn't help, sir. I guess it's this way, Colonel Lehman. I want a transfer. I want out of Special Forces."

Lehman looked at Sutter a long moment before saying, "We'll sorely miss you. You're one of the finest platoon leaders I have. I'm a little shocked, Frank. I didn't expect this. But I guess a man has only so much killing in him. After that, he begins to get desensitized and becomes apathetic ... or brutal. You'd be no good to us either way."

"I don't like this either, sir. My quitting. I'd hate to think that I don't have what it takes. But I guess I'll have to face that possibility."

"Maybe it's good that you don't have what it takes.

Maybe if more people felt like you, there wouldn't be any need for terror or retaliation against it. But that may be blue-sky utopianism. Have you ever heard of E. B. White?"

"No, sir."

"A twentieth century journalist, essayist. I was reading an essay of his the other night, on what they used to call 'disarmament' back then. The idea of everyone chucking his gun in a big hole and covering it up. Actually, the issue revolved around nuclear weapons. But it applies to total disarmament as well. I can't quote verbatim—and with White the exact words are of utmost importance— but his idea was that disarmament was an unstable state. Like a boulder precariously balanced on the crest of a hill. The slightest displacement, the slightest tendency of any of the parties involved to hedge their bets, to make the slightest move that could be interpreted as a threat, and the rock rolls down to either gully, where the kinetic situation is again stable. It doesn't pick itself up and roll uphill again, except with great effort. And then it rolls right back down again. But even implementing disarmament wouldn't be easy. Say world peace was declared and everyone was in agreement that this was a good thing. We all throw our weapons into a hole. But how many would say, "Well, wait a minute. What would it hurt if I kept a few weapons? Just a few, in case someone is cheating." So, everyone holds back a little. There's an instant arms race, to see who can cheat the most. Again, an inherently unstable dynamic."

"I'd like to read that essay, sir."

"I'll photocopy it and send it along to you through channels. But enough theory. There's got to be a way you can serve your country using your abilities to the fullest. I'm not going to throw you to any dogface unit that needs another warm body. I have a special job for you. Not working for Special Forces. You'll remain with SF but be detached for duty with OSO."

"Office of Secret Operations? You're going to make me a prairie dog, sir? I'm no spy."

"They'll make you into one."

"Sir, I don't understand. The spy business is the dirtiest business there is."

"Where you're going there will be no killing. You won't be able to. You'll be gathering information on the Republic. That's the other thing we have to worry about, Frank. Here's this enigma on one side of us, occupying a third of what used to be our country, and we haven't been able to crack it yet. We don't know how it started, or who started it. All we know is that twenty years ago, all communication with the eastern part of the country was mysteriously cut off. We do know the place is an utter dictatorship, but we don't know who's dictating. The population is as complacent as a flock of lambs. The place has to be wired with some kind of mind control system. We have to find out what and we have to find out if it represents a threat to us. And we have to ferret out the origin of this thing. Whatever it is. For years the crazy rumor was that some kind of space aliens had taken over. We know now that's fantasy. But someone's in charge of the Republic. We have to find out who."

"Why me, sir?"

"You fit the job description. They want someone with outstanding physical characteristics, a military background— and something else. They want someone with a streak of independence. A stubborn streak. Someone who simply doesn't follow orders blindly. That's you, Frank. You've always been a bit of a misfit."

"I don't think so."

"You see? Sometimes you're argumentative to a point just short of insubordination. Your record speaks for itself. In fact you came to SF because you transferred from unit to unit. You were looking for something. Something that suited you. We cut our people a lot of slack in Special Forces. It was an environment that was made for you."

"I can't deny it. If it weren't for the other problem . . ."

"You're a rare combination of personality traits, Frank. I think OSO can make a good secret operative out of you. With your okay, I'll process the detachment papers immediately. Remember, on paper you'll still be one of us. If it works out, we'll make it a permanent transfer later. Meanwhile, stick around the base, take it easy. You'll leave for Mattoon as quick as the paperwork comes through."

"Yes, sir."

Colonel Lehman smiled. "And thanks for all the good work you did for me, Frank. As I said, you're one of our best."

"Sorry I let you down, sir."

"You don't think I've lost sleep over the same soul-searching? It isn't just young men who are troubled. I'm pushing fifty and I haven't figured it all out yet."

"Won't they muster you out fairly soon, sir?"

"Eventually, if another truce is declared. But not until then. They need me. Then I can finally get in some real fishing."

"I still don't think I'd make a very good spy, sir."

≽ Chapter One ≼

Frank Sutter had jumped off airplanes before (perfectly good ones that aren't even on fire, as the old paratrooper joke had it), but he had never done so without a parachute.

It was a big plane, a huge, lumbering flying boxcar of a cargo plane, jet-powered, dating from the last century. It still flew well. True and steady with a steady throb of power. The engines were louder than usual as they worked harder to keep the plane up at this low altitude and at greatly reduced airspeed. The back cargo bay doors were wide open to the night, and wind whistled through the bay. The plane would do a partial power stall to reduce speed to almost nothing, and he, Frank Sutter, secret agent—or secret fool?—would jump out the back end of the thing.

With his hand glider, of course. Such was the fear of the Republic that the CUS high military brass would not authorize a flight over its territory. Too many mysterious disappearances had occurred over the years. True, most had been on the ground and had involved infantry personnel, but the brass weren't taking any more chances. A mythology had grown up about the Republic. The Republic's defensive system had mind-control beams, or some such. They could make you into a zombie and a turncoat at will. How it was done was anyone's guess. Gas, microbes, invisible rays, you name it, whatever delivery system could be imagined, the Republic was reputed to have it, operational. Did the brass believe the myths? Probably not, but they *still* weren't taking any chances.

So, the plane would fly close to the border (fuzzily delineated) and let loose its human bird to fly to roost on its own power. Rather, gravity's power. He would be taking a long glide path into rough country. Once down, he would disassemble the glider, bury it, and strike out toward the nearest habitation. What his next course of action would be was not entirely clear.

"I wish we could say that the Republic is only an enigma wrapped in mystery," Victoria Slater, OSO's Chief of Information and Research, liked to say. "It's that, plus it's hidden inside a Chinese puzzle."

The mystery had begun some three decades before, when a series of social upheavals rocked the big cities of the eastern United States. Wave after wave of sabotage rocked the nation. Power stations blew up and transmissions lines were severed. A nuclear plant in Connecticut suffered a partial meltdown. An insurrection in Washington, D.C. uprooted the government temporarily. Congress reconvened in Philadelphia, where it had all started, for a while, but then had to pick up and move again as terrorist bombs exploded in major cities. With security too tight at targets—such as the World Trade Center—that had been attacked in the last century, the bombers concentrated their attentions on sites that lay unsuspecting and unprotected. These attacks culminated in the titanic collapse of the Chrysler Building in Manhattan, brought down by carefully placed demolition charges. A thousand office workers died along with over five hundred pedestrians.

A months-long period of confusion set in. A series of revolutionary governments declared themselves in this interim, one after the other, headed by various ad-hoc revolutionary cabals. These "coups" were announced every time one gang of thugs succeeded in shooting their way into the Washington studios of the Access News Network and booting the last group out. Then new edicts would go out over the communications network of the world. Almost as an afterthought, Capitol Hill became a battle ground for competing groups of insurrectionists. The White House had been destroyed almost at the outset by a concerted hand-launched missile attack.

During all this turmoil there was still a legitimate Congress of the United States, duly elected, and a President, also elected. But they ended up in Peoria, Illinois.

The instability reached a peak in the spring of that eventful year. All communication was cut off. Commercial TV stations stopped broadcasting, cable TV channels went out, and the blackout continued for weeks. A flood of refugees surged west.

Then, mysteriously, something else began to intrude. The violence abruptly stopped. Guerrilla groups threw down their arms and gave up. No one knew what it was or who was behind it. The revolutionary edicts stopped, and Washington, D.C. suffered a total news blackout for a month. When communications were finally reestablished, some vast sea change had come over the eastern U.S. Bland news announcers proclaimed the birth of something enigmatically called the "Republic of Innerverse," some kind of utopian scheme without any readily identifiable political stance except bromides invoking "social cooperation" and "the harmony of community."

But what community?

The mission dispatcher approached him. "Showtime!" he said with a smile.

"Right."

Sutter positioned himself under the delta-winged glider and grasped the cross-bar of the triangular control frame. He was already in his prone harness, a sling that would support his body from shoulders to knees and allow him to hang and fly in a prone position, head forward. The dispatcher connected the hook at the end of the harness's suspending strap to a loop on the keel above, and Sutter was now part of his flimsy aircraft. His body and its position would provide the center of gravity and its movements would control the craft.

The dispatcher was talking again, but Sutter couldn't hear him over the rush of air out the back of the bay. Sutter tapped his helmet, and the dispatcher's voice came through the earpiece.

"We're circling the launch point now," the dispatcher said. "Any time you're ready, give me the nod, and wait for my signal. Remember, stay clear of the bay doors. Jump straight out. And try to relax."

Sutter gave an ironic grunt. Relax? Easy when you're jumping out of a perfectly good airplane with a gizmo that looked like something out of ancient silent-movie footage of the earliest attempts at flight, back in the days when crackpot inventors jerry-rigged kite affairs and bird-winged, aerodynamically dubious contrivances that usually proved instant death for the brave but foolish "aviators." Sure. And how many hobbyists had been killed by these high-tech but essentially primitive sport gliders over the years in the best of conditions, let alone at night and out the back of a jet transport?

On top of all that, he was jumping into a mystery.

Who ran the Republic? Who were the government? And what was Innerverse?

It was difficult to say. Satellite photos showed Washington, D.C. to be a virtual ghost town, its population fled. Most government buildings were ruins. No government had ever announced itself. All was quiet. For the most part, radio and TV broadcasting in the Republic had ceased, supplanted by, it was suspected, closed computer networks. A vast, eerie silence descended. And it had been that way for some thirty years.

There seemed to be no central control point, no nexus of decision-making. Yet decisions were made, and a country of sorts had grown out of the ruins. A country without a leader or a legislature, a country that sent no ambassadors to foreign lands, a country that barely spoke to its neighbors. There was something calling itself the Committee for International Understanding that would periodically broadcast on short wave radio. It seemed to speak for the country, but it issued no policy statements. All that came over the air were bland voices reciting tepid philosophical musings about peace and harmony.

Extending from the Canadian border to the Gulf of Mexico, the Republic of Innerverse was a island cut off from the rest of the continent, and from the world.

The dispatcher pulled on a hanging overhead cord, and the glider dropped free of its suspension cable. Sutter now bore the weight of the glider. The frame was of titanium alloy tubing and weighed practically nothing. The airfoil's fabric, colored black though sheer enough to be translucent, was like gossamer.

He centered the glider in the cargo bay. The dispatcher reached to Sutter's helmet and slid down the photon-multiplier night-sight goggles. To Sutter's eyes the bay, dim in ordinary light, now looked as bright as day. Light from the outside spilled in as well, not as brightly. There was no moon, so it was starlight he was seeing, or light spilling into the sky from the nearest large city. Superimposed over his field of view was an array of readouts—altitude, artificial horizon, airspeed, and stall warning, a light plane's instrument panel in miniature.

He tapped his throat mike to activate it. "Ready."

"Okay. Dispatcher to pilot, we're ready to launch."

"Roger," the pilot's voice came over the craft's intercom. "Stand by."

The dispatcher planted his feet wide, raised his right hand and held it up.

The plane's engines groaned as the craft's nose rose sharply. Sutter bent his knees and braced himself with one foot forward to prevent his moving toward the open bay doors prematurely. He had practiced the launch many times. It was difficult to maintain position right before the stall, but he had always managed to hang on before. The maneuver was necessary to reduce turbulence at the back of the aircraft. Turbulence was death to a hang glider. He would have to go into a dive immediately upon exiting anyway, to get quickly away from any instability. It would be tricky, for the plane would quickly go into its own dive in the other direction in order to recover from its partial stall. The jetwash could be difficult to avoid.

The engines suddenly died, and the dispatcher's arm came down sharply.

"Go!"

Sutter began running toward the rear of the cargo bay. Everything went well up until the last second.

A cold, tumbling eddy of wind found its way into the bay and gave the glider an unwanted and premature lift. Sutter yanked down on the control frame but could not prevent his feet from leaving the deck. He was flying inside the bay, not a thing he wanted to do. He pulled himself halfway up through the control triangle, trying to get the glider's nose down, but it was no use.

He had only a second to react, and then he and the glider were out the back of the bay into free and not very turbulent air, but not before a wrenching jolt shook the glider's thin metal-tube frame. Wincing, Sutter could guess what had happened. The king post—a short length of tubing sticking vertically up above the nylon cloth of the sail, serving as an anchor for four rigging lines connected to the four corners of the craft—had hit the overhead edge of the bay before exiting. On this design, adapted for military use, the king post did not stick up as far as on civilian models. Unfortunately, it had been just far enough.

But everything seemed to be fine. The craft was sailing, and he was in control. He looked up and checked the "Jesus bolt," a pin that secured a complicated clamp that connected the wings' crosstube brace to the delta-shaped control frame. That bolt shears, and the pilot drops (presumably yelling "Jesus!"), and it's all over. But the bolt looked all right, and Sutter's heart began to beat regularly again. The king post could have taken a beating. It had hit hard enough to bend, but even badly bent, it could do its job if the rigging wires were still secured to it.

But Sutter couldn't see through the sail well enough to assess what shape it was in. No matter. Everything was okay so far.

Sutter had gone into his dive immediately, heading for quieter air. As he pushed the control bar slowly forward to level off gradually, he heard the jet transport's engines whine, as the aircraft struggling to regain lift. The plane did its own dive to get out of the stall, and then the noise of its engines dwindled. It banked steeply, turned, and droned away into the night.

The drone faded to nothing, and Sutter was flying alone with only the gentle, steady fluttering of the glider's nylon airfoil as accompaniment. Presently, though, there was another sound, a faint beeping in his helmet's earpiece, telling him he was pointed in the wrong direction. He would have to turn until the beeping died, which event would inform him he was heading due east, in the right direction.

Turns in a hang glider are best done slowly and widely. Sutter proceeded to take the conservative approach.

The latest weather report had surface winds coming in from the southwest at a moderate speed. Heading east, he would be sailing with the wind, and would have to execute another 180 degree turn in order to land safely, into the wind.

Land where? That was up to him. Several likely landing areas had been scouted and suggested, but it was problematic if he could find them in the dark, even with the night-vision goggles.

He scanned a terrain painted in weird, murky blacks and grainy grays. It looked uninhabited. No army bivouacs were in evidence. This was technically a war zone, though there had never been a war as such. The border between the Central United States and the Republic had never heard a shot fired, but two whole divisions of the CUS Army had mysteriously disappeared beyond the border very near here. All the more mysterious because there was really no "enemy." The Republic had no armed forces of any sort. But they had something. No one knew what. Satellite recon had found abandoned CUS tanks, trunks and equipment. No sign of any soldiers.

It had been a short "war." A few tentative incursions into enemy territory ("Manifest destiny, in reverse, from west to east," as one commentator had put it), and then ... nothing. Radio phones went silent, no explanation. Alerts went out and were not answered. Two whole divisions, lost forever, silently and inexplicably.

"Of course it's some kind of mind control," Colonel Slocum had said at Sutter's briefing. "We know that, and we suspect various techniques, but we've no idea which one is being used. It's chemical, that's a good bet. Well, Sutter, we've shot you up with all the counteractive drugs we can think of. You've undergone psychotherapy and we've taught you how to resist brainwashing. You've come through pretty good. One of the best subjects in the experiments we've run. You're also an ornery individual, a misfit. Not easily yoked or controlled. But you're going up against a complete unknown."

The eerie topography below echoed that sentiment. Parts of what was in his field of vision looked like the surface of the moon, but that was probably an artifact. He could see trees and clearings. The problem was that the terrain was a little more hilly than he would like it. But they had wanted to have him enter at a point that was as close to Washington, D.C. as possible. Below was what was once West Virginia, a mountainous state indeed. Fortunately the area below was situated in the panhandle of the state, which made it more like eastern Ohio. Nevertheless, it was still dangerously hilly for trying to land a hang glider at night.

Worse, there was no one down there to help him once he was down. There was no underground, no resistance movement, or at least none that the OSO knew about. There were presumably no OSO operatives active in the Republic. The four operatives who had gone before Sutter had never reported back, and all attempts at reaching them by radio had failed.

No resistance, no underground, no spies. What method of tyranny could control a society as tightly as that?

To find some answers to all the mysteries was Frank Sutter's mission.

Pushing the control frame gently to the right, he induced the craft to begin its wide turn to the left. He would do well to conserve altitude at this point. He had a long way to go before he crossed no-man's land completely and was well into Republic territory. It would be embarrassing to come down in the middle of a UCS army camp. He'd have lots of explaining to do, if he didn't get shot first. Fortunately, as there had never been actual fighting here, the troops wouldn't be so jumpy. Still, it would be touch and go.

He didn't have to navigate. Another beep would sound in his helmet when he had crossed the border. Signals from navigation satellites, which his helmet could pick up and process, made this possible.

He didn't have to do anything but fly. The turn was going well. He checked the readouts. Altitude was holding up nicely, and the artificial horizon tilted at just the proper angle.

The navigation warning beep stopped, and he slowly brought the control bar to center position again, leveling off and flying straight again. So far, so good.

Now he would glide until he heard the second beep (pitched lower than the nav's tone), whereupon he would start looking for likely landing sites. He would fly no farther than he had to, even if it meant a long walk to the nearest habitation. He had a small backpack with enough provisions to last three days, plus a tent and everything he needed to survive in rough country. It was late spring and the weather was balmy, but he was dressed for any weather down to a little below freezing. In a holster strapped to his side was a 9 millimeter semiautomatic pistol. A snub-nosed .38-caliber revolver hid in a shoulder holster inside his jacket, which, along with a bowie knife strapped to his right calf, were all that he had in the way of armaments.

He wouldn't have to find any thermals. The glide path had been figured fairly accurately. If all went according to plan, he would have enough altitude to fly far over the border, with enough margin of safety in height to circle and land safely.

If all went according to plan.

Planning. All intelligence reports showed that the Republic, after a slow start, was run rather efficiently and had a working economy. It did no foreign trade whatsoever, so it had to make everything at home. Satellite photos showed factories and assembly plants, their workers beavering away. Agriculture bulked on a big scale, with huge state farms in evidence. They looked efficient and well thought out. The Republic had all the appurtenances and physical plant of a modern industrial state, and it had a recognizable managerial apparatus. Whoever was running things liked to maintain a low profile, but there seemed to be the usual hierarchy of managers, supervisors, planners, and bureaucrats, and they all issued orders, myriads of them, to this and that underling, all the way down the line. What was not in evidence was the Republic's government. There was no head of state, no legislative body, no courts, no police, no army. This was not possible in the world that Frank Sutter or anyone else knew. But the Republic was almost literally a world unto itself.

He did not hear anything untoward at first, only a slight increase in the steady fluttering of the airfoil above him. Gradually the anomaly registered on his consciousness and he looked up. He saw nothing but stars through the translucent black fabric. He suspected something was amiss, however. The right side of the airfoil looked a little more active than the left.

Then, without further warning, the bottom fell out of everything. He heard the heartbreaking sound of ripping fabric and a helpless flapping like the wings of some great wounded bird. The glider lurched to the left, going into an uncontrollable, unrecoverable spin.

A chorus of beeping went off inside his helmet, and red dots flashed on the display panel. He could do little but push at the control frame to try to get the nose up, but that course of action seemed only to increase the rate of descent.

The next few minutes were of panic and increasing desperation, the wind whooshing through his helmet, the beepers beeping, the red warning lights like angry red bugs attacking his eyes. He shifted his body this way and that, trying different angles of attack, trying anything that would stop his downward death spiral.

And something finally worked. Somehow the glider came out of its spin and continued into a flat dive. This was more controllable. The ground was coming up fast, too fast to be able to choose where to land—to crash, for that was now his only option. It remained to be seen how he would crash, how fast, and into what.

Lights up ahead, no time to form a cognitive estimation of what it was . . . a farm? Some big buildings, a few smaller ones. One was all lit up from inside . . . recognizable, but . . . Greenery inside.

More ripping. The king post was fine but the bump against the bulkhead had probably stressed the fabric and produced a small tear, which was now a huge tear. And getting bigger by the second.

He was coming in fast, heading directly for whatever that big building was. He had to either go over it or land short. It didn't look good for the former option. His glide angle was too steep. But putting the nose down now would send him crashing to the earth.

But he had to make a decision. Either land short or hit the damned building, and the damned building looked to be made entirely of glass. Green things . . . a hothouse?

He nosed down, rotating his body out of prone position, legs down, to take the shock.

He wasn't so bad off, there was still half an airfoil over him, there still was lift. . . .

Another heart-rending tear, like rags being sorted, like the most embarrassing moment in your life, there goes the tux and you'll miss the wedding or the prom, and there's your ass hanging out, and just like that, gone was the lift, the glider had no damned lift at all, and he dropped like a rock, but the fall was short and he hit with both feet and it hurt like hell, and he was running, running, still holding the damned glider up like some stupid kite, like a kid on the beach, and just when he thought that he had made it, he had really made it, though his leg hurt like hell, shooting pain up into his groin, the world flipped, turned upside down, the glider upset and began to come apart, its tubing going clatter clatter clatter and more ripping, still that damn ripping, but he didn't care any more, it could rip all it damned well wanted to, but now he was upside down and being dragged through vegetation, and something else, sticks, lots of sticks sticking up and jabbing him, and green leafy crap in his face, and a smell, a familiar smell, very strong in his nostrils along with the dirt that packed in there . . . tomatoes! Tomato plants, millions of them and all piling up in front of him, a huge jumbled jungle of green, reeking, smelling of wet dirt and whatever the hell makes tomato plants smell that way, but he couldn't stop, couldn't stop the dragging and the clattering even by grabbing onto the plants and the sticks, and then with a resounding crash and a great tinkling of glass suddenly and mercifully it all came to an end.

≽ Chapter Two ≼

He lay there in pain until some people came and took him away. They injected him with painkillers and he fell into a dreamlike trance. He came to full consciousness slowly, over days, and gradually a picture formed. He was in the picture. And the picture was one of him in a hospital room.

Over time, slow time, the picture faded and became reality. He was in a hospital room, in a bed. White walls, bare floor, a white sheet draping him. A bank of machines stood near the bed. A single IV dripped from its tree to his right. The tube ran into his right arm. The arm was in a sling and it hurt a bit. But not much. It was his right shoulder that was sore.

The room had no windows and was almost featureless, except for some lettering on the wall opposite the bed.

DISCIPLINE COMES FROM WITHIN

He tried to sit up and found that he could, but a dull pain began in his right leg. Wires running from the machine to his head and chest tugged. He eased back, then tried again.

He was thirsty. A small table beside the bed held a pitcher and a glass.

With his left arm, awkwardly, he poured himself a glass of water. It was cold and good.

29

He looked around.

Well, what the hell gives here? He hadn't expected a hospital room. A cell, yes. An interrogation room. A torture chamber. Anything but this. Was he badly hurt? He didn't feel badly hurt. Just banged up. Maybe they thought he carried some disease from the outside.

He looked at the wires and the machines. Maybe this was a torture chamber.

Presently a young man in a white coat came into the room carrying a clipboard. He was tall and had a lantern jaw.

"You seem to be doing fine," the man said pleasantly.

Frank took another drink, then sat back against the pillow. "Fairly well."

"It's miraculous that you weren't injured more than you were. The people at the hydroponics station said you demolished the greenhouse. All that glass, and just a few nicks and cuts. Remarkable."

"I'm lucky. Any internal injuries?"

"No, but you did fracture your right fibula rather badly. It was shattered. But we've patched you up. We kept you out while the work was done."

"Work?" Frank said.

"Repair work. Inside your leg. The bone's as good as new now. The surrounding tissue's bruised and you'll have soreness for a few weeks, but we'll give you something for that, too. Oh, you also had a slight concussion. But that was nothing."

"If I'm okay, what am I doing here?"

"We've taken a good look at you. Ran some tests."

"Looks like. And what did you find, may I ask?"

The man looked up and smiled.

"Oh, nothing much. You're in perfect health physically. Mentally, fine. Spiritually, not so good, though."

"Yeah? What's wrong in that department?"

"You don't have Innerverse."

"I see. What's that?"

"A guide to right behavior. Nothing more than that."

"And I don't have it."

"Didn't have it. We corrected that."

"That's nice."

The man stepped to the machines and noted readings, entering them into the device.

"Is that standard procedure when you find someone without this Innerverse stuff?"

"Pretty much."

"I see. What did the police say about me?"

"Police?"

"I was brought here by the police, wasn't I?"

"No, you were referred to us by the Citizens' Committee on Solidarity."

"They're not the police?"

"There are no 'police,' citizen. That's a very old-fashioned concept."

"No police?"

"No. They're not needed."

"Who brought me in?"

"The Citizens' Committee for Constant Struggle."

"You mean the army?"

"Not an army. We don't need an army."

"You don't need police, you don't need an army"

"But there is need for constant struggle until the whole world is set right. But when the whole world has Innerverse, then there won't be any need for constant struggle either."

"I see. It's all so clear now."

The man smiled. "It will be. Hungry?"

"No. Actually, I have a date for lunch. So, if you'll get this tube out of my arm—"

"You can't leave."

"No? Is the Citizens' Committee for Constant Struggle outside the door?"

The man shook his head.

"Are you going to stop me?"

He shook his head again.

"Right."

Frank began yanking off the tape that held the ends of the wires.

"You're not allowed to do that," the man said.

"You seem like a nice enough guy, but up yours."

The white-coated man shrugged. "It's useless. You have Innerverse."

"I've got exactly nothing inside me, pal. I'm hungry as hell."

"It might take a while for the systems to establish themselves."

"Sorry, can't wait."

Wincing, Frank plucked the needle-end of the IV out of his wrist and cast it aside. Blood welled from the hole, and he stanched the bleeding with a sheet. The flow stopped quickly enough, and he got unsteadily out of bed. He was naked.

"I suppose it wouldn't do any good to ask for my clothes."

"They may be in the storage closet near the unit station."

"Thanks."

Frank left the room. The hall outside looked like a conventional hospital floor but most of the rooms were unoccupied. He saw the unit station, a glassed-in office with monitoring instruments. Two female nurses sat inside. They looked up in surprise when he appeared.

"Excuse me, ladies," he said.

He tried a narrow door and found a broom closet. A door across the hall proved to be a room with metal shelves holding a number of boxes. He rummaged in these and found the slacks and shirt that he had had on under his jumpsuit. He got dressed in a hurry.

Finished, he peered out of the storage room. The nurses had gone back to whatever it was they'd been doing. Neither of them looked to be making frantic phone calls or sending out alarms. He left the room and walked down the corridor, keeping close to the wall.

He reached the entrance to a stairwell and entered.

It hit him at the top of the steps. First it was just a strange feeling, turning quickly to low-grade nausea. As he went down the stairs, anxiety welled up. It was instant and all-consuming. Stunned, he collapsed on the landing, shaking and sweating.

He remained there for several minutes, totally immobilized, the walls closing in, nameless terrors chewing at him.

At length he was able to climb back up the stairs. He staggered back to the room and collapsed on the bed.

After a while he became aware that someone had entered the room. He turned over and sat up. It was the doctor—or was he just a technician?—and a woman dressed in a shapeless gray suit.

"Hello," the woman said brightly. "How are you feeling?" She wore no makeup and had lines at the corners of her gray eyes. Her salt-and-pepper hair was drawn up into a bun.

"What kind of drug is it?" he asked.

"We didn't give you any drugs," the doctor said.

"You have Innerverse," the woman said. "It tells you when you're doing something wrong."

"What was I doing wrong?"

"You were leaving against medical advice," the woman said. She smiled again. "I'm from the Citizens' Committee for Social Improvement, Orientation Sub-Committee. My cognomen is M-D-E-T-F-G. My omnicode is one-dash-seven-oh-nine-oh-six-three-one-two-eight."

"Don't you have a name?"

"You can call me M-1."

"Mine's B–7," the medic said.

The woman read from a small recording device: "And *your* cognomen is B-K-F-V-G-D. Your omnicode is—"

He waved her silent. "Never mind. Just tell me what you did to me. What is Innerverse?"

"It's a guide to behavior. It tells you—"

"I *know* that. What *is* it?"

"Can you explain it to him, B-7?"

"Sure. When I said we didn't give you any drugs, I was telling the truth. What we did inject you with was a solution, but in that solution were tiny little machines."

"Machines?"

"Call them machines, that's what they are, in part. Some of them are no bigger than a bacterium, and most of them are smaller. They're constructed at a very small level of magnitude, the molecular level. Instead of big mechanical parts of metal or plastic, they have very small parts, some as small as atoms. In fact, some of the parts are atoms. Most of these machines are self-controlled, while others are controlled by computers that aren't much bigger than the machines. The computers have the same kind of atomic and molecular parts. But they're computers all the same."

"What do the machines do?"

"Lots of things. But mainly they monitor things in your blood and lymph. Watch your emotional states, look for telltale chemical signs."

Frank said, "Signs of what?"

"Well, for instance, when you do something that you shouldn't be doing, your body reacts in certain ways. It changes chemically and electrically. When the monitoring machines detect these changes, they send signals to your glands to secrete certain things. They also send signals to the brain."

"I understand," Frank said. "So, if I don't do what I'm told, this automatic punishment system goes online."

"Oh, it's not punishment. It's your own body's shame and guilt for doing the socially unacceptable thing. The reactions are just amplified, that's all."

"Oh, yes. I got that much."

"If you didn't feel any shame or guilt, Innerverse couldn't affect you."

"I feel absolutely no shame or guilt, friend. Stop bullshitting."

"Of course you feel it. You have to. You had the reaction, didn't you? Innerverse was speaking to you."

Frank had no answer.

"It will take time for you to understand completely," M-1 said.

"How can machines that small do anything?"

"If there were only a few of them, they couldn't do much. But there are millions of them in your body. And they can replicate themselves endlessly. A single bacterium can't do you any harm. But after it makes endless copies of itself, you have an infection."

"You'll get used to it," the woman said. "In time, Innerverse won't need to guide you at all. You'll guide yourself."

"I bet I will, if I know what's good for me."

She grinned expansively. "You're learning already! I'm so pleased. It will make my job so much easier!"

"Glad to oblige. What's going to be done with me?"

The man looked at him curiously. "Done?"

"For entering your country illegally. It was an accident. I was hang gliding near the border, and I got lost, and the glider was—"

He chuckled. "We know you're a spy."

Frank closed his mouth and breathed out. "Spy?" he said as innocently as he could manage. "That's crazy. I was—"

"We know what you are, we know why you were sent. Constant Struggle says that a number of your countrymen have come before you. You're the first we've seen at this facility. But, to answer your question about what's going to be done with you—the answer is, nothing. Absolutely nothing."

"I won't be charged as a spy?"

"No. Not as far as I know."

"But you said you knew I was one."

"We do. But it doesn't matter what you are. You have Innerverse now. That's all that need be done, my friend. Citizen."

"Then, you're going to send me back home?" Frank asked with faint hope.

"Why, no," the woman said. "You're a Citizen of the Republic now. The Republic of Innerverse. You're brand new and don't know the ropes yet, but we'll teach you. There's a little Orientation course. That's my job. First, though, you'll get well."

"Innerverse will take care of that, too." The man told him.

"It will?"

"Sure. Who do you think fixed your leg for you? Repaired that bone in less than twenty-four hours? It was done by bone-repair machines, little ones, inside your body. One of the many things Innerverse does for people. It keeps them healthy and cures them if they get sick or injured."

"What doesn't Innerverse do?" Frank asked ironically.

"Not much."

≥ Chapter Three ≤

Orientation was perfunctory. There was no political incul-
cation, no long harangue; there was no indoctrination per
se, no attempt at persuading him of the rightness of any
ideological point of view. He was simply issued clothing—
an ugly blue all-weather jacket with baggy trousers of the
same coarse material, probably a cheap synthetic weave—
and a sheet of paper with some instructions on it. The
instructions said to report to a certain address, his new
residence. He was to remain there until he was issued new
instructions, which he would receive via his "domestic
commscreen." That, along with a few slogans ("Conscience is an Inner Voice"—a deliberate pun?), was all
there was to Orientation.

Banners with slogans draped every building facade,
hung from every cornice. "To Love is to Obey" said one.
There were others: "Good Citizens are Happy Citizens."
And: "Duty Lies Within." There were nonideological
signs, but these only advertised quasi-ideological events—
rallies, marches, "Self-Criticism Roundtables," and such
like.

There were no billboards advertising products or ser-
vices. He walked the streets reading posters in storefront
windows and on kiosks. He could not get a sense of who
was running things. He expected to see giant blow-ups of
some dictatorial face, or direct references to a political
party or revolutionary cabal.

But there was nothing, no one. Innerverse ran things. But who ran Innerverse?

The people he passed all smiled, hurrying to some duty or another. It was a strange smile, incongruously detached, irrelevant to any real sense of well-being. It was not forced, yet not quite real.

He stopped to ask directions of a traffic director—not a policeman; the man wore only a white brassard and was unarmed. He told Sutter to take an omnibus with a certain number and to get off at Complex 502 on the Boulevard of Social Concern.

"Put a smile on your face," the man told him.

Ignoring the order, Sutter walked on.

It was not long before the first pangs of nausea began. He forced a smile, and his stomach rumbled, then quieted. He felt better almost instantly. Justice was that speedy. His own body was judge and jury, its verdict not open to appeal.

There were few stores or shops. Most storefronts were boarded up or had their windows used as billboards. Here and there a door was open with no sign above saying what was going on inside. He stopped at one such place and found a store with a few undifferentiated shoes inside bins. Another store offered socks and underwear. There wasn't much stock in any store he visited. The places looked ransacked, and no salespeople were about. He continued walking.

Traffic was limited to trucks, buses, and official-looking vehicles. No bicycles or powered two-wheeled conveyances. The sidewalks were crowded, as they would be on any workday in any major city around the world. This was downtown, the area between the rivers. There were hundreds of office buildings and thousands of workers. Everyone was dressed pretty much as he was, in the same utilitarian outfit.

He passed what looked like a restaurant. He went back and looked in the window. The place was a cafeteria. His stomach had calmed down and he was hungry again. Very hungry. His instructions had not told him about food or about getting it, and he had no money.

Yet he went in. It was mid-morning and there were no lines. He watched a woman at the counter load her tray and walk to a table. He could see no checkout station, no cashier. He decided to take a chance. He took a tray and slid it along the runners.

Nothing looked very good. He passed green gelatin and wilted salads. Farther along an attendant was ladling what looked like chicken stew into a container. He asked for some of that, and got a small bowl full of gray goop. He took slices of bread and a cup of what appeared to be custard or vanilla pudding. There was little else to choose from. He got himself coffee but no cream, as that commodity was not in evidence. No sugar either. He found a seat.

The stew, if that's what it was, was awful, tasting of cornstarch paste and unidentifiable flavorings. The vegetables were tasteless, and the "meat" was not chicken but something like bean curd, and as appetizing. He forced it down. The bread had the flavor of cardboard. He spat out the first mouthfuls of ersatz custard and sipped the coffee surrogate, which carried the heavy aftertaste of chlorine. Or was it detergent?

He looked at the wall above the counter.

SUICIDE IS UNSOCIAL.

Of course; a simple way out, and one Innerverse probably had a hard time thwarting. In fact, any attendant discomfort on contemplating or attempting the act of suicide would only serve as a goad to go through with it. He wondered if they'd figured on that. Perhaps nausea and anxiety were merely the first tier in the hierarchy of punishments. What topped the pyramid? Unendurable pain, such that you simply could not finish the act if you attempted it? In that case, why the admonitions against suicide? Curious.

Gloomily, he wondered if suicide was the only way out.

He left half the coffee in the cup and went out to the street. He now knew why the stores needed no salespeople. Citizens simply walked in and took what was needed. They took exactly as much as they needed and no more, or Innerverse would punish. Dandy way to run a distribution system. No money necessary. It was the age-old utopian dream: a moneyless economy immune from the laws of supply and demand, based on mutual cooperation and individual restraint. Inevitably such a system would breed chronic shortages, but who would complain?

Who *could* complain?

He caught the bulky omnibus on Conscience Avenue, a thoroughfare that ran to the river and crossed a bridge. On the other shore the bus turned left and entered a section of the city that probably had been known as the South Side, he guessed, roughly judging compass points by the sun. In this universe it was nameless and consisted mostly of high-rises and little parks.

The Boulevard of Social Concern was the main street, leading past numerous groups of buildings, signs designating each complex by number. He saw 501 go by, and made his way to the front of the bus.

The driver beamed at him. "We're getting happier every day, citizen."

"Aren't we, though?"

He paid for the irony with a twinge or two of gastric pain.

Building C of Complex 502 looked increasingly shabbier the closer he got to it. Intended to be lean and functional, it looked only weathered and threadbare. The raw, unpainted concrete was cracked and streaked with water stains, and the tiny windows made the place look more like a prison than an apartment building. The surrounding grounds were clear of trash but looked desolate. The grass was stunted and looked dead, gone brown and dry.

He passed through a cracked glass door and entered the lobby. It was empty except for a few stacked fiberglass chairs and an underused bulletin board. He waited for the elevator.

The elevator never came. His apartment number, so the instruction sheet said, was 502-C-346. He found a stairwell and went up to the third floor.

The door to 346 was open. There was no lock.

It was a one-room apartment with two small windows and walls of unpainted concrete block. The floor was bare concrete. The place was perfunctorily furnished: a cot, one table, one chair, and a small settee. A lidless toilet stood in a corner next to a small sink. There was a kitchen of sorts—a hotplate and a cabinet. No refrigerator, no kitchen sink. The walls were devoid of decoration and there were no curtains on the windows.

Set in the wall in front of the settee was an oblong screen. It displayed:

MESSAGE WAITING
TOUCH SCREEN TO START

He was sorry he had looked at it. It was an order, and if he disobeyed . . . He managed to put off activating the message until a synthesized voice came out of the speaker below it.

"There is a message waiting for you. Touch the screen to start the message. Touch twice if you want the visual display only and no audio."

He touched twice. The screen came to life.

Cognomen: BKFVGD
Omnicode: 2-093487438
Message: You are late. You must not tarry when you are told to report somewhere. Do not hurry, but do not waste time. Step right along. Tardiness is unsocial. Innerverse will remind you of this in the future.

Your program for the rest of the day is as follows:

1. In your free moments, familiarize yourself with our new living facility. Report any deficiencies to your Residential Complex Supervisor's office.

2. Watch the one-hour Information Special that will follow this message. You must watch at least two Information Special programs per day, and at least one hour of general programming, for a total of three hours of screen viewing time per day. This routine must be followed always, except on designated Special Days. The viewing schedule will be altered on these days to permit various activities: parades, Solidarity Meetings, etc.

TOUCH SCREEN TO CONTINUE MESSAGE

He brushed the screen with his finger and more lettering filled the lighted oblong.

3. Report to your building refectory for dinner. You also have the option of eating in. You may procure food at your nearest Grocery Outlet.

4. After dinner, watch the Information Special program that will start at 19:00.

5. After the program you have one hour free time until Lights Out. You may continue to watch general programming or you may sit and get in touch with Innerverse. Remember: peace is constant struggle.

6. At Lights Out you will go to bed and sleep for eight (8) hours. You will awake refreshed and happy, ready to face the challenges of the new day.

Your Schedule Tomorrow:

Tomorrow you will report at 8:00 to the Committee on Employment, Job Training Sub-Committee, Building 1, Complex 122, Dedication Drive. Be prompt. Watch this screen tomorrow for further details. That is all.

You may proceed with implementation of the rest of today's schedule.

He had already familiarized himself with his "living facility."

He sat down. What would happen if he got on a bus, went to the edge of the city, got off, and kept walking? Perhaps this direct approach would work if he could keep his mind occupied somehow, if he could in some way not dwell on the fact that he was doing something forbidden.

But was that possible? He had his doubts. No, his unconscious reactions would not escape Innerverse. And there was nothing he could do about his unconscious—or "subconscious," if you wanted to use the popular term.

Yet there had to be a way. Somehow the monitoring process would have to be defeated, or at least misled or disabled, until he could get to a radio and call for help. But were there radios? There had to be, he thought, a shortwave radio somewhere in this country. In some government office somewhere.

He was becoming nauseated.

He was dismayed but not surprised. Innerverse was probably extending and refining its control of his bodily functions. Eventually, even stray rebellious thoughts would be punished. It was a powerful system of oppression, self-perfecting and self-perpetuating, more effective than any secret police force or surveillance system.

The screen brightened and a program came on. He sat and watched, trying to let the banal content—something about happy agricultural workers meeting new higher quotas—occupy the front part of his mind while he continued his scheming in the shadows.

The ploy seemed to work, but he could not come up with any solutions. For the moment he was stuck in this strange world.

When the program ended, something like a panel quiz show came on. Since he was under no compulsion to watch it, he looked for controls on the screen. There were none. He had to let it play.

He didn't relish the prospect of another cafeteria meal, so he went out to look for a food store.

He walked several blocks before encountering what passed for a business district. Finding what he took to be a supermarket, he went in.

The place was virtually devoid of stock. The shelves held little but empty packing cartons. There were only a few items. There must have been an adequate potato harvest this year. Even at that much of the stock was mushy and nearly rotten, alive with sprouting eyes. He found a few that were edible. There were no shopping carts or bags, so he broke off the sprouts and stuffed the spuds in his pocket. He found canned goods. Most were vegetables, but he did come up with a lone can of BEANS (BAKED).

That was enough to get him through a day and keep him out of the awful cafeterias. As usual there was no paying for anything, so he walked out of the store.

On his way home he found himself following a woman. She was blond, her hair done in the unflattering pageboy style that seemed prevalent. Her figure—from what he could make of it through the baggy clothes—was trim and attractive. He drew abreast of her and glanced at her face.

She wore no makeup. Her eyes were pale blue and her lips thin. She had a pronounced chin and an upturned nose. On the whole she was not unattractive.

He wondered how reproduction was handled here. Were there married couples, families? He somehow doubted it. Mating centers, the offspring raised by the state. Worse, insemination centers supplied by mandatory donations. He had seen no children at all. Were they all sequestered in crèches? The thought of tiny children being inoculated with diabolical mind-controlling bacteria made him shiver.

He walked on ahead of her. She followed him when he turned into the complex.

In the lobby he pretended to read the bulletin board

while waiting for her. When she passed him on the way to the stairwell he grinned.

"Good evening," he said.

She gave him a brilliant smile. "Every day we're getting better and better!"

"It's great, isn't it?" he replied.

"Oh, yes. Oh, yes."

She entered the stairwell, and the warped, ill-fitting door thumped in closing behind her.

His eyes wandered over the bulletin board. One posting, hand-written in a scrawl, read:

> *troubled citizen w.*
> *unsocail thougts wants to*
> *join "self-critisism group"*
> *help me citizens! Apt. 678*

He wondered how such "thougts" were possible, but obviously they were. Innerverse's control might not be as complete as he had surmised. Bugs in the system? Programming errors in the tiny biological computers?

Perhaps there were random glitches, but he doubted that they were anything but rare. How long could he hope to go on thinking such blatantly unsocial thoughts as he was thinking right now?

He would have to do something very quickly.

≽ Chapter Four ≼

The next day dawned gray and dismal. A thick cloud cover had moved in, matching his mood.

He took an omnibus to the "Employment Committee" building, back in town, across the river. He reported in the nick of time to avoid getting a stomach-lashing for tardiness and was curtly instructed to cool his heels in the waiting room. He sat in a hard plastic and metal chair for two and a half hours before his name was called. There were other people waiting with him, but the sign above the door forbade all conversation.

He was shown to an office where a pasty-faced young man sat behind a metal desk. The usual decor here: stenciled slogans on bare concrete block, a dented filing cabinet, a wastebasket. In one corner a large dustball lay huddled like a frightened gray hare. Some janitor had no doubt got a bellyache for shirking that duty.

"Yours is an unusual case," the man said. "You're an Outperson. Worse, you're an enemy of Innerverse." A toothy smile. "Or you were."

"Were," Frank said.

"Innerverse can have no enemies."

"That's right," Frank said blandly. It was true, after all.

"And properly shouldn't. When the whole world has Innerverse, everyone will wonder how anyone could have been against it."

"Of course."

"No crime, no poverty, no disease. The ancient scourges of mankind wiped out forever."

Frank studied at him. That last utterance had the sound of a recitation from memory. The young man looked down at the papers on his desk.

"So, you're with us now," he said. "No problems, right?"

"Right!" Frank said enthusiastically.

The man smiled again. His teeth were very white. "Great. That's wonderful. Better and better."

And Frank felt better for saying it. Positive reinforcement as well as negative? Why, of course. It made sense. Obeying orders made you feel good. Disobeying made you feel bad. Simple.

They assigned him to a hospital to work as an orderly. The place was different from the place where he'd been incarcerated. The atmosphere was decidedly low-tech. The floor he was assigned to was a cardiac unit, but there were no continuous monitoring instruments in use. Nurses wheeled bulky EKG machines around from patient to patient to get periodic readings. Doctors (if that's what they were, though they were probably more on the order of highly-trained paramedics) relied on tried-and-true devices and methods: stethoscopes, pulse-taking, and so forth.

The place was dingy, plaster cracking on ill-painted walls. It was clean, though, because he cleaned it, pushing brooms and slapping mops around. The patients wore pasted smiles but were generally miserable, as the medical care was terrible and the food was worse than in the cafeterias.

He'd keep trying to come up with a plan, to find a way of exploiting the glitches, the defects in the system. Innerverse's control was marginally less than total. The system was essentially a technological approach to totalitarianism. While political methods of repression could approach complete efficiency, no technology could. The anguished note on the bulletin board proved that things could go awry. Either the control system could not penetrate to the forebrain and control thoughts, or the tiny controlling computers could malfunction. He did not know which was the case; either way it was a ray of hope.

He could still think, but there was no telling for how long. The people around him seemed to be under more complete control than he was, but this could have been an illusion. He had quickly learned to curb his tongue, to act the part. Speech was behavior, and here behavior was controlled by a quickly responding mechanism of "reinforcements," to use the behaviorist jargon that he'd learned in his briefings. Most of these reinforcements were "negative," i.e. tending to punish. But some were positive in the sense that compliance with accepted modes of behavior was just as quickly rewarded with surcease from psychic and physical pain. He wasn't sure about full positive reinforcement. He hadn't felt any thrill or unnatural pleasures when obeying orders. Innerverse was like a drug, he reminded himself. It could do things drugs could do, and it could no doubt reward with pleasure as easily as it punished with pain. But perhaps pleasure was not in the scheme of things in the Republic of Innerverse.

A republic of pain.

Perhaps his thoughts would continue to be his own, but thoughts wouldn't help his body, which was dangling like a marionette on biochemical strings.

The contrastingly backward technology of the hospital led him to think. He watched nurses take oral and rectal temperatures with old-fashioned mercury thermometers, the standby of home medicine chests for ages. Even with the dumb technology, minimum sanitary measures were followed. Those thermometers were sterilized, and for a thermometer the only way to do that was immersion in alcohol; for oral purposes that meant ethyl alcohol, ethanol. Methanol, wood alcohol, was poisonous.

If his unconscious bodily mechanisms were being monitored internally, was there something he could ingest that would suppress those mechanisms? Drugs, maybe. Drugs were here, and he could get to them, but what sort of drugs would suppress autonomic responses? Tranquilizers? Maybe, but he doubted that any in use here would be effective enough. Narcotics? Possibly. But he was naturally wary of those. After all, overdosing was as easy as falling off a ghetto stoop.

Narcotics were easily available, in the sense that there were no physical barriers. The drug cabinets had no lock. In this society locks were unneeded. And for that reason he couldn't touch them. He couldn't approach the cabinets with the intention of stealing drugs without risking intervention by Innerverse.

But the thermometers made him think. He had seen no taverns, no liquor stores. As far as he knew this society was Teetotal. Why? Perhaps because the effects of booze could thwart Innerverse.

There was probably a bottle of ethanol in the drug cabinet, and if not there in the supply lockers. But the question was, could he steal the alcohol?

No. The same constraints applied, or would be applied. He couldn't even risk thinking about it too much.

Back to square one. He ruefully half-entertained thoughts of sidling up to the bottle, eyes averted, whistling innocently, then grabbing it and chugging as much as he could before Innerverse grabbed his gut and squeezed. But the ploy was absurd. He couldn't very well plan to do something without knowing he was going to do it. There was no one to fool but himself.

Was there no way out besides hoping for his internal police force to go on the fritz?

He might have to face up to the possibility that there was no way out of this. The thought of it was numbing. An eternity here?

What about the OSO? He had missed several radio check-ins by now. They surely would know something had gone wrong. Surely they'd do something. Come and get him.

Surely.

The thought of a commando team, faces dark with burnt cork, submachine guns rattling, bursting into this world . . . well, it was ridiculous. Incongruous. OSO would never authorize such a risky mission. They had lost four previous operatives here, and he would no doubt be the last one. The only thing to do would be to throw up a Maginot Line along the border and hope the Republic would never invade. For if it did, there would be no contest. The Republic would win hands down, without firing a shot.

It made him think. Why hadn't this happened already? What was keeping the Republic from swallowing up the rest of the world?

He went home after his first day, made himself boiled potatoes—no salt, no pepper, no butter—ate, then sat down to log screen time. While he watched, he thought. At length he resolved on a course of action. Absurd an idea as it was, tomorrow he would try stealing the bottle and downing as much alcohol as he could, neat, before the shakes got to him. He wouldn't try to fool himself or Innerverse, he would just do it and try to fight the pain, the fear, the shakes. He simply could not think of anything else to try.

The resolution enabled him to sit through the evening's "entertainment" without too much distress. Afterward, he was restless. He decided to go out for a walk. As far as he knew it was allowed. Anything that was not specifically forbidden, he could do. Or so he conjectured.

Maybe he would keep walking. He'd had about enough of this place.

Then he considered what might happen if he tried to escape. He had refrained from daring another escape attempt out of simple fear. He did not want to experience again the excruciating psychic pain, the unbearable sense of impending doom, the unremitting terror that he had felt under Innerverse's lash. The very thought of it made his stomach spasm.

Then his plan of grabbing alcohol was doomed from

the start. He would not be able to stand up to Innerverse's wrath.

This instantly depressed him.

No, he wasn't quite ready to face it again, and the bottle-grabbing notion now struck him as stupid and rash. In time, maybe. For now about all he could risk was taking a walk.

He was on the stairway between the second and third floors when she came through the door opening on the landing. He almost bumped into her. It was the woman he'd seen last night.

She seemed startled at first, then burst into the forced smile she'd given him before. "Hello, citizen!"

"Hi," he said. Then he blurted, "I'm going out for a stroll. Want to walk with me?"

The smile disappeared, and she gave him a penetrating stare.

He stood there, letting her gauge him, take his measure. She seemed to be weighing the risk, trying to figure whether this was a test, or a trap. Could she trust him? Should she dare? All this she spoke with her eyes, and he was vastly relieved to hear it. It was the first evidence he'd had of humanity, of conscious volition, behind the universal facade of robotlike obedience.

"Yes," she said finally.

They walked out of the building together.

The night was cool and the city was quiet. Too quiet. It was not yet Lights Out, but along the stark faces of the high-rises there were more dark windows than lighted ones. A musky, watery smell came on a breeze from the river. There was little traffic on the boulevard. No one else was about. It was late.

"When did it stop?" she asked after they had walked in silence for a stretch.

"When did what stop?"

"Innerverse."

"It hasn't."

She halted and looked at him. "You just haven't realized it yet. It's gone."

He shrugged. "I haven't tried to do anything unsocial yet."

"You're doing it now."

"I didn't know evening walks were forbidden."

"They're not. There's no need to forbid it. No one does anything that's not on his daily schedule. It's too risky. Don't you know that?"

"No," he said. "I'm new here."

"Were you an Outperson?"

"Yeah. If that means a foreigner."

"An Outperson is someone without Innerverse. The whole world doesn't have Innerverse yet."

He had wondered about how much of the planet Innerverse had under its control already, albeit covertly. Did Innerverse have secret operatives all over the globe? Of course he could not hope to know about that. Nor could he think of any way to find out.

"What do you know about Outpersons?" he asked.

"Nothing," she said. "We haven't been able to get any accurate news for years."

"Who's 'we?' "

She started walking again. "People who've lost Innerverse."

"So not everyone's controlled."

"No, not everyone." She gave him a glum look. "But it might as well be everyone. There are so few. You're one, even if you don't know it yet."

"How do you know that you don't have Innerverse any more?"

"Because I can do anything I want. Go for walks in the evening, take an extra portion of food, not watch the screen when I don't want to. I almost never do any more."

"No wonder. It's awful stuff."

She smiled. "See? You wouldn't be able to say that if you hadn't lost it."

He shook his head. "I wish you were right. But they

just shot me up with the gunk the other day. Can it fail that quickly?''

"We don't know. Most maladapts lose Innerverse in their late teens. That's when I lost mine. I'm twenty-six now. And they haven't caught on yet."

"Is there danger that you'll be found out?"

"Oh, of course. There's always that danger. But you get used to it. The thing is, though Innerverse is inactive, habits are hard to break. I don't do anything really unsocial. Just little things.''

They turned a corner and walked toward the river.

He asked, "Why does Innerverse sometimes fail?"

"We don't know that. We think that the body's defense system overcomes it, like it was an infection. Maybe maladapts have better defense systems than most people.''

"Just like some people have spontaneous remissions from cancer, maybe.''

"Yeah, maybe.'

They walked on until they came to a small park by the river's edge. There was a bench, and they sat. Lights on the other shore reflected as long wavering lines on the water. There were no boats on the river, no barges. This town was a quiet administrative center.

"I usually come here at nights when the weather's nice," she said. "I like to watch the river go by. It comes from somewhere and goes somewhere, away from here. I like to think about taking a little boat and going out on the water, and letting the river carry me away. I'd never leave the boat. I'd just fish, lie in the sun, do nothing all day."

"What do you do all day?"

"I sit and type on a keyboard. I key in data, and then I ask the computer to report on the data, and it spews out all kinds of stuff at me.''

"Sounds like fun. Tell me this. How many other maladapts are there?''

"I only know two, but there are more. Don't ask me

their cognomen-omnicodes, because I don't trust you well enough yet. You might be Innerverse.''

"You mean I might be a police agent?"

"There are no police. But I've heard of people being arrested by the Committee for Constant Struggle."

"The army."

"Yes. They sometimes use agents to trick people. Or so I've heard. It may be all lies, though. You never know. You can never know what's truth and what isn't."

"Let me ask you something very basic and crucial. Who's in charge of the government? Who runs this whole nightmare?"

"I don't know. We've been trying to figure it out for years. All we know is that there's Innerverse."

"But someone invented Innerverse. Someone used it to control people. Who was it?"

She shrugged.

He asked, "You're not old enough to remember a time without Innerverse?"

"No."

"Aren't there any history books?"

"What's a history book? What's a book?"

He looked out across the river. Darkness and silence and slow-moving water.

Her hand sought his.

"Let's go back," she said. "My place."

"Are you sure?"

She giggled. "I've had an order to get pregnant for months now. I've been ignoring it. Couldn't find anyone I wanted to get pregnant with."

Now he knew how the business of reproduction was gone about. An order was issued, an order was obeyed.

Light came through the lone window and made a trapezoid on the bare floor beside the bed. Lying on his side, he studied it. He liked its lambent geometry, its two-dimensional clarity.

"Are you awake?" she asked.

"Yes." He rolled over to face her.

She asked him, "What are you thinking?"

"Of how to get out of this place."

"This place? You mean the living complex?"

"This world."

"How can you get out of the world? That's silly."

"It seems like another planet."

"A different world," she said dreamily. "Do you think there are worlds other than this one?"

"Maybe. But I'm not interested in reaching them. I just want to get out of the country and back home."

"How would you do that?"

"I don't know. Walk, take a bus. Steal a vehicle. It doesn't matter. The main question in my mind is, can I do it without Innerverse interfering?"

"You should be able to. You wouldn't be able to sleep with me if you still had Innerverse."

"How can you get pregnant if no one is able to sleep with you?"

"If they had an order, they could."

"You need an order?"

"Sure. You didn't find the order to impregnate someone on your schedule, did you?"

"No."

"Well, then. You wouldn't be able to sleep with me unless Innerverse was dead inside you."

"Then that means there's nothing preventing me from leaving."

"Not if you don't have Innerverse."

"But I don't understand. Just today I was thinking about doing something to get the hell out of here, and the nausea hit me on schedule. Do you think I just lost Innerverse this evening? Can it happen that quick?"

"I don't know. It happened to me gradually."

"Okay, so there's such a thing as partial control."

"I'm pretty sure. I've always thought that there are lots of people who are that way. I mean, with Innerverse not fully in charge."

"What makes you think that?"

"Nothing I can put a finger on. A look in their eyes, the way they look at you. The way they act."

It suddenly struck him that he didn't even know this woman's name. Wait—she didn't have a name, only a nonsensical and dehumanizing jumble of letters and numbers. He really didn't want to know what her cognomen was, much less her omnicode.

"Alice."

She said, "What did you say?"

"I just gave you a name. Alice. You look like one."

" 'Alice.' That's pretty."

"So are you."

"That's unsocial. No one is better looking than anyone else."

"That's a lie. Alice, listen. I'm going to leave here and I want to take you with me. Do you want to come?"

"Go with you?"

"Yes."

"To this other place, this other world you talked about?"

"Yes. Do you want to come with me?"

She was silent for a long time.

Then she said: "You know, I was thinking about doing it tonight. Jumping into the river."

"You wanted to kill yourself?"

"Yes."

"Tonight?"

"Yes. But I think about it a lot. Just jumping in and letting the water carry me away."

"Drowning."

"Of course. Killing yourself is the most unsocial thing you can do, and I wanted to do it tonight. And then ... I met you. And now you want to take me away."

"Come with me, Alice."

She inhaled deeply and sighed. "Yes, I'll go with you."

"Let's leave now."

She kissed him. "Tomorrow. Let's try to get me pregnant again."

"All right, Alice. By the way, my name is Frank."

"Frank." She laughed. "Frank. It sounds funny."

"Laugh all you want. It sounds wonderful."

≫ Chapter Five ≪

Not at all sure his body had overcome Innerverse, he thought up experiments to test the hypothesis. As he lay there with Alice, he thought about escaping, dwelled on it in detail.

It took him a while to imagine some details. He hadn't a clue how to begin. Then he got the notion that he might steal a car. Trouble was, he had seen few vehicles of any sort.

It was over a minute before the acidic claw of nausea began to get its grip on his middle.

That was good. At first the punishment had come instantly. Now, it was delayed. That was some progress.

He tried to stop thinking of the escape, but of course could not. And the nausea grew, and when it became strong enough to prevent him thinking of anything else, only then did it peak and begin to subside.

He belched. Nothing ever came up. He had never vomited, which led him to suspect that the nausea wasn't "real" in the sense that his stomach was really upset. Perhaps the nanomachines worked on the mind directly, producing phantom sensations.

The night was unnaturally quiet. He strained to hear an auto horn, a train whistle, anything signifying that there was some life out there. But he heard nothing but an occasional creak of a structural beam or the whine of a ventilation fan.

He felt better, but there was no question that Innerverse was still inside him. It was a good bet that it was on the defensive, but he was still in thrall. But the thought that Alice was immune buoyed him, somehow. Innerverse wasn't omnipotent, and that was reassuring.

He rolled over, put an arm around Alice, and went to sleep.

It was still dark when they boarded an omnibus heading for the suburbs. The sky was starless and the streets were almost deserted. A lone street-cleaning machine—a robot, apparently, with no operator in sight—whirred its way along the curb, the only denizen stirring. The omnibus driver gave them a cheery smile when they got on.

"Getting an early start, eh?" she said. "Your shop storming for a quota overfulfillment?"

"Better and better!" Frank said.

"Every day!" Alice piped.

Frank's hand had instinctively reached into his pocket for fare, and he took comfort that the reflex was still there. The two days he'd been here seemed the longest stretch of time he had ever experienced.

He held Alice's hand out of the driver's sight as they rode. The rows of high-rise buildings continued for several miles then thinned out, the gaps filled by older structures, some that were once single-family homes, with the look for having been carved up into apartments. Frank doubted that the luxury of single family homes—were there families at all?—were rare in the Republic. There were many vacant lots with old foundations still standing. The city had a ragged look, as if it were being cleared for new development. As in all totalitarian societies, the past must be obliterated and the present erected over top of it. Soon the landscape would hold nothing but faceless monoliths.

Dawn came, shading the sky purple.

"Do you know how far out the last stop is?"

Alice shook her head. "I've never ridden this line."

The city gave way to suburbs. There were a few factories and more high-rises, but no houses. There were some old boarded-up apartment buildings.

"Do you know the population of the Republic?"

Alice said, "The population? How many citizens? I don't know."

"Did it ever strike you that there weren't a lot of people, that there were less and less as time went on?"

"Well, not really. What made you ask?"

"Housing doesn't seem to be a problem. Or is that because of heroic construction-worker efforts?"

Alice shrugged. "I've never thought of it."

They passed light-industrial parks, warehouses, yards full of building materials, lots with parked earth-moving equipment. Everything looked dreary and forlorn.

They rode for about fifteen minutes, passing through the last of suburbs. Finally the omnibus pulled over to the side of the road.

"End of the line," the driver announced.

They got off and walked along the road. There were overgrown fields to either side, trees bordering them.

"Let's cut across and get into the woods," Frank said.

Dew drenched their shoes as they made their way through the tall grass.

"Do you know where we're going?" she asked.

"Only generally. We have to move west. We're miles from the border, though. We'll have to hitch a ride or steal a vehicle."

"We'll get there," she said gayly.

"Don't be so goddamned optimistic. I'm sick of the smiles, the phony cheeriness."

"Sorry."

He drew her to him and hugged her. "I'm sorry. I shouldn't have snapped at you."

"It's all right," she said.

"No, it's not. You're the only ray of light in all this darkness. You shouldn't exist. I—"

She drew back from him. "What's the matter?"

He halted. "It's starting."

"Innerverse?"

He nodded. "Nausea. There was a little on the bus but I was hoping it was just nervousness. Let's keep walking."

The woods were green and cool, alive with morning birdsong. They followed a deer path through thin maple trees and dense undergrowth: ferns, laurel, wild raspberry bushes, mayapple plants.

"What are you feeling?" she asked.

"Fear," he said.

"Bad?"

"Yes, getting worse."

She held his hand tightly. They came out of the woods and crossed a hayfield, entering the trees on the other side. A slope led down to the road, which had curved to the right and crossed in front of them.

"Let's chance the road awhile," he said.

They walked about a quarter mile before encountering a garage with numerous official-looking vehicles parked in front of it. Most were trucks, but there were two cars, nondescript gray sedans. He led her across the parking lot to one of them. He tried the driver's door—it was unlocked.

"Get in," he said.

The interior was stripped-down and functional, the dashboard made of unpainted metal with minimum instrumentation. The car had a standard transmission with a floor shift. As he had hoped, the key was in the ignition.

He looked around the lot. No one was about. He depressed the clutch pedal and turned the key. The engine coughed, turned over and started chugging and rattling.

He struggled with the gear shift.

"What's the matter?" she said.

"Feel weak. The nausea. Can you drive?"

"No. I never learned."

"Of course not. I'll be . . . fine."

He got it into reverse and backed out of the parking slot. Jamming the lever into first gear, he started across the lot for the road.

A man in greasy overalls came out of the garage, stopping when he saw the car pulling out. He yelled something.

Frank floored the accelerator pedal, spinning tires on the gravel. He drove off the lot, swerving onto the road with only a cursory glance to see if traffic was coming. The engine yowled but didn't put out much power. He kept his foot to the floor, though, and the speedometer soon read eighty—miles or kilometers or something else, he didn't know. He kept at that speed until it was apparent that they weren't being chased.

He slowed down.

"Well," Frank said, "the guy is sure to call the . . . the what? Would he call the army?"

"He might report the incident to the local Committee for the Investigation of Unsocial Behavior," she said. "They might call Constant Struggle."

"Does Constant Struggle patrol the countryside?"

"I don't know."

"That's who picked me up. What were they doing out there? Do you have any idea?"

"No, Frank. I don't."

"Tell me this. Have you ever seen Constant Struggle use force on anyone?"

"No. But I know they come for people."

"They come for people? You mean, they come to take people away?"

"Yes. Maladapts, if they find out they're maladapts."

"What happens to maladapts?"

"I don't know."

"Did you ever know a maladapt who got taken in?"

"Yes, two."

"And did you ever see them again?"

"No."

"Well, that settles that. Are there any prison camps? Internment camps?"

"I don't know, Frank. No one knows about that kind of thing."

"I guess not. But it's my guess that they simply liquidate maladapts."

"Liquidate?"

"They kill them."

"Oh," Alice said in a small voice. "That's probably right, though no one's ever been able to find out."

"Try to eliminate them genetically, so in the future there'll be fewer."

"That's terrible," Alice said.

"Yeah." He coughed. "Oh God, I gotta throw up." He swallowed bile.

"Pull over, Frank," she said.

"No, don't want to take the chance. If I have to puke I'll do it out the window. Hope you don't mind."

"I don't mind."

"The thing is the anxiety, the fear. It's not as powerful as it was that first day, but it's getting to me."

"I don't understand, Frank. You shouldn't have Innerverse at all. You're a maladapt."

"I don't think so. But if so, maybe this is psychological? Psychosomatic? I hope."

"If you're not a maladapt, maybe you have something that's fighting Innerverse."

"I don't know what it could be."

"You must have something."

The road went into a series of turns and the motion sickened him even more. He slowed down, swallowing the lubricating mucus that had worked its way up his esophagus, preparing the way for the return of his breakfast of near-rotten potatoes. Then the road straightened again, his stomach rumbled and the breakfast stayed down. He belched.

"Excuse me. Alice, have the maladapts ever gotten together to do something?"

"Like what?"

"Like a revolution? Guerrilla activity?"

"I don't know what you mean."

"Any attempt to bring down the system. To fight Innerverse."

"But how do you fight something that's inside people?"

She had a point. He belched again, feeling a little better. The road went serpentine once more, climbing a grade. Woods were dense to either side, an occasional connecting dirt road the only break.

"I did see one thing, though, a few years ago. I was at a rally and all of a sudden a woman—I didn't know her—stood up and began screaming, 'Can't you see we're all slaves? Wake up, people! We're slaves and we'll stay slaves forever if none of you do something!' She kept yelling and crying and screaming until some people dragged her away. I think it was a bunch of Constant Struggle people, but I'm not sure."

"All right, what that tells me is that there is physical force used in this society. Control is not complete. That means . . ."

At the top of the hill the woods cleared and they passed through an abandoned hamlet, its weathered houses and stores boarded up and deserted.

The nausea was making a comeback, rising in yet another wave. His heart fluttered like a wounded bird. The anxiety was something alive in him, scrabbling to get out, wanting to scream, to run away.

The road was blocked off ahead with a red paint-slapped wooden barrier. The sign on it said simply ROAD CLOSED. There was no detour.

He smashed through the barrier. Shards of wood fell off the hood and windshield. He was loath to get out and walk just yet. It would be risky traveling an interdicted road, but he wasn't ready to give up the car. Piece of junk though it was, it was something he could control. It obeyed his wishes, responded to the dictates of his body and will. It was power. He felt that if he let go of the steering wheel he would cave in and become some whimpering creature seeking only the alleviation of pain. He was afraid that he would give up and go back, do anything to make the hurt stop, even turn Alice in if it would help. The possibility of that scared him even more than the thought of being caught. He was feeling the lash right now. Would there be greater punishment if he was apprehended? Worse than this? He couldn't imagine it.

He realized he had speeded up. The speedometer read eighty-five. The fuel tank was half full, so no worry there. There was no water temperature gauge, no battery charge meter, but he wasn't particularly concerned with those readings. The car, clunky as it was, seemed to be in passable condition.

He screeched around a turn, braking in and accelerating out. They raced through another ghost village. Why were these sites abandoned? A matter of population decline, or was it part of a plan to redistribute population? Get people out of the countryside and into compounds of high-rises so as to be more easily controlled? Perhaps. There were precedents in Earth history, though sometimes the flow went the other way, from the cities to the country. But dictatorships were notorious for shunting masses of people around, bulldozing villages, deporting ethnic groups. The only people you'd need in the country would be personnel to work the fields of the huge state-run farms, like those he'd seen from the air, and those workers would live in residence complexes. There were no independent farmers, so no quaint farming villages were necessary.

He heard the whine of turbine engines above. He craned his neck to look. A flitter, a vertical takeoff and landing craft, was following, swooping low.

He floored the accelerator, taking the next bend fast enough so that the car went up on two wheels. The vehicle's weight was obviously ill-distributed. Any good car would have taken the curve in stride. He cursed the industrial system that produced such shoddy design and manufacture. It felt good to get angry. Anger fought back the anxiety. Maybe that's what was keeping him going.

"STOP YOUR VEHICLE IMMEDIATELY! PULL OVER TO THE SIDE OF THE ROAD!"

The voice boomed from a loudspeaker on the craft. He pressed his foot against the metal floor.

"PULL OVER OR YOU WILL BE FIRED UPON!"

He glanced at Alice. She looked amazingly calm. What would be her fate? They would probably shoot her up with new nanocomputers, better ones. No more evening walks, no more filching an extra dessert. Not even those peccadilloes would be allowed her then. Would it be better for her to surrender, or to die in a mad attempt to gain her freedom?

"What should I do, Alice?"

She looked at him with defiance in her eyes. As if she'd been reading his mind she said, "Don't let them take us. I'd rather die."

The VTOL fired, the sound like the buzzing of a chain saw. Dust rose from the shoulder. The miss had been deliberate. Frank began swerving all over the road. The craft's guns sounded again, and this time the miss might not have been intentional. Another bend came up, trees intervening between the car and the craft. The gunship veered away.

He looked ahead for cover, for a road to turn into, a building to hide behind, anything. There was nothing but dense forest to either side of the road, which was temporarily to the good, because the gunship had to keep well above the high trees and had a bad firing angle.

"Alice, get down."

She obeyed, tucking herself down between the dashboard and the seat.

The trees gave out and they were in wide-open country. He started weaving again. He couldn't see the gunship but could hear its vacuum-sweeper roar. The forest picked up again about a tenth of a mile down the road, and he decided to trade defensive maneuvering for time. He mashed the pedal and drove straight, hoping to make it to cover before the craft could maneuver for a killing shot.

There wasn't time. When he saw the craft again it was coming straight for him, its gun pods chattering. Asphalt exploded from the road, then the windshield shattered as the gunship whooshed overhead.

He spat out glass. It took him a few seconds to realize that he was miraculously unhurt. Wind from the rent in the glass tore at his face.

"Are you okay?" he yelled.

Alice nodded.

The car reached the trees and he thought that they had gotten through with no extensive damage, but telltale white smoke trailing from the hood told him otherwise. Slugs had probably hit the radiator.

He rolled another quarter mile before a red light appeared on the instrument panel. Engine overheating. A bullet must have taken out a water line. White smoke was billowing out of the hood now. Another red light came on—oil pressure dropping. He wouldn't be able to go another mile at this rate.

The right berm graded off to a steep drop, leading down to woods. He made a decision. He braked and pulled off the road, skidding to a stop.

"Get out!" he told her.

She did, and he put the transmission in neutral, got out, and let the car roll down the slight grade, steering to the right as he walked with the car. The car crossed the berm and headed for the edge. He closed the door and let it go. It rolled down the embankment and crashed through a wall of underbrush, and when it stopped at the bottom of the gully it was wheel-deep in a creek and was very hard to see from the road.

He took Alice's hand and led her down the embankment. She slipped on the loose shale and slid most of the way on the seat of her pants. At the bottom he hoisted her up and they splashed through the creek, ducking into woods.

They clambered up a hill. There was no trail and they had to force their way through weeds and nettle. At the top they went straight until they came to the end of the woods and the edge of an overgrown hayfield.

They went to the left, keeping well inside the tree line. For the next few minutes they ran, trying to get as far from the road as possible.

When they heard the craft, they hid underneath a pine tree. The gunship whined irritably above them, searching the woods. The loudspeaker blared, but the words were indistinguishable. The craft continued its pattern for a good ten minutes before giving up and going away.

They listened to the engine sounds die in the distance. Presently, birds began singing again. A cricket chirped nearby.

They were lying on their bellies on a bed of brown pine needles. He rolled to his side and looked at her.

"You okay?"

She smiled. "Yes. How are you?"

"Adrenalin must do something. I feel better now."

"Good."

"But our situation isn't. We're still a long way from where we want to go, and now they're looking for us."

"We'll make it," she said.

"Yeah, even I'm beginning to believe it."

≽ Chapter Six ≼

There was now no doubt that the Republic resorted to physical force when necessary, and had the means to do so. But Sutter did not know the size and dimensions of that force. Was there a secret army?

Perhaps those UCS invasion troops hadn't mysteriously disappeared at all, but were stopped and overwhelmed by Republican conventional defense forces, not some secret weapon, and not by Innerverse. If this were true, the OSO would be mightily interested to know the size and deployment of those conventional forces.

He couldn't accept it. If there had been a battle, telltale signs would have been in evidence. Satellites would have picked up the flashes of explosions, etc.

No. It was a good bet the flitter that had attacked them was part of a paramilitary force, probably a combined police and paramilitary force. Very small, but effective in concert with Innerverse.

After all, how big a police or militia did you need to keep a rein on a nation of zombies? Aside from a few maladapts like Alice, everyone, having no choice, pretty much kept his nose clean.

Were there other lapses of control, from time to time? Sutter wondered about the incident Alice related, the woman screaming at a solidarity meeting. A sudden failure of Innerverse? Or had it been the sudden onset of schizophrenia? Perhaps Innerverse was not omnipotent on the medical front. Suppose that there were illnesses that it could not overcome. That seemed a good bet, unless medicine in the Republic had taken great leaps ahead of the rest of the world. As far as Sutter knew, cancer and heart disease still led all other afflictions in gathering their yearly harvest of humanity. And there was still practically nothing to be done about serious mental disease.

Okay, it probably wasn't omnipotent. And maybe Innerverse was defective, either in whole or in part. Likely in part. That would explain Sutter's partial immunity, or resistance, or whatever you'd call it.

It was getting unseasonably chilly. A cool spring breeze blew in from the west carrying with it the remembrance of winter and the threat of rain. It was late April and there was still the chance of a cruel sudden freeze at night. Sutter deemed it necessary to find shelter for the night. And not some lean-to, either.

But there were no structures immediately about. What was about were woods—lovely, dark, and deep, but not very inviting with the threat of rain and cold. Branches, budded but barely leaved, ticked and clattered above. Sutter breathed in deeply. Spring. Still cold, yet there was the earthy smell of renewal in the air. The thought of the endless cycle of the seasons gave him comfort. The earth went on, benignly oblivious to what men did.

Too bad the weather hadn't stayed balmy since his arrival.

They walked through tall trees, white pine mixed with oak and beech, Sutter noted. And a few maples. A Midwest boy learns his trees; out on the prairie they are few and far between. Undergrowth was thickening up, but it did not yet provide much cover. The woods were still mostly winter-bare. That would mean that a careful aerial search by flitters might turn up a fugitive couple quite easily, with a little luck. Sutter and Alice had been lucky before. All the more reason to find a roof to put over their heads.

*   *   *

They walked for a good two miles. Neither said very much. Sutter would have enjoyed the walk were it not worrisome to be out in the open.

Then, suddenly, Alice stumbled and yelped, dancing on one foot.

"Sprain something?" Sutter asked.

"Ow, darn it. That hurt."

He sat her down and examined her left ankle, palpating it.

"Oh, that feels good."

"I don't think you sprained anything. Just turned your ankle."

"Oh, keep doing that. My feet are killing me."

Sutter massaged her small foot. It was a nice foot, as feet go. He nursed no foot fetish but he'd always liked women's feet. Usually small, delicate and pretty, against men's, often big and flat and ugly. He suddenly thought of the dead Mexican commando girl. One dainty bare foot sticking out of the filth . . .

He squelched thoughts of the past, put Alice's shoe (God, and what a unattractive, ill-made shoe!) back on her foot, and stood her up.

"Okay?" he asked.

"Okay. I like walking with you. I like walking through the woods. It's so nice. I've never done it before."

"Never?"

"No."

"You've spent all your life in the city?"

"Yes."

"Never even went on a picnic?"

"What's a picnic?"

They walked on. Briefly, the sun came out, peeking through the heavy cloud cover, and the woods became dappled in golden light. Cathedral shafts of light came down and emblazoned a clearing, which the couple skirted, keeping to the deer path that wound around it.

They walked another half-mile before the woods ended abruptly.

A cornfield.

"A farm," Sutter said. "One of the state's, do you think?"

Alice shook her head, "I don't know. I went to an agricultural station on a field trip once but it was one of the ones with greenhouses."

"Are all state farms like that? Don't they grow things in fields?"

"I don't know, really, but the ones I've heard of all do other kinds of farming, 'nonobtrusive,' is what they call it. It's better. It doesn't disturb the earth or other living things that way."

That could explain the paucity of foodstuffs, Sutter thought. If food production was limited to "nonobtrusive" farming or other alternative agricultural techniques.

"How can you grow food 'nonobtrusively'," Sutter wondered aloud.

"Oh, by increasing the amount of food that you can get out of the ground. Intensive agriculture, they call it, instead of this old-fashioned way. See how much land it takes up?"

"Yeah. But it works."

"Sure. It does."

"Then not all agriculture is collectivized or state-run? Is this true, Alice?"

"I don't know. I thought all farms were run by the state."

But apparently that was wrong. The cornfield ran down over a hill, and Sutter climbed two branches up a tree to see over the crest. He glimpsed a shingled roof.

"Farmhouse down there," he said, jumping down.

"It could be a state farm," Alice said. "What should we do?"

"Are you cold?"

"I was before, until the sun came out."

"Well, it'll be dark by eighteen thirty. And it'll get cold tonight. And we'll be hungry. Let's check out that farmhouse."

"Okay."

They came out of the woods and walked over the corn-rows, withered, gray-white stalks crunching under their feet.

"This field is due to be plowed soon, if it's a working farm."

"Can you tell if it is?"

"This looks like last summer's corn."

The farmhouse sat in a hollow of three forested hills. A ramshackle barn stood across a circular turnaround of a dirt road that skirted the cornfield and connected a paved road that wound up the near hill. There was a dreariness to the place, a look of disuse and lack of upkeep. The yard was not mowed, and piles of undifferentiated junk lay heaped to both sides of the barn.

The house looked dark and deserted.

Sutter said, "If those damned boring documentaries are to be believed, there are teams of farm workers that go out to fields and then return home to dormitories at night. Right?"

"Yes."

"But are they working this farm at this time, is the question. They should be. It's planting time. But maybe we have a few days. At any rate, we should be safe for the night."

"I wish I knew more," Alice said. "I don't know very much, do I?"

"In this society, you're lucky if you know the time of day. You have a government that deals wholesale in secrecy. I take that back. I don't know if you have a government at all."

"I don't really know what a government is," Alice said glumly. "Another thing I don't know."

"Never mind. Let's see if we can break into this place. Hope it's not wired with alarms."

The house was two-storied with wood siding of grayish white. It had been kept up fairly well, but had weathered some. All windows were intact, and the doors locked. The house was wired for power, and after a quick search Sutter concluded that the place had no alarm system. But he couldn't be sure. If it were a state-owned farm, it should be protected.

Sutter considered searching the barn first for tools. A crowbar would get them through the front door in a hurry, but he didn't want to leave traces of their visit. The lock was an antiquated thing, and he thought he could pick it with a short length of wire. After scouting the ground around the front porch without finding anything suitable, he took a few steps toward the barn, turned his head to tell Alice, and stopped. With both hands, easily, Alice was lifting the front window, a large double-hung affair. She turned her head and gave him a mischievous smile.

He laughed. "I never thought of the obvious. Have you done much housebreaking, Alice?"

"Never, but I saw this window was lifted a bit. Come on."

He followed her through the window and shut it behind him.

The house was dark even in daylight. Most of the shades were drawn. They had entered a parlor—a front room, shabbily furnished, its walls dark with grime. Still, it looked livable, somehow, though it didn't look lived in. An odor of dust permeated the place. There were three bedrooms upstairs, but only one had a bed in it, along with a battered dresser and a night table holding a candlestick, no candle. The kitchen had an ancient coal stove, a sink with a pump, and little else. The cupboards were empty, as was the larder.

The place was deserted. However, Sutter got an odd feeling that whoever had lived in this house last had tidied up before leaving. However humble the living conditions, this was not squalor. Perhaps the occupants expected to return? And if these occupants were agricultural workers. . . .

Sutter searched every cabinet in the kitchen, finding

nothing. "We need something to eat," he said. "Maybe we can forage something back in the woods."

And maybe those survival courses he took would prove their worth. But the thought of eating wild mushrooms and roots made his already-queasy stomach twinge.

He saw another door. "Let's check the cellar."

The dank, musty cellar turned out to be a cornucopia of jars of preserves, barrels of apples, and bins of grain and potatoes.

They feasted on apples and canned peaches and drank the peach juice left in the cans. There was no coal to fire the stove, so the other provender was unusable for now, but Sutter was determined to have hot food tomorrow—porridge or potatoes or even some fresh meat if he could kill some—and went out for firewood. He found two logs in a long-neglected woodpile near the house, and foraged in some nearby brush for dry kindling. He gathered enough just before rain started to fall, along with night.

The house was completely dark when he reentered, and quiet. He called out for Alice and she answered from upstairs.

"I'm in bed."

He smiled, and went up after fetching matches from the kitchen, lighting his way up the steep, narrow stairs.

She was in bed, bare shoulders sticking out above the covers. He went to the night table and tried lighting the hurricane lamp, after finding to his surprise that there was liquid in the tank on the bottom of the thing. The wick smoldered, spat a few sparks, then lit up, painting the room in orange light. He undressed in a hurry, and, shivering, got in under the tattered covers. The bedclothes smelled the tiniest bit of must and mildew but it was tolerable. He waited until he had warmed up a bit and then wrapped Alice in his arms.

The rain made a soothing patter on the roof. For the first time in a week Sutter felt safe and content.

"How are you feeling?" she asked.

"Mostly okay. Funny, I haven't thought about the nausea in a while. I guess ... I'm *hoping* I've licked Innerverse.''

"No one ever wins against Innerverse," she said. "You just hold out against it."

"Maybe," he said.

"But you must be Immune," Alice said. "That's good. You're like me now."

"I still don't know why I'm immune," he said.

"Nobody knows why. Doesn't matter. Just hold me."

"I will, my darling Alice. I will."

She reached down and handled his already tumescent penis. "I want you to put it in me."

"I'll do that, too."

"I'll do whatever you want and we can make love all night."

"Most of the night. We need sleep."

"We'll sleep all day. Let's never leave here. Let's live here, you and me, forever." She threw her other arm around him, hugged him tight, almost desperately, pressing her head against his chest.

"Forever."

The last thing he heard before finally falling asleep was Alice's gentle breathing and the sound of rain on the roof.

➢ Chapter Seven ◁

"Frank, wake up. Frank?"

Morning hit his eyes. Squinting, he raised his head and nearly bumped his nose against the barrel-end of a shotgun.

The barrel wavered slowly in front of his face. Still straining to see, Frank Sutter looked beyond it to the person holding the gun, trying to bring the image into focus.

It was an elderly man with sparse white hair, skin like yellowed parchment, and sharp blue eyes. He looked over seventy. Behind him stood a woman of about the same age.

"Hello," was all Frank could think to say.

"Who are you?" the man demanded.

"Frank Sutter."

"What are you doing in our house?"

"Sorry. We needed a place to stay last night. We broke in. We took some food. Are you with the Citizen's Committee?"

He snorted. "Nope. This is our place and we don't like people breaking in."

"Look, we're very sorry. We didn't mean any harm. We were in trouble. You say you own this farm?"

"Yeah. Leastwise, the damned government lets us work it. For them, not for us, though they let us keep some stuff."

Despite the gruffness, the man's manner was refreshing to Sutter.

"You don't have Innerverse, do you?"

The man sneered. "Damned right. I'm no zombie. Neither is the missus, here."

"Why not?"

"Damned if I know, though I think it's because we was too old at the time this fool business started. They need us farmers. Their damned state farms are no damned good, so they let some of us alone so's we could feed the bastards."

Frank felt a wave of relief. "I'm glad to meet you, Mr. . . . ?"

"Name's Erickson."

"Mr. Erickson. And that's Mrs. Erickson?"

"You still haven't told me who you are. You don't look like a zombie."

"You can tell?"

"Something funny about the eyes. You don't have it. Neither does she."

"You're right. She doesn't. She's immune, and I think I'm immune, too. Though we're not sure. We ran away."

"Immune. Yeah, I've run into a couple of those. Not many. You say you ran away? Well, you must've licked the devil inside you."

"I'm not a citizen. I'm a spy. I'm an undercover operative for government of the Central United States."

Erickson lowered the shotgun. "I'll be damned. You mean someone in the outside world is actually doing something about this mess we got here? I'd-a give up hope. It's been thirty rotten years. What the hell took you so long?"

"Nobody understands the situation here, Mr. Erickson. They seem to have no idea at all about Innerverse."

Erickson sighed. "I don't blame 'em, I guess. Who the hell could imagine such a thing. Well, anyway. I'm glad to see you. Far as you're breaking in, seeing as what you are—if you are what you say you are—you're welcome in my house anytime, and welcome to stay. Though it's gonna be hard keeping the zombies from knowing, unless we're real cagey about it.''

Frank made a motion to get out of bed but suddenly remembered his nakedness. ''Uh, I'd like to talk with you . . .''

''Wait a minute, let us get out of your way, here. Take your time, come downstairs when you're ready, we'll have breakfast for you.''

''Thank you, thank you very much.''

The elderly couple left and closed the bedroom door.

Frank looked at Alice and smiled. ''Our luck seems to be holding.''

She threw her arms about him and he went over onto his back again.

''Whoa. Can't have a replay of last night, unfortunately. No time.''

''No, I'm just so happy. I've never been happy, really happy.''

''I know, dear. It's not a happy world. Let's get dressed.''

Breakfast was simple, but good: smoked bacon, scratch biscuits spread with bacon drippings—or peach preserves, or strawberry preserves—hard-cured smoked ham, summer sausage, and a brewed grain beverage. The ham and bacon were good, and the sausage had a flavor all its own, hinting at sage and rosemary and other things. Heated up, it was delicious. All the foodstuffs were of a kind that could be stored for long periods without refrigeration. Sutter wolfed it all down. It was the first decent meal he'd had in a week.

The grain beverage was fair, much better than the swill Frank had choked down in the cafeteria.

''There hasn't been any coffee to be had here in thirty years,'' Erickson said. ''Getting harder to get stuff all the time. Meat, for instance. Government's phasing out meat production of all kinds. One day there'll be no beef cattle, no hogs, no nothing. And then they'll go after poultry. I got that bacon trading with other independent farmers, and the missus made the pork sausage herself out of scraps we got from two friends of ours that work in probably the last slaughterhouse there'll ever be in this area.''

"I still don't quite understand why you don't have Innerverse," Frank said.

"Never had it.''

"I thought they inoculated everyone with Innerverse.''

"Most everyone. But when this thing started, seemed like they decided to spare the older folks. We was over forty then. Like I said, I don't understand it myself, but they let us alone. I figure they needed to leave some independent people, especially farmers. They got some strange notions about farming, I'll tell you. No wonder half the population is starving.''

"Is it? I didn't see any evidence of it in the city.''

"No, they eat, but what they eat is hog slop. Nobody eats a proper diet anymore. No meat, no dairy, no nothing but that vegetable glop that comes out of vats in the food processing plants.''

"I saw fresh vegetables being grown, though I didn't see much in the stores.''

"Hell, half of it rots before it gets to the store, and what's left gets grabbed up the first day it hits the shelves. Yeah, they raise all kinds of stuff at those agricultural stations, those damned silly hothouses and hydro . . . whatever they call it.''

"Hydroponics?''

"Yeah, but they got all sorts of other ways of growing every damned fool thing they can think of, except food people want to eat.''

"Vegetables are supposed to be healthier, I guess.''

"Sure, they're healthy, and you need 'em. But by God, you gotta eat other things. The puzzle of the whole thing is that fresh vegetables is what they always run short of. I never did figure it out.''

Sutter said, "Mr. Erickson, this house was empty last night. How long have you and Mrs. Erickson been away?"

"All winter. They only let us live here during growing season. We have an apartment about ten miles away. Rat trap of a place."

"We live for when we can come here," Mrs. Erickson said, still busy at the stove, frying up more sausage. "When they let us come here." She was a large, gray-haired, buxom woman with a pleasant smile.

"But they're not going to let us do it forever," Mr. Erickson said. "One of these days they're going to tell us this will be our last season on the farm. They'll take it over, and that'll be that. Neither of us have much time left, but we'd like to spend it in peace, living on this place. After all, damn it, it's ours. It was my dad's and his dad's before that. It ain't right. It just ain't right." He shook his head wearily.

"I don't understand something," Frank said. "You don't have Innerverse. Why don't you up and leave?"

"We wouldn't get far. The damned army—I call it the army, but it's more like police and army combined—they'd turn us right back. We first tried to leave back when the strange stuff started."

"What happened to you?"

"Nothing. In any other country around the world, in any other dictatorship, they'd do the decent thing and shoot you. Not this damned hell of a country. They'd just make you a zombie like the rest." Erickson inclined his head toward his wife. "They told us that, told us what they'd do if we try to escape. And they keep reminding us now and then what they'd do to Controls who try to leave. They call us Controls, people that they didn't inoculate back at the start. Funny, calling us that. We're *not* controlled, and most everybody else is. Well, Sarah and I vowed we wouldn't let them. I still have a gun, and we'd use it. On ourselves. We'd rather die than be slaves."

"They never threatened to kill you?"

"Nope. Never. They say the government is the way it

is to eliminate the need for violence entirely. That's what they say.''

"Well, somebody shot at us," Sutter said.

"Do they know you're a spy?"

"Yeah."

"Maybe that's why."

"Must be. But that means they still have uses for violence."

"Oh, I never believed 'em about that no-violence stuff. That's flapdoodle. Anytime they want to kill us, me and Sarah, that's fine. Like I said, we'd rather die than be slaves."

Mr. Erickson took a long drink of grain brew. "All the same, we don't want to provoke 'em, either. As long as they leave us pretty much alone and let us stay on our land."

"You don't think you could make it across the border? It's not far."

"No. Oh, we could make tracks, and we could get fairly close, but sooner or later some snoop would look at us and say, who are those people, they don't belong here, and call some damned Citizen's Committee or another. And we'd get reported, and that'd be all she wrote. Another thing about this hellhole is that nobody, but nobody can mind their own God damned business. They snitch, they tattle, they poke their big noses in. Damned bunch of busy-bodies. Have some more sausage, Alice."

"Thank you. Oh, this is good. I've never had real meat before. Just stuff that's supposed to taste like it, only it tastes awful."

Mr. Erickson gave Sutter a wry look. "See?"

"Believe me," Sutter said with a laugh, "I've sampled what passes for food in the Republic. I know all about it. I got sick just about every time I ate."

"Damned shame."

"Tell me this, Mr. Erickson. You were around back when this all started. How exactly did it start?"

"You mean Innerverse? Hard to say. Sarah and I kept

as low as we could during the riots and all, not that anything much happened around here. Except one day the
army showed up in Sturkeyville and took over, and they
set up inoculation stations, to combat the cholera and the
typhoid fever, they said. Bubonic plague, too. They said
that broke out in the west. All this stuff was going around,
they told us. They inoculated most everybody under the
age of forty, including our son and daughter. Jim had just
turned twenty and Susan was eighteen, I think. And they
put up posters about a new government, a permanent government, and they called it Innerverse. Nobody knew what
in the hell they were talking about. Well, we found out in
time. The young people started to act funny as hell, Jim
and Susan included. Did everything that the government
told them to do, followed orders to the letter, no com-
plaints. It was odd. Real odd. And I still don't really
understand what exactly they did to them.''

"Does the word 'nanotechnology' mean anything to
you?''

"Yup, but don't know what it means. What does it
mean?''

"I'm not entirely sure myself," Sutter told him. "But
generally speaking, it's tiny little machines that get inside
you and control you.''

Erickson nodded. "Yeah, that sounds about right. I
guess that's the way I've heard it, now that I think about
it. Though I never understood how you could make machines tiny enough to get inside a human body.''

"Have you ever found out anything about where the
machines come from?''

"Nope. For years everybody thought it was space
aliens.''

"Do you think that's who's behind it?''

"No, don't think that any more. Used to, but I haven't
seen any space aliens.''

Sutter was thoughtful. "I wonder if aliens come in very
small sizes.''

"Could be," Erickson said. "Maybe they do. I give up

thinking about it long ago. Don't matter to me who's behind it. Whoever they are, I'd like 'em dead. They oughtn't to do this to people. Ain't right.''

Sutter nodded, chewing biscuit. He washed it down with the grain beverage and was done eating.

"You say the army showed up," Sutter said, "but you haven't seen it since. There must still be an army today."

"But you never see 'em. That's the real hell of it. You never see anyone in authority. You never see guns. You never see tanks. You don't see a damned thing, but those faces, those zombie faces, smiling all the time and being so damned happy about this and that and everything. Makes you sick, all that happiness, 'cause it's all phony. They ain't happy, no happier than Sarah and me. And we ain't happy at all.''

"You've never seen any display of force since Innerverse took over?"

"Not even a police car. Don't know what happened to the police. We've heard stories, though. We've heard stories of police coming at night to take people away. People . . . I'm afraid to say it—like Alice, here. People that the little buggers don't have a hold of.''

Sutter nodded. "And in all that time since they took over, you've never had a clue as to who's behind it all.''

"Heard stories, like I said. First it was the Devil. Then it was space critters.''

"The Devil?"

"What you call the Antichrist. Like in the Bible, in Revelations. We all thought it was the end of the world back then, with all the fighting in the cities, people killing each other, and the diseases going around, and the government shot to hell. Well, some of the more religious folk started saying that the end of the world was here. The Tribulations. I was ready to believe it. And then when the army showed up and everything quieted down so sudden, it seemed like something happened, like someone come on the scene. The religious folks started saying it was the Antichrist. And then . . . this is funny, not so long after that, they switched to saying it was Jesus come again. They flip-flopped real quick. With all that sudden peace, it must be the peace of Jesus, they said. The Kingdom, they called it. Most of us didn't know what to think. And then it started getting so peaceful it was downright peculiar. Something not right about it. That's when somebody, I don't know who, said it was space critters. And then . . . nothing. Jesus never came down from the clouds. Nobody knew what the hell it was, and it's been that way ever since."

Sutter took a pensive drink of the last of his beverage. "Thanks, Mr. Erickson. You've told me a lot."

Mrs. Erickson asked, "What do you plan to do, Frank?"

Frank shrugged. "We don't have a plan right now. We have to cross the border into the Central States. I have to report back on what I've found out."

"You say you're a spy. Are you with the CIA?"

"The CIA ceased to exist years ago. Intelligence is mostly handled by the military now. That's the way it should be, I think. My outfit is called the Office of Secret Operations. OSO. We report directly to the Joint Chiefs of Staff, who report directly to the President."

"Damn. There's still a President of the United States?"

"Has been all along."

"Congress?"

Frank sighed. "Yeah, we still have them, too. Don't think they've changed much over the years. Still squabbling and generally gumming up the works."

"I'd kiss every one of 'em now," Mr. Erickson said. "I'd give my right arm to sit in the gallery and watch the United States Congress go about its business. Thought they were one with the dodo. They don't tell us *anything* here. No news. No news at all. Damn, it's been bad." He wiped a sudden tear from his eye.

"Don't worry. We'll do something sooner or later," Sutter assured him.

"We got but little time left, me and the wife. You'd better get to it soon."

"We'll give it a try. But I have to get back first and report. How we're going to do that is a problem, though. We have to steal another vehicle. Trouble is, there's so little traffic—"

"If you stole one, they'd catch you for sure," Mr. Erickson said. "But if you had your own—"

"Eh?"

"We have an old truck in the barn. Hasn't run in years, but it could be made to run, 'cause I have the right parts stowed away. Some of 'em are buried, like the distributor and other stuff. But I can get 'em pretty quick and put that truck engine back together. We've been saving it for a quick getaway, but your getting back is more important."

"Wouldn't want to leave you here without any chance of escaping someday."

"Don't you worry about us. Like I said, Sarah and I are determined not to let 'em take us. We're old—I'm nearly eighty, did you know that?"

Sutter was mildly astonished. "You don't look it."

"We've lived our lives, no regrets. If they come for us, for helping you out, that'll be the end. That right, Sarah?"

"Like we always said, John." Sarah told him, sitting down at the table to eat. She beamed at Frank and Alice. "Like we always said."

⋙ Chapter Eight ⋘

The truck was an ancient Ford pickup, dented and battered, afflicted with rust spots, but essentially intact, for all that its paint had faded from red to a dull red-orange. It was propped up on concrete blocks, no tires, no battery, no ignition wiring. The model year must have dated to the 1980's or before. Though hardly expert on antique vehicles, Sutter deemed its vintage very possibly before 1980.

All the missing vital parts were well hidden away, as Erickson claimed, but it took him little time to retrieve everything needed. He allowed it would take him a day, with help, to get the vehicle running again. Gasoline and oil were on hand.

The toughest job was mounting tires, fetched from the barn's cellar, on wheels that had been stored in a tool shed. There was a tire-mounting anvil to facilitate the job, but it took work.

"These front tires are worn pretty bad, but it's not likely to snow this time of year," Mr. Erickson said. "Just take it easy on rainy roads. Take those bends real slow."

"Right. You say your farmhands could show up any day? We should come up with a story of some kind."

"You're my son, and Alice is my daughter. Simple. They won't know, though they might wonder what you're doing here. We'll have to say that I took ill. They let families visit sometimes."

"Sometimes?"

"Yeah. Ordinary family ties aren't thought much of these days, at least not around here. We're all one big family, they say."

"Do you ever see your son and daughter?"

"Every once in a while. They usually don't come here, usually the apartment. Tell you the truth, I don't like seeing them, ever since they got sucked up into whatever it is that's controlling them."

"It's uncomfortable for you?"

"Yeah. You got to watch what you say to them. I think it's that happy talk they talk all the time, that bothers me. 'Getting better and better,' and all that bosh. Gets to me. Half the time I wind up wishing they'd leave as soon as they come. Damned shame, but that's the way it is."

"I hope we can leave before anyone shows up."

"We'll try. I got a message in the house says the hands won't show up for another two days. They usually stick real close to schedules."

"I know it."

"So, it's up to us to get you two motoring before day after tomorrow. Help me with this jack."

"Sure. I'll need to be looking at a map at some point."

"Got all you need up the house. Fastest way would be to take the old Interstate, if it's still open. West. But . . ."

Sutter thought of the flitter and its chattering gun pods. "Too easy to be spotted. We'd probably be the only thing on that road heading west."

"That's what I was thinking," Mr. Erickson said. "Then you take back roads, and I got some fairly good maps. Only thing, they're thirty years out of date. No telling what roads are still open."

"I'd rather take our chances on the back roads than risk an empty highway."

"You'd be right. But no one's gonna know that you're in this truck, remember that. They're probably still looking for that buggy you heisted."

"If they haven't found where we abandoned it."

"Now, where did I put that distributor cap?"

They worked well into the night. No farm hands showed up, nor any by the next morning. Frank and Alice spent another night in the Erickson's big double bed, the old couple taking the spare bedroom. They didn't make love, just held each other all night, Frank listening to the quiet cheeping of frogs courting in a pond or marsh somewhere out there. At least he thought it was frogs. Or toads, or whatever raises a soft din in the spring night.

Everyone was up by six. Mr. Erickson and Frank went out to the barn to run a final check on the old pickup. The valves clicked like an old alarm clock but the engine ran smoothly enough.

"I timed that sucker pretty well," Mr. Erickson said. "I think I have a can of gunk to seal up those valves, too."

Mrs. Erickson loaded the cab with an assortment of victuals: hams, preserves, fresh biscuits, sausage, apples, and potatoes, and onions.

"You can roast these over an open fire," she said of the last two items. "If you want to risk a fire."

"Maybe we can find another unoccupied house," Frank said.

"You gotta watch who you run into," Mr. Erickson said. "You can't trust no one. You lucked out with us, but . . ."

"I know. Well, we owe you our lives."

"Don't you never mind about that. Glad to help. Here, you might need this."

Erickson pulled an automatic pistol out of his jacket and handed it to Frank. Then he fetched out a cardboard box and handed it over, too.

"Ammo for it. That's all I got. Just enough to fill the clip twice."

Sutter examined the weapon. It was a Glock 9-millimeter, semi-automatic. Light, sturdy, and dependable.

"My dad's old gun. Good luck to you."

"Thanks, hope I won't need to use it."

"Okay," Mr. Erickson said. "Remember, you got enough gas for about seven hundred miles if you take it steady. Twenty in the tank, two ten-gallon jerry cans in the back. Take 'er easy, and check these lashings on the cans once in the while. You don't want 'em to come loose.''

"Right."

"Very nice to have you stay with us." Mrs. Erickson said. "Come back when the world is right again."

"We will," said Alice as she hugged Mrs. Erickson.

"God willing, it will be right someday," Mr. Erickson said, clasping Frank's hand.

Frank smiled at him. "You're sure there is a God, aren't you?"

Erickson nodded. "I've seen the devil. If there's a devil, I figure there must be a God."

The countryside was webbed with red and blue lines, a thousand two-lane asphalt roads, going every which way. At least that's how it appeared on their tattered, yellowed map. But after traveling only two hours, Frank and Alice came to the glum realization that most of those little blue and red lines were fictitious.

You could see where a road had been; the cut banks were still visible, but the roadway itself was a ribbon of new growth between taller trees, interspersed with patches of bare asphalt or concrete. Most roads were completely overgrown, the pavement broken up into rubble.

The still-existing roads were in poor shape, if they hadn't been abandoned long ago to gravel or just dirt. But most of them were passable. The government needed to keep some roads open, it seemed—though, obviously, a high-speed efficient highway system was a thing of the past in the Republic. Sutter wondered how foodstuffs and other necessities were transported around the country, to the cities. He concluded that most cities were more or less self-sufficient. Crazy system, he thought. If you didn't have something locally, you didn't have it at all. Rather limits one's diet and other discretionary choices. But self-sufficiency has its advantages. From the point of view of military strategy, cities could withstand sieges much better. It would be harder for an enemy to disrupt the country with strategic bombing.

But the more Frank thought about it, the more he deemed the extreme decentralization part of a wilder philosophical point of view. Transportation consumes energy, and energy is expensive. Eliminate the need for a nation on wheels and you save piles of money, not to mention saving the natural world from some nasty pollution.

Almost the same thing had happened in the Central States. When the reserves of overseas oil had finally run dry, the old mobile ways had died a quick death. Tractor-semitrailers still plied the highways, but their numbers were far, far fewer than in trucking's heyday, in the last century. The permanent energy shortage had brought about the rebirth of the railroads, now the pride of the Central States. Brightly painted stock of the Illinois Central Railroad rolled out of Chicago on meticulously maintained track that stayed meticulous all the way down to New Orleans and all the way out to Denver. Railroad accidents were few and far between.

And the trains rolled on time, or heads did.

He had not seen a train or heard mention of any railroads so far in the Republic of Innerverse. But surely there were trains here. How else did they move heavy equipment? Raw materials? Whatever oil was needed?

Unless they didn't move anything at all. But that was silly, was it not?

They had to move something.

"It's so pretty," Alice said. "I've never seen so many trees in one place."

"This is a very wild part of the country. I'm from the Midwest and you don't see this kind of vegetation much."

"What's it like, your part of the country?"

"It's another country, Alice. It's the United Central States of America. What you're looking at used to be part of the old United States. Which neither of us remembers."

"No."

"They tell you much about how it used to be?"

"No. Except that it was all part of the Old Way."

"What's that?"

"The way things used to be. The way things were done. The Old Way."

"And Innerverse is the New Way?"

"Yes. A new way of living and working and organizing. A New Society."

"I got a taste of that sort of propaganda, from the tube."

"What's propaganda?"

"You get only one side of an issue."

"I see. I never thought about it, but I guess there could be two sides of something. People look at things different ways."

"Exactly. But with Innerverse, like you said, there's only one way. Propaganda."

"That's not good."

"No."

"People should leave people alone, mostly," Alice said. "Except when they need help."

"Good plan to follow. You know, seems to be I remember the phrase 'New Society' from history." Sutter thought about it. "No, it was New . . . oh, something. Or the Great Society? I dunno. I get those mixed up. You weren't even taught history and you probably know about as much as I do." Sutter laughed sardonically. "Anyway, I know that this isn't the first time that somebody threw away the old deck and brought out a brand new one. 'New Deal,' that was it. Roosevelt. But it wasn't anything like Innerverse. Something different. But so was the original American Revolution. That was something radical, different. A whole new way of working things. That part of history I know fairly well. Washington, Jefferson, Adams, Kennedy. . . ."

"You must know a lot." Alice was impressed.

"Public school education. It's pretty indifferent, really.

Spotty as hell. I got fairly good grades, then I went to college. University of Illinois.''

"What's college?''

He looked at her. "It's amazing ... I'm sorry, but I can't understand how they could keep so many people in the dark for so long.''

"It's easy with Innerverse," she said simply.

"Right. I know only too well.''

"Don't you like me anymore?''

He reached over and caressed her short blond hair. "Alice, honey, don't ever say that again.''

"Ok, I won't.''

➢ Chapter Nine ≼

The blue car started following them near what had once been Morgantown. Frank had decided to dip south and cross the border from West Virginia, after hitting any number of dead ends heading west in Pennsylvania. It seemed that no roads went west in that state. Or perhaps those that formerly did were cut off.

He had no reason to believe that West Virginia would be different, but there was not much else to do but try. If it was no go down here, they'd head back north again and drive all the way to the last dead end, abandon the truck and go on foot. They had enough provisions, and he thought they could carry enough to survive. The problem of shelter might ease with milder weather, which seemed to be in the offing. Nights would still be cold, though. Well, they'd have to do it somehow. There was no going back.

The truck had a simple feature that greatly aided navigation: on the dash there was mounted a cheap, plastic ball compass. No need to stop and take readings with the pocket compass Mr. Erickson had given him.

The chances of their making it across the border seemed good.

But if there was a Republican army, and it was lurking near the border, sight unseen, that might be another problem.

However, the immediate problem was that blue car. It

appeared to be some kind of official government vehicle. Had that dreary, dull-painted look about it. But not a cop car or a military vehicle. It could simply be a nosy citizen.

Frank sped up a little, took the next bend on the fast side, then gave a glance to the rear view mirror.

The car seemed to be pacing him.

"What kind of vehicle is that, Alice?"

She had been looking through the back window.

"I don't recognize it as anything special," she said. "It looks like the kind of car my boss drives."

"He rates a car?"

"It's a she. Yes, she has one. You have to be pretty high up in rating. CW-fourteen or higher."

"CW? Citizen . . . ?"

"Citizen Worker. We're all Citizen Workers, but with different ratings."

"What's yours?"

"Nine. Pretty high up, but I had a ways to go."

"That means whoever that is must be pretty high up. An official, probably. And it looks as though he's taken an official interest in us. Or she."

Frank braked a bit, still looking at the rear view. "He. Yeah, looks like a man. One man. Okay, I don't think we're going to have any immediate trouble."

Suddenly the car sped up and drew up almost to the truck's bumper. A horn sounded.

"Spoke too soon."

Frank poked his head out his window, looking up and down the road. "Nobody about."

"You're stopping?" Alice said, puzzled.

"No choice. Can't outrun him. So . . ."

"Frank, if we just keep on going, maybe—"

"I don't see him with a radio in there. But sooner or later he'd just stop and report us."

"Frank, I'm scared."

"Don't worry about it. I think I can talk my way out of it."

Frank pulled the truck onto the rutted dirt shoulder and

turned off the engine. The car pulled up behind and its motor died. Frank watched the man get out of the car and begin to walk toward the truck. He was dressed in the standard dingy blue utility suit.

Frank opened the door and got out, grinning.

The man raised a hand. "Hello, Citizens!" His smile was bright and cheery.

"Better and better, Citizen," Frank told him. "Always better."

"Reason I stopped you, I wanted—"

Frank's first shot caught the man in the right pectoral. He stopped as if he'd run into something, then began to stagger backwards, his face registering vague surprise.

Frank squeezed off another shot, aiming carefully for the sternum. The man fell over backward and sprawled in the mud. Frank took a few steps and watched him, tucking the Glock back into the inside pocket of the denim jacket that Mrs. Erickson had insisted on giving him.

The man's mouth was open, his eyes staring skyward. Frank watched as the man's chest heaved violently and then, suddenly, went still. The legs twitched a few times and a gurgling sound issued from the dead throat.

Frank looked up and down the road. Nothing. He got back into the truck.

Alice had watched the event with interest. Her blue eyes were wide open.

"I've never seen someone kill anyone before."

"So, how was it?"

"Didn't look like anything. I expected more blood."

"There usually isn't, at least not right away. I must say, you're taking it calmly."

"It wasn't anything, really. That gun made a loud noise, though. It made me jump. I didn't know you were going to do it."

"I had to. He could have just wanted to tell me the back tires were low . . . but they aren't, of course. No, he wanted to ask questions, and we don't have answers. The only thing I'm thinking about is whether to take his car.

But when he doesn't report on time for the next item of his agenda, they'll know something's bad, and an all-points bulletin might go out, and they'll be looking for an official car that's going somewhere that doesn't look official. Damn it, hard to decide what to do when you just don't know anything about the situation you're in." He shook his head. "No, we stay with the truck, but we have to ditch the body and the car. Come on, help."

They dragged the man back to his car and dumped him in the back seat. They got in and Frank drove down the road a piece, found a dirt turn-off to the right, and took it. He eased the car off the narrow trail, into the bushes. They both slid out the driver's door, and Frank re-arranged brush around the car until it was hard to spot standing only a few feet away.

They hiked back to the truck, got in, and drove on. No other vehicles had passed during the interlude.

"Have any idea what he was, Alice? What kind of official, what his job was?"

Alice shook her head. "Hard to tell. You can't tell much by looking at people. We all dress the same. No class distinctions."

"Right. Everybody's equal."

"It's better that way, I guess. Better than the old way, when some people had better clothing than others. There are some things about Innerverse that aren't so bad."

"There's always something good to say about almost anything. But I'd like to know about that guy. I sure hope he wasn't just being friendly. No good deed goes unpunished."

"He's better off," Alice said grimly. "Anything's better than Innerverse. I know I just said there were some good things, but it's not worth it. Not worth the unhappiness. The emptiness. The feeling that . . . that there's no purpose in living. That's the thing I couldn't stand. But it's all right now. I'm leaving this place. And I love you."

She threw her arms about him and kissed him on the cheek.

"I love you. God, we're like some trigger-happy hood and his moll. We just killed a man. I did."

"We did. I was with you."

"Don't tell me you like it."

"No, I was afraid and a little sick. I feel sorry for him, in a way, but like I said, he's better off."

"I hope so. I'll never know. I'm tired of killing people."

"Are you? Did it make you sick?"

"You mean Innerverse sick? No. Funny enough."

"You're Immune, you know. That proves it. You couldn't have done it if Innerverse was still inside you."

"How does Innerverse know what I'm going to do before I do it?"

"It reads your soul. When you want to kill someone you're angry with that person. Innerverse reads the anger."

"I shot him in cold blood, honey. I'm capable of it. How did Innerverse know I was going to do it?"

"It only takes a second to sense what you're going to do," Alice said.

"But what's it sensing? Must be some subliminal reaction. When you kill, even in cold blood, there must be a whole hell of a lot of things going on in the nervous system, in the brain, and that stuff happens real fast. I think I understand. Amazing, really."

"Innerverse doesn't allow any strong emotions. Not even extreme happiness. It keeps you on an even keel. You don't swing from one extreme to another. Sometimes I wish that part of it was working in me. I got so unbearably unhappy sometimes."

"Everyone on an even keel. No ups, no downs. No happiness, and no unhappiness either. Trouble is, that's not life."

"No, it isn't. It's death. That man you shot was already dead."

"Anyway, good to know I finally licked the damn thing. I haven't felt any pain or nausea for a good long time."

"I'm glad, too. I want you and me to be the same."
"Looks like we are. Two desperate fugitives."

They stopped to eat late that afternoon, pulling well off the road, among a copse of tall pine. They ate the biscuits and little else. Neither was very hungry, though Frank had a sudden craving for a beer. He suppressed it and kept watching the road.

"Well, should we try to find someplace for the night, or push on?"

Alice shrugged. "I want to get across into your country as soon as possible. I don't want to stay another night here."

"Absolutely. We drive on. We'd be there already if we had a straight road. Ooops, looks like rain."

A few viscid drops had spattered the windshield. Frank and Alice watched them form tiny branching rivulets and run down the glass.

"With any luck it won't be a downpour. Anyway, I won't stop for anything. I just wish we could find a damned road that goes some distance west."

They found such at the next intersection, a junction. The western stretch of road looked in fair shape as far as they could see, which was not far, but it did look promising. Frank wheeled left and sped down the road.

Rain began a steady beat against the roof of the truck's cab.

Dark clouds were moving above the trees, and the countryside was darkening fast. In short order rain began to hammer at the windshield, a sudden wind flattening the water into sheets. Frank searched the dash for a control for the windshield wipers. He found none. But there was a lever on the steering column that has no function he could readily see. He pulled it down, and it clicked, and he heard a mechanical groan come from the front of the dashboard. Wipers came up and swept the windshield, once, twice. Once again.

And did no good at all.

"Worn blades in the wipers," Frank said. He flicked on the high beams and strained to see through the distorting refractions of swirling water.

"I can't see a thing," Alice said.

"Me neither, but we gotta push on. With any luck it'll blow over."

The rainstorm moved in from the west, crashing with thunder, spinning wicked webs of lightning. Rain lashed the road and wind whipped the trees crazily.

"Getting sorry we didn't take the car," Frank said ruefully. "Damn, this is worse than I thought."

The high beams sent back blank white light, reflecting off the sheets of rain. It looked like a cold rain, with drops that might contain a grain of hail. It ticked against the metal of the truck body. He took the beat of the wipers up another notch, maximum speed, but that did little good.

He pulled over.

"Wait till it passes. It's heading east."

He put his arms around Alice and they waited. He kissed her a few times and fondled her breasts. She grinned and put her tongue in his ear.

"This is cozy," he said, "but let's hope it blows over soon."

It did not. If anything, a harder rain began falling, making a steady rattle against the truck and raising a din in the treetops. In the headlights, splashes jumped out of puddles along the shoulders ahead, sparkling and glistening.

"Really coming down," Frank said. "Wish I knew what to do."

"You can't drive in this."

"You're right. Not without windshield wipers. We either have to find some quick, steal 'em, or put up for the night."

"Where would we steal some?"

"No likely victims in sight. Guess we put up. There was a sign back a little ways. Old one, falling apart. It said RESORT, I think."

"What's that?"

"Could be an old hotel. Hope so. There was a road going off to the right. Let's try it."

Frank swung the truck around and headed back the way they'd come. He drove for about half a minute.

"Damn, missed it, I think. You could barely see it, as I remember."

Frank found a wide section of shoulder to turn around again. He slowed to a crawl and peered out through the sheets of rain.

"See anything, Alice?"

"No . . . wait . . . No, that's . . . oh, is this it?"

Frank stopped dead.

"I think . . . Yes! Resort . . . what does that say? Franklin Springs Resort. Never heard of the place. But let's see what's up the road."

It was barely a road, a gravel path hung over with flailing trees. The overhang held off the worst of the downpour, though, and visibility went up a degree or two. The headlights showed up the twisting and turning well. At some points the gravel gave way to huge puddles and stretches of mud. But the old pickup splashed and spun its way through these easily enough. Then a few big rocks supplied some nasty shocks, and Frank slowed. Something was looming through the trees.

"A big house," Alice said.

It was big, whatever it was. An old Victorian hotel, as it turned out, many-gabled and capacious, but in a startling state of disrepair, as seen by lightning flash. One whole section of roof had collapsed.

"No one could be here," Frank said.

The place was entirely dark. Shutters flapped and eaves dripped.

"Christ, looks like something out of a horror movie."

"Frank, this place scares me."

"What I said."

≽ Chapter Ten ≼

Pistol in hand, Frank kicked the front door of the old hotel, and it swung open to reveal nothing but darkness inside. Alice snapped a flashlight on and shined the beam through the doorway.

"Place is big enough to hide an army," he said.

"Looks like no one's home."

"Hasn't been anyone home here for decades."

They walked cautiously into a large foyer that had a counter running along the far wall. To the left a sweeping staircase mounted to a wide landing. Behind the counter, a doorway led to a back office.

"The lobby," Frank said.

The room still had an opulent charm to it. Moldy red damask covered the walls. As Alice played the flashlight's beam around the place, the staircase's brass railing glinted and light sparkled in the cut glass of a big chandelier hanging from the middle of the ceiling.

"Bed and breakfast," Frank said. "All I want's a bed. First, though, let's see what's over here."

The room to the right was the bar and dining room. Half the roof was off. But most of the tables and chairs were still set up, as if waiting for ghostly clientele.

"I think the rain's stopping."

Frank cocked an ear. It was letting up a little.

"Now, upstairs."

"Frank, I'm afraid."

102

"You want to sleep in the truck?"

"I don't mind."

"Let me check upstairs first."

"I'm going with you."

"Okay. Stay close. Watch where you step."

"Yes, Frank."

"Just keep the light pointed ahead."

"Nice rug. I've never seen carpeting like that."

"Used to be a nice place."

"These stairs creak."

"Shush. If there is somebody here . . ."

"Sorry."

They mounted the stairs, feet quiet on the plush carpeting. The stairs groaned alarmingly under them. Frank stopped, bouncing on the balls of his feet. The old wood complained again, then ceased.

"Hope this staircase is sound."

"You think?"

"Step lightly."

They continued and reached the landing, at the far end of which a doorway gave onto a long hallway.

"Hell, we can't check every room in this place."

"We only need one."

"If there's anyone here, they've heard us for sure. But they're not making a sound."

Frank felt guilty, taking chances like this. He should be in here by himself, checking the place. But the rambling hotel had looked entirely deserted from the outside.

Derelicts squatting here? Did this society have derelicts? He didn't know. It seemed unlikely. Then who could be lurking about? Surely not the police or army.

Immunes? Runaway "Controls"? In either of those cases there was probably nothing to fear.

"Pick a room, any room."

"Frank, open that door."

"Sure."

With one foot, Frank eased the door open. Alice shined the flashlight into the room.

It was a typical hotel room with two windows, both broken, empty but for debris on the floor.

"Something tells me this place has been stripped, long ago."

"Try this one."

The big door creaked almost comically. Inside was a bedframe with no mattress. More litter.

"A little better. Let's check them all."

Five minutes later they came across a room with a mattressed bed. There was nothing else but some dust on the floor. The windows were intact. The bed looked dry.

"I'll get the blankets."

"Frank, don't leave me."

"Never, dear." Frank walked to the bed and sat on it. The mattress sagged deeply. "I don't know how much sleep we can get on this."

"I'm so tired I could sleep standing up. Forget the blankets."

Alice lay down beside him and hugged him.

"Gotta hide the truck."

"Do you have to?"

"Have to. Get up, Alice."

"Frank, I'm so tired."

"Let's do it or we'll never get up till morning."

Alice yawned.

Then she said, "Kiss me."

He did, and afterward he jumped up and dragged her off the bed to her feet. She giggled.

They walked back down the sumptuous, creaking staircase and went outside. The rain had let up considerably, but the lightning was still active far off, throwing huge blue flames up at the sky. Frank started the truck and followed a brick driveway to the side of the hotel, where a garage stood with its door open, as if waiting for them.

"This will do nicely."

He eased the truck inside. They got out. Frank waited till Alice had got some things, and then pulled down the rotting but still intact garage door. It slid down into place and blocked any view of the truck inside.

"Good enough."

On the way back up to the room, Frank shut the front door and wedged a strip of baseboard between the bottom edge and the floor. That would impede any intruder. Though it was an empty gesture, as he had not even checked the back of the place for entrances. He decided to throw caution to the winds. It would take him an hour to thoroughly case the joint. There were probably any number of ways to get in and he wasn't going to go bumbling around in the dark and rain.

They spread blankets and crawled into bed and listened to the sounds the ramshackle building made, turning their heads to every creak and shudder.

Presently, they relaxed a little. The rain continued, softly and steadily.

"Do you think we'll ever get to your country, Frank?"

"Yeah. Don't worry about it. I'll get you out."

"What will we do?"

"Do?"

"Can I live with you?"

"Uh . . . well, we'll see."

"I'd like that."

Frank realized she was like a child in many ways. But somehow her simplicity was attractive. It reassured him. She was a normal, uncomplicated human being, not some smiling automation. The horror of this "Republic" reared its head anew for him as the thought of the millions of people in it and their hopeless plight.

He had not given any deliberation to Alice's fate when they reached safety. What was he going to do with her? Then, slowly, he came to realize that he did want to live with her. He felt responsible. He wondered if she could live on her own, make her own decisions, after a lifetime of having every decision made for her. And what about her countrymen? They were in the same boat. If and when

Innerverse passed, would they all be marionettes without strings, lifeless, helpless?

Something crashed in the next room and Alice yelped.

Frank sprang out of bed and went to the door, pistol in hand. After poking his head out into the hallway, he moved to the door of the next room down the hallway, paused, and listened.

Then he stepped back a little, kicked the door open, and dashed into the room.

No one was there. There was a bed in this room too, plus a chest of drawers. A pile of rubble lay in the middle of the floor. Frank looked up. Half the ceiling plaster had fallen. Water dripped from a gaping hole over the bed.

"The place is literally falling apart," Frank said as he crawled back into bed.

"That scared me."

"This is a scary place. I don't think I can sleep, tell you the truth."

"Let's leave."

"Okay. Rain's let up enough, I think. But it's going to be hell trying to find our way in the dark."

"I don't like this place."

"Neither do I. But we'd better try to get a few hours' sleep anyway. There's no one here, Alice. No one. It's an old empty rotting house. Maybe a rat or two is all we have for company."

"I don't mind a rat or two," Alice said.

"Do you believe in ghosts?"

"Ghosts? No. They don't scare me."

"But do you believe in them? Do they teach any kind of religion here? Not that ghosts have anything to do with religion, but were you taught a belief in any kind of afterlife or spiritual universe?"

"Spiritual universe?"

"I mean religion."

"No. Religion is antisocial."

"Uh-huh. Yeah, well . . ."

A wind made a low moaning through the eaves somewhere, then was silent.

"Place has many voices," Frank said.

"Hope it doesn't crash down on us," Alice said.

"It won't. Water damage in that other room. Leaks."

As if on cue, water began dripping to the floor not far from the bed.

They both laughed.

"Many voices," Alice said.

"Does that bother you? Want to move to another room?"

Alice snuggled closer. "I want to stay right here."

"Okay."

Frank's ears were now attuned to other sounds of dripping throughout the place, off in far rooms, below, above. The roof must be a sieve, he thought. Rats wouldn't live in a place like this.

Lightning lit up the windows, etching the pattern of the panes on the wall in stark geometry.

Frank counted the seconds until the thunder arrived. The storm was moving off.

He thought of home, his father's farm, just a few miles from Peoria. For some reason, the memory of the smell of mown hay came to him. And the feel of the hot sun in August when he would walk through the cornfields inspecting the tall stalks and their almost bursting yellow cobs. Field corn mostly, with about a quarter acre of sweet corn for eating. Nothing better than sweet corn fresh from the field, mere minutes from stalk to boiling pot, and then eating it with fresh butter melting around the corners of your mouth, the cob burning your fingers, still too hot to hold. Mrs. Erickson's biscuits had reminded him of home. His mother had been a fabulous cook. He felt a sudden pang, missing her all over again, now, thinking of her, of his loss. She had died of uterine cancer the day after his twelfth birthday. He remembered the funeral, the finality of it all, the painful thump as one end of the coffin hit the bottom of the grave after a pallbearer lost his grip on the rope. But Mom hadn't felt a thing, had she? He remembered thinking that, she didn't feel that. She's not there, she's not in there, not really. She's in heaven. But he'd wondered where that was, puzzled over its exact location—heaven, a place of rest, a wonderful place to be—up there, in the sky? How was that possible? How did that work, exactly? As a child he had not known—no one had explained the concept in detail—and still did not know. But the notion had comforted him. Still, the coffin's dropping had been a painful if momentary contretemps, that hollow thud going through him and making him wince, another spasm of hurt in a hurtful proceeding.

And Dad all alone all those years. Never remarried. Never would, he had always maintained. He was near seventy now.

It took a few seconds for Frank to realize that the light playing on the wall now was not lightning.

Headlights.

"Alice."

Alice gave a start and raised her head.

"We have company. Get up, honey."

Whoever it was arrived in a clamor: engines raced, horns blared, male laughter rang out, raucous and obscene in the darkness.

Frank knelt at the window and peered over the sill. Six vehicles had arrived, five camouflage-painted. Along with an olive drab civilian automobile, there were two small trucks and three jeeps. Men and women got out of them, but only the men were in paramilitary uniform—camouflage print fatigues, fatigue hats, and combat boots. The women wore civilian dress. He watched as one of the men picked up a woman from behind, whooped and shouted, "Party time!"

Some escorted—herded would be better—the women toward the front door. A few of the men carried rifles at the ready. There were six men and eight women in all.

Frank waddled back to the bed. "Let's try to get out the back way."

They heard banging against the front door as they ran from the room. Frank halted as soon as he heard voices in the house. He began to step quietly. They groped down the hallway in the dark, heading away from the stairs.

Voices filled the hotel and footsteps thumped everywhere, chasing Frank and Alice into the gloomy recesses. As footsteps came up the grand staircase, Frank thought furiously of what to do. He flipped up the safety catch on the Glock but he did not want to try shooting their way out. That was sure suicide.

But it seemed the only way.

"Frank, stairs!"

He looked. In the dimness, he could see them. But the stairs went up, not down.

They followed the narrow stairwell upward. It went up one flight into a large space under a sloping roof, an octagonal cupola appointed with long mullioned windows, the floorspace crowded with stacked boxes. They made their way through the stacks to a window.

"We can climb down a tree and get to the garage," Frank said. "Can you climb down a tree?"

"I never did, but I'll try."

But what would they do then? Frank would have to wait for a particularly noisy moment to pull the truck out of the garage and sneak across the parking lot to the road. The revelers were making noise enough. Gales of rowdy laughter rent the night.

Voices in the hallway downstairs, tramping footsteps all over. Doors thumped open, orders rang out.

"Up there!"

Footsteps mounted the stairs to the attic, and just as Frank and Alice had ensconced themselves behind a stack of crates, flashlight beams played around them.

A cough. "Dusty as shit up here."

"Aw, there's no one in the whole damn place. Go tell the Lieutenant, and let's get at those babes. I'm ready for 'em."

"I'm with you, Sergeant."

The two soldiers retreated down the stairs again. Frank and Alice knelt in silence, listening to sounds of merry-making echo through the ruined hotel. There came a rebellious whoop, answered by another. Glass shattered. A woman shrieked. Whether it was in laughter or terror, Frank couldn't tell.

"Alice, is it rape, or . . . do you know where they got those women?"

"I've heard of it. They come in the night to take you. But it never happened to anyone I know."

"Rape?"

"Yes. When you get an order to get pregnant, you're supposed to go with them."

"So that's how it's done?"

"Not all the time. If it happens, you just do it. You let them. Otherwise, it can be with just any man."

"The government permits gang rape?"

"I guess."

Frank shook his head. "How does Innerverse let them do it? I thought . . ."

Alice shrugged. "I don't know."

Then again, Frank mused, if they were following orders, why not? Innerverse was a mechanism for enforcing obedience to orders. Theoretically, it didn't matter what those orders were.

But those men down there weren't doing some solemn duty. They were enjoying themselves. What they were doing they did with enthusiasm. It was not the usual tenor of the Republic.

Those men were not controlled.

Neither were they "Controls," old folks who had been spared Innerverse originally. These were young men.

And they did not have Innerverse.

≽ Chapter Eleven ≼

"We've got to find a back way out," Frank whispered.

"Maybe there's none," Alice said.

"There's gotta be. Let's go. Tip-toes, now."

Slowly, agonizingly slowly, and with scrupulous caution, they made their way back down to the second floor. By the sounds, Frank judged that the carryings-on were taking place in the lobby and the bar.

He asked himself why soldiers on a spree would choose this wreck as a likely site for an orgy. Because a building this old would have no monitoring devices built in? That sounded reasonable. Then what they were doing was not officially condoned? All this was difficult to sort out.

Or impossible to sort out.

But, then, nothing made sense in this place. It was unreal, all of it.

Frank took the flashlight from Alice and flicked it on when they had groped down the hallway far enough from the front stairwell to risk it. He cupped his hand over the lens first, and the flashlight's muffled beam lighted up the hall ahead in feeble pinkish red. Then he took his hand away.

Suddenly, things looked markedly different.

"Oops."

A fire had taken out most the rest of the first floor. Over a wide area the flooring was completely gone, leaving a blackened grate of charred joists. A few wall studs on the second floor were left as well, some hanging without support. There was not much other structure remaining. Above, the roof was burned away.

A lightning strike on another stormy night long ago, a sudden fire. When the flames took out the roof the rain came in and killed the fire. And this was the result, a half-burned hulk.

The floor below held the remains of what looked like a ballroom or large meeting room.

Frank let the flash's beam sweep the far reaches of the burned area. Near where the flooring started again was a staircase leading down to another, smaller foyer and a door.

But how to reach it?

Frank searched the intervening grille of joists. Most looked completely carbonized. But a thick, sturdy structural wood beam ran right through the middle of them. It was charred, but looked essentially sound. On the far end of the ballroom a load-bearing plaster wall (perhaps of plaster and asbestos) stood more or less untouched by the fire, bearing up the beam's other exposed end.

He leaned toward Alice's ear. "Ever walk a tightrope?"

Grimacing, totally serious, she shook her head.

He smiled. "We'll have to walk across that beam."

"Oh, Frank." She looked down fearfully.

"We'll do it together. Else we have to stay up here until they leave. From the sound of 'em, they'll hang around till morning."

"Let's stay. We'll hide."

"They could find the truck. Or they could suddenly decide to move the party to another room."

Alice looked nervously across the charred chasm. "Okay. Let's do it."

"That's my girl. Watch me first, then I'll come back."

Frank gave her the flash, and, as a second thought, the pistol, thinking it might make him top-heavy. Besides, he could do little shooting if caught out on the beam. She put the gun inside a deep inner pocket of her jacket.

He gingerly placed one gum-soled shoe on the beam and made it bear some of his weight. It didn't bend and it didn't creak. He gave the beam his full weight, and when he was satisfied it was sound, lifted his other foot away from the burnt edge of the flooring, placed it one step out on the beam and balanced himself, arms straight out and waving to counterbalance. The upper surface of the beam itself was about eight inches across. It really was not difficult to walk on and required little in the way of a circus balancing act. Fear was the worst impediment.

He walked out about six or seven feet, balanced, then carefully worked his way back. Alice reached and hauled him in.

"Easy," he said.

She looked doubtful.

"I'll hold your hand all the way. It's just across here to that wall. See where the flooring starts up again? We'll have to stay on the beam until we're sure the floor's good, then we go down those stairs and out the door."

"Okay, Frank. I'm scared."

"We'll make it."

They inched out together, hand in hand, Alice doing a fair job of balancing, Frank in the lead. When they got out to a point of no return, however, she began to get inhibitingly fearful. Below lay the ruins of a wood dance floor, and beneath that, viewed through ragged holes, lay a basement of block and stone compartments housing hulks of furnaces and pipes and other ugly stuff that did not look comfortable to land on.

"Don't look down, honey," he whispered hoarsely.

"Frank, I'm going to fall," she said anxiously, tugging him back.

"No, you're not. Come on."

"Frank, I can't . . ."

"No going back, Alice, honey. I've got you."

She didn't scream when she misstepped and fell, and Frank somehow held onto her. He caught himself with one arm hooked over the beam, and they hung in the air for a few seconds, Alice swinging pendulum-like, Frank holding her like an orangutan mother saving her baby from a nasty fall from the treetops.

The beam groaned, flakes of carbon falling from it like black snow.

"Climb up," Frank said through gritted teeth. "Climb up on me."

She did, and the sleeve of the seam of his jacket sleeve ripped halfway. But she managed to reach the beam and hauled herself painfully up. With his strong right arm, Frank boosted her and she ended up sitting up precariously on the beam. Frank then chinned himself, threw one leg over, raised himself and straddled it.

The beam warned them ominously, creaking and clicking, but it held.

They remained in that position until they caught their breath. Then Frank persuaded her to try inching her way across in a sitting position, sidesaddle, as it were. She did this, and it seemed to suit her better. He saddled along behind, thinking that he should have thought of this method first.

They reached the other edge of the flooring. He pushed her on ahead, telling her to spread herself out. He followed, and soon they were on all fours. Presently, satisfied that they were on sound footing, Frank stood.

He pulled Alice to her feet.

"You okay?"

"Yeah."

"Got the flash?"

"Here it is."

"Frank, we nearly fell down there."

"But we didn't. Good girl, you're doing fine. Now, all we have to do—"

She suddenly threw her arms around him and kissed him.

"I love you, Frank."

"I love you, Alice. Now, are you sure you're okay, you didn't hurt yourself?"

"No."

"Great. Okay, just down these stairs, and we're out of here. Wait."

"What?"

"Let me go first."

"Okay."

"You can never tell." Frank walked two steps down from the landing.

With stunning suddenness, the staircase collapsed under his feet and he fell into darkness. He heard nothing, and in a second he knew nothing.

He heard voices first, and he listened to them.

"Where the hell did they come from?"

"Who knows. Two Immunes, I guess."

"Unless he's the UCS spy."

"Think so? He's got nothing on him says who he is."

"No one has anything on them unless they're Controls. You know that."

"But he must be Immune. How come they didn't just kill him?"

"They didn't know in time. Shot him up with the bugs, and it seemed to take, if I remember the report. Then he got Immune."

"Yeah? I never heard of it happening that quick. Anyway, what do we do with him?"

"Bring him in."

"What the fuck for? He's dead meat. There was a kill order.

"Yeah? Well, then, shoot the bastard. What do I give a shit?"

"Let's have some fun with him first."

"I'm going to have some fun with her first."

"Jesus, don't you ever get enough? You just got done porking eight in a row. This guy's amazing."

"You can never get enough. Besides, this one's real good lookin'. The others are fucking dogs."

"You'd fuck a dog if there wasn't anything else around."

"Fuck you. Hey, you fuck who you want and I'll fuck who I want, you dog-faced dickhead. Don't tell me what to do."

"All right, all right, go ahead and do her."

"I'm gonna do her right. Turn around honey, get your ass up nice. That's it."

He didn't want to open his eyes but he had to. He was lying on a long narrow table and something was wrapped tightly about his chest and legs. He could not move his arms. He looked to his left, then his right. The right view took in three soldiers, their backs turned to him. They were watching a fourth man mount a semi-clothed Alice from behind.

"Stop it," Frank said weakly.

Two of the three turned around.

"Hey, he's up," said one.

"Hey, Spy Guy. You've been giving everyone the run-around, haven't you?"

"Leave her alone," Frank said. "She did nothing."

"She and you killed an Area Inspector."

"I did. I shot him. She didn't do anything."

"Well, hey . . . Sergeant? This guy says we should leave his girlfriend alone."

Sergeant was busy, but he turned his head and leered. "Wait a minute, pal, I'll be done here real quick, and then I'll get to you."

"He's the Minute Man," one of the three quipped. They laughed. "That's all it takes with the Sergeant."

Two more soldiers entered the scene.

"Hey, you guys all pooped out, or what?"

"Who are they?"

"The guy's the UCS spy. I guess she's Immune or she wouldn't be with him."

"So, we terminate both of them?"

"Sergeant wants to do it in the fun way."

"Aw, come on, Sergeant, I don't want to get into that

shit. You always gotta do something like that. Let's just shoot 'em and take the girls back. Jeez, it's gettin' late.''

"The fun way," Sergeant said, panting. "First him, and then her."

"Well, I don't have to watch. I'm going out for a walk."

"You get back here, Private, and watch this interrogation of the prisoner."

"Shit, if they'd wanted him interrogated, they would have done it themselves."

"You'll obey orders, dickface. Get back here. You, too, Rogers."

"Yes, Sergeant."

. Sergeant stood up and hiked up his pants. "Not bad, but I've had better. Thanks, honeybunch." He kicked Alice's rump and she went flat on the floor, sobbing.

"That's nothing to what's coming at you later, baby. I got something special all thought out for you. Rogers, run out to the jeep and bring back those wirecutters."

"Wirecutters?"

"You heard me."

"You got a sick mind, Sergeant."

"How do you know what I'm thinking? You must be thinking of it yourself. You ever hear of Chinese torture? The Death of a Thousand Cuts? Huh? Well, we ain't got time for a thousand, but I'm gonna take this joker apart piece by piece. Startin' with these little toes of his."

"I thought you were going to interrogate him."

"Sure I am. Then I'm going to take him apart."

"So, ask him a question."

"Who's giving orders around here? I outrank you."

"Yeah, you do. So what? What if I tell the Lieutenant?"

"He's out cold, dead drunk."

"What if I file a report?"

"You gotta report yourself to do it, asshole."

"A little unauthorized screwing isn't so much. You're gonna torture the guy."

"Yeah, so what? I'm gonna torture him. Ain't nothing in our standing orders . . ."

"The shit there ain't. 'No deliberate cruelty will be tolerated.' You want to get cut off from Innerpause maintenance?"

"Hey, fuck you. I'm sorry I asked you along with us. You're an asshole."

"Yeah?"

"Yeah, and if you want me to prove it, I'll meet you outside in five minutes. You can hide anywhere, asshole, and I'll come for you."

"All right, do anything you want to him. What do I care. I'm going to inform the Lieutenant."

"Go ahead. You need Innerpause, all right, dickface. You need Innerpause right up your fucking faggot asshole."

"What a guy!"

"Hey, any day you think you can take me out, dickhead."

"Fuck you."

"Here're the cutters, Sergeant."

"Thanks. Now, let's get to this. Lost a shoe, did you, Spy Guy?"

Frank felt his right little toe being handled daintily.

"A thousand cuts. Let's see, we got ten toes. Take that other shoe off. And then we go for the fingers, right? And then the balls."

They all laughed.

"One ball at a time, and then the pecker, and . . ."

"He's not going to care whether he lives or dies after that, Sergeant."

A face appeared above him. It was the Corporal, a smirk on his pimply face.

"Oh, yes he will. You'll see. Now, let's get this little piggy set up."

Frank's body spasmed at the sudden pain. It was like nothing he'd ever felt before, a sharp burning that increased to unbearable intensity. He let out a yell.

The Corporal's face registered a strange amalgam of mirth and feigned disgust. "Ewwwww. God, I don't believe you did that. Sergeant, you are one sick motherfucker."

The Sergeant let out an evil cackle. "That's just the start. He yells pretty good. Let's see if he yells louder the bigger the toes get."

"You're not going to do that to her, are you?"

"Why not? 'Course, maybe I won't start with her tocs."

The Corporal giggled. "God, you are sick. I don't believe you."

The burning pain started again. Frank let out another yell but managed to clench his teeth and bite off the end of it. The burning washed over him in waves, and he felt faint, weak from the ensuing shock. His vision dimmed. He blinked his eyes, and the face in front of it was blurry, but a smarmy smile came through.

"Zat hurt, buddy?"

"You bastards."

"Number three toe," the Scrgeant sang.

Again, the pain, and this time it pierced him to the core. His body shook and spasmed.

"Aw, enough of this. Let's cut his balls off."

The Corporal winced. "Ewwww, Sergeant, please. My God, I don't know if I can't stand to see that."

"Cut through his pants, there. Shit, we shoulda took 'em off first."

He heard ripping and felt a tug on his trousers. He knew what they were going to do but he couldn't anticipate. The pain was still there, a burning that didn't ccase.

"You gonna cut 'em right off?"

"Naw. Let's see what he does when we cut one in half. There they are. Hey, he's pretty well-equipped. Shame."

"You are one sick, perverted bastard." It was the voice from before.

"Shut up. You can't talk to me like that. You want to see what it's like to have your balls cut off, dickface?"

"Hey, take it easy. I thought you were going to interrogate this prisoner."

"I said back off, Jeters."

Frank tilted his head. At his feet stood the Sergeant and another man of equal rank, to judge by his shoulder stripes. Both were big men.

"This has gone far enough. I demand that you let me take the prisoner back to headquarters for questioning or bind him for Walden."

The Sergeant balled his fist and struck Jeters across the jaw and Jeters went tumbling.

"So much for that," the Sergeant said. "Now." He brought the wirecutters up.

The Sergeant brought his big face up close, breath like a sepulcher with a fresh-rotted corpse. "Hi, fella. You got a choice. I can cut this here ball in two, or you can have your dick off. Dick'll be less painful. What'll it be?"

"That's nice, what the Sergeant's doing for you," the Corporal said.

The Sergeant leaned back. "What'll it be, Spy Guy? Dick or balls?"

The Sergeant's head exploded, a gout of blood erupting from it like a sudden cockscomb. He fell across Frank's body. The room lit up with flashes of light and loud gunshots, one after another in quick succession. The Corporal fell, and then Rogers and the remaining man.

Frank tried to focus his vision. Someone was walking toward him, gun in both hands, hands outstretched.

It was Alice, still naked from the waist down. Tears streaked her face, but her face was hard, her eyes hot with anger.

"Frank, oh my God. Oh my god, Frank, look what they did to you."

"Alice, Jesus, it was you. How did—?

"I forgot I had the gun, Frank. I forgot I had it. I didn't know how to use it, but I remembered what you did."

"Jesus, but how did you know how to shoot like that?"

"I just kept pulling this thing, here," Alice said. "And it kept jumping up real hard. So I had to bear down on it and I kept squeezing the little thing here, just like you did, Frank. I watched you. Just like you did it, and I killed them, Frank. I killed them all."

⩾ Chapter Twelve ⩽

Other than having lost three toes, Frank was in fair shape. He had a massive headache and most likely a concussion. However, that the fall hadn't done him more damage was nothing less than miraculous.

"Must have landed on my feet, somehow. Lucky I didn't break a leg."

"I thought you were dead," Alice said.

"How long was I out?"

"Frank, I don't know. I can't remember. It seemed like forever."

After she cut Frank loose from the strong metallic tape that bound him, Alice had to strip one of the corpses and use the cloth for bandages to staunch Frank's bleeding. By the time the blood stopped flowing, he had lost quite a bit, but not a catastrophic amount. Wincing, his right foot a bulge of bandages, he stood up unsteadily, using a length of board as a crutch. If it hadn't been for all the blood, he would have looked almost comic, like some man with gout in an old silent comedy.

He deliberated about finishing off the comatose lieutenant and the one called Jeters. The lieutenant, passed out in a booth in the hotel's bar, had a weak pulse. On the table lay bottles of pills and other drug paraphernalia, and Frank deduced that the man had mixed the wrong chemicals. Jeters had hit his head in falling and remained unconscious, although his vital signs were robust.

He decided to spare them both. Frank decided that killing them would be of no utility whatsoever. Word was out already.

Besides, Jeters did not deserve to die.

"Where are the women?" Frank asked.

"In the army truck. They're just sitting in the back, there. They look kind of . . . stunned. They asked me if we were supposed to take them home."

"Nothing we can do for them. Let's get the hell going."

Alice watched him limp along. "Frank, dear, are you sure you're in any shape to drive?"

"We have to get out of here."

There was no time for Frank to recuperate in leisure. Alice helped him to hobble to the truck. As she could not drive, Frank fought off fatigue, strained against weakness, and drove as best he could.

Alice's ordeal had done her no physical damage, but there was a residue of fright and shock in her eyes. Frank hugged her, and she gave him a bleak smile. She would never be the same.

There was not much left of the night. Frank concluded that either they had slept a few hours before the soldiers' arrival at the hotel or he must have been out quite a while after the fall. He had no sense of having fallen asleep before hearing the soldiers' arrival. Be that as it may, in a few hours, day dawned gray and muted, but no rain fell.

"End of the line," Frank said on seeing the sign up ahead.

"ROAD CLOSED," Alice read. "What now, Frank?"

"I'm damned if any roads go west from here. I have no idea where we are at the moment." He fumbled with the map.

"I don't see how you can read those things."

"I'm having trouble focusing my eyes. Trouble thinking." He leaned his head against the window. "Damned headache. We don't have anything for it, either."

"Wait." Alice opened the glove compartment and

brought out a plastic box with a red cross on it. "Mrs. Erickson said this would come in handy."

"First aid! They thought of everything."

Frank rummaged in the small box and came up with a small tin of aspirin. "I don't know if I should be taking aspirin with this head injury, but I've got to do something about the pain. Have that water bottle handy?"

Alice gave it to him and he washed four pills down.

"Does your foot still hurt?"

"Funny, not as much as my head. But the aspirin will help that, too. Should."

"Frank, you can't walk with that foot."

Frank looked around. "No. I'm going to go back to that junction we passed and head farther south. There has to be a road that gets closer to the border. Has to be."

They have an army, he thought. Don't they need roads to the damned border?

He swung the truck around and headed back up the road, and took the first right, a road that began to twine through the hollows of steep hills.

"Compass is keeping southeast," Frank complained. "Don't tell me this road doesn't go west either."

They drove all morning, and the road tantalized him with feints southwest, but it was fooling. He saw an old sign for a small town (God only knew if it still existed), checked the map, and found that he hadn't made any progress west at all.

"This is getting to me," Frank said. "I'm getting ticked off. Really ticked."

"Maybe they blocked them all off because of us," Alice said.

"No, it's part of an old plan. It's to keep the Controls from leaving. Make it hard as possible for them. The zombies they don't worry about. Maybe it's to keep the army here. They're not zombies."

"What's a zombie, anyway?"

Frank smiled. "You've never seen any movies, have you?"

"Movies? You mean screen programs?"

"No, movies."

"What are they?"

"Like stuff on the screen, only it's fiction. For entertainment. Not some damned documentary."

"For entertainment. No, I've never seen a movie. All the stuff we watch is for education."

"All you have is instructional media," Frank said. "Nothing else. Some people are always complaining about how worthless mass entertainment is. If they only knew how deadly dull 'worthwhile' fare can be."

"It's the worst," Alice said. "Of course I stopped watching the screen years ago, when I didn't have to anymore."

"You were lucky. If I had to watch a month's worth of documentaries on heroic worker efforts I think I'd go bonkers."

"Frank, what's fiction?"

"Stories that are made up. Not true."

Alice frowned. "Why would anyone tell such stories?"

"For entertainment."

"But . . ."

"It's hard to understand. You'll see."

"Will I, Frank? I want to see some fiction."

"Or you can read it. I haven't seen a book since I got here."

"There are books. But they're no fun to read."

"Of course not. Who the hell dreamed up this place? What kind of wet blanket, what kind of killjoy could dream up a so-called utopia that's totally clean of any simple pleasure that human beings can have?"

Alice shrugged. "Nobody's ever told us. There's just Innerverse."

"Yeah, Innerverse is all there is."

"But, my God, it's a nightmare. They even screwed up sex. Now, that takes some doing."

"They didn't screw it up for us, Frank."

"One good thing. Do you still want me after what happened, after what those men did to you?"

"Why wouldn't I still want you?"

"I don't know. I'm sorry. It's just that I'm afraid you might start hating men. I'm one."

"Why would I hate all men because of what a few men did? Now you're talking crazy, Frank."

"Okay, good. Sorry."

"Don't be sorry, you didn't do anything. Anyway, they're dead now. All of them. And I did it. And I'm glad I did. It felt good to kill them."

"Don't get bloodthirsty."

"I don't feel like doing it to anybody else. Just to people that hurt me. I wish I could do it to whoever invented Innerverse."

"I'll second that. Maybe we can find them someday. Starting to rain again."

The rain started out light but steadily got worse until it came down in torrents, sluicing across the road and creating instant lakes in the gullies and dales. Frank bravely splashed through a couple of these, then slowed down and cautiously forded the next one, for fear of shorting out the truck's ignition. But apparently he hadn't been cautious enough. The engine coughed and threatened to stall.

The truck rolled to a stop and Frank pumped the accelerator, his right foot throbbing.

"Damn."

"What's wrong?"

"Water in the ignition system."

"Oh. Can we dry it."

"Don't worry, it'll shake it off and start going again. I think."

The old truck engine choked and sputtered, then finally renewed its commitment to keep running.

"This is ridiculous," Frank said as the rain seemed to redouble its efforts to flood the gully they were in. "Let's get to higher ground and stay there for a bit."

Frank ran the truck up the next hill and pulled over at the crest.

"I'm hungry," he said. "Let's eat something."

They finished off the biscuits and cured ham and washed it down with water from a plastic squeeze bottle. All the while the rain came down in floods. Frank had rarely seen a downpour this intense.

"This food is so good," Alice said, lifting the water bottle to her lips.

"Stale biscuits, chewy meat, and water. Yeah, it's better than anything in the whole damned country. Finish up, kid. We gotta get moving. Seems to be letting up . . . oh, shit."

Alice got a face full of water as Frank gunned the truck's engine and peeled out.

"What is it?"

"Something coming down the road. Looks like trouble."

Alice looked back through the rear window. "Just a car."

"No such thing as 'just a car' in this place. Any clue what kind of official it could be?"

"No. Probably some administrator."

"It's a woman this time, I think."

Alice asked, "Do we have to kill her?"

The car, a gray nondescript sedan, sped past without even slowing down.

Frank stared after it.

"Well, she saw us. Glad she didn't stop. I don't relish another shooting."

"I would have done it."

Frank looked into her eyes. "Alice, it's a little disturbing to me that you've taken a liking to that sort of thing."

She looked away. "I don't exactly like it. It's a strange feeling. For years I've been angry. Very angry and hurt inside. Frustrated. Being a prisoner, being told what to do, every day the same prison, the same orders, the same hopelessness. And all the while wanting to lash out, wanting to destroy it all. At night sometimes I'd lie there and think of slow ways to kill my boss. And her boss. And the next one up, until I got to the top, whoever it is up there. And then I'd kill him or her and the whole thing would come crashing down. I'd feel guilty about it, about thinking like that. But it didn't bother me all that much, entertaining thoughts like that. Why should they live to rule over me, to make me miserable all the time? I felt it was my right to smash the state, or try doing it. And if I couldn't do anything about it, I could think about it. There was nothing wrong in that. Is there, Frank? Is there anything wrong in fighting against the state?''

"Of course not. It makes me worry a little, though, when and if Innerverse finally goes, and everybody is suddenly free to do what they want, after years of repression. What kind of mass mayhem will break out? Good chance it won't be very pretty.''

"Maybe not.''

"Chaos, maybe. I hope we in the west are up to holding the country together.''

A throb of pain suddenly went through Frank's head, and he pressed his fingers against his temples. "Yow.''

"Are you all right?''

"It's fading. Shit, that aspirin didn't do much good. And I took a handful of them.''

"You probably shouldn't take any more.''

"No. Wish I had a hit of codeine or something stronger. Really should get my noggin X-rayed, but that's out of the question till we get back home.''

"Home? You mean your country?''

"Yeah.''

"It'll be my home, too, won't it, Frank?''

"Yes, Alice. It'll be our home. I'll take you to the farm.''

She smiled. "I'd like that.''

Frank started the engine. "I'm going to find a side road

up ahead, and pull over. I need a nap. A short one, and then we'll get moving again.''

"Okay, Frank. You take a nap, and then we'll go home.''

≽ Chapter Thirteen ≼

The nap turned into a three-hour snooze. Exhausted, Alice conked out, too. They slept undisturbed. Frank had chosen the rest stop carefully, practically crashing the truck into a bramble of bushes and weeds well off the road. They were well-hidden.

They awoke bleary-eyed; Frank still had a headache. It was early evening. Frank chewed some smoked sausage while Alice ate a whole jar of peaches.

Alice asked, "You're not hungry?"

"Not really. This rotten headache. Lost my appetite. Ready to move on?"

"Sure."

As if on cue, the rain began again.

"Whole damned storm front must be moving across this region. Won't be long until dark. And we're still no closer to the border."

"Frank I don't want to spend another night here. I don't want to find another shack and try to sleep. Let's keep driving."

"Right. We'll sleep in the truck if we have to. It doesn't look too bad. I'm going to drive until I'm absolutely sure we're as close as possible to the border. Then we'll have to walk it."

Alice looked down at Frank's bundled right foot and frowned.

"Yeah, I know. It's crazy. But I'll have to do it. We're

130

getting nowhere, and we're running out of fuel. Still have
about five gallons left in the truck and there're the jerry
cans, but this heap must get less than ten miles to the
gallon. It's guzzling gasoline. Needed more than Mr. Erickson could handle in the way of an overhaul. So, we're
going to have to hoof it eventually. Better we pick the
time to bail out rather than run out of gas in the middle
of nowhere."

"But you can't possibly walk very far," Alice
protested.

"I can walk. It hurts like hell, but I can walk. Maybe
we'll luck out and find a road west. Luck's been horrible
so far. Bound to change."

But he didn't believe it.

They drove until dark without finding any hint of a road
that went west. Frank's headache got worse, and he felt
progressively more rotten as the night wore on. Rain beat
incessantly against the windshield and visibility was poor.
The slick tires reduced the truck to snail speed on turns,
and the pathetically inefficient engine could only crawl
up hills.

After an hour of agonizing non-progress, Frank pulled
over, got out the flashlight, unfolded the old road map,
and had a look.

He turned the map this way and that, then refolded it
and opened it up again in a different configuration. All
the blue and red lines seemed to take on a life of their
own, like a colony of worms, squiggling and wiggling and
doing things that roads ordinarily refrain from doing. His
vision blurred, and a bolt of pain shot through his cranium.

Groaning, he rubbed his eyes and shook his head.

"Frank, what is it?"

"I'm all right."

"You look terrible, Frank."

Alice reached out and placed her palm on his forehead.
"You're warm, How do you feel?"

"I fell like a pile of dog waste. Must be the head injury.

Only thing is get to a doctor. A hospital. But not on this side of the line, that's for sure.''

"Maybe we should give ourselves up."

He looked at her hard. "You don't mean that."

"I'm worried about you. I'd rather die, Frank, but I don't want you to die. Maybe you should give yourself up so they can take care of you."

"No," he said with finality. "I'll be okay. I don't want you to worry. It's just a headache, and maybe with all this dampness I've caught something. But neither a bump on the head nor a cold's going to prevent me from getting back across the border. Okay?''

"Okay. If you say so."

"I say so. Give me a smile."

She smiled wanly.

"Better. Kiss."

She kissed him. Frank put the transmission into first gear.

He shifted back into neutral. "Forgot. Let's see if that map makes any sense at all."

Reapplying the flashlight and his tired eyes to the map again, he saw even less than before.

Frank sighed and let the map drop. "Don't have a clue where we are. We're lost, totally lost."

Alice took a look at the map, brow furrowed. "These names don't mean anything to me."

"They wouldn't. Half of them have probably been changed, and there's no reason you would know this area of the country anyway."

"What road are we on?"

"I'm fairly sure we're on this one," he said, pointing, "but exactly where, I don't know. Haven't seen a sign in hours. They don't believe in signs here, apparently."

"The only signs you ever see are old," Alice said.

"Yeah, if they haven't rotted away completely. See this thick line here? That's an Interstate highway, or used to be. Big road. It might still be open. It'll take us Southwest, and maybe somewhere down around here we can pick up an old dirt road that gets us to the Kentucky border. It's a long drive, though."

"Let's do it."

"We either have to save fuel somehow or find more. We've passed a couple of old service stations, closed up years ago, and every time I've wondered if they're a few gallons of gas left in those old underground tanks. Of course, to draw it up we'd need a pump ..." Frank suddenly sighed again and rubbed his eyes. "Oh hell. Let's just keep on this road. South. We have to hit something sooner or later."

He drove on into the night, fighting the pain and the mounting fatigue. The rain finally let up, which helped, but the pain seemed to make up the difference. A dull ache throbbed at the back of his head. It was not a kind of headache that he recognized or that had afflicted him before. It was an agonizing, pounding ache that seemed to echo inside his head.

His temperature rose. He felt hot and clammy, and his clothes stuck to him like paste. The road was endless, offering repetitions on a single theme: road lined with scraggly trees, black indeterminate sky. Road, trees, sky, nothing more, no change, no variation, broken only by taking his eyes from the road and looking at blond Alice and her pretty face, her furrowed, worried brow. He reached out and brought her closer, held her as he drove.

"Frank, you're hot. You're burning up."

And the road continued, uphill and down, winding left, then right, through an eternal night of mountains and overgrown side roads and splintered road signs and broken pavement.

He drove for about a half hour more before he realized it was all he could take.

"Gotta stop, Alice. My head is killing me."

"Pull over and we'll sleep again. Our nap wasn't all that long and we didn't get any last night."

"I'm sick, babe. Got to stretch out, get some rest. Let's see what's up this road."

"Frank, I'm scared again."

"No one will bother us, I promise. I'll shoot anything that comes near us. Shoot first, apologize afterward."

The road led up a hill and leveled out. To the right lay an expansive clear area of crumbled asphalt. Frank recognized it as the remains of a parking lot long gone to weed and grass. In the middle of the lot sat a large building that had once been a store, its windows and doors boarded over. At the entrance to the lot stood a tall rusted metal pole, at the top of which were the ruins of a plastic sign, the sort that lights up, but the lettering was shattered beyond readability.

Alice surveyed is disapprovingly. "What is this place?"

"Ames, Wal-Mart, you name it."

"Huh?"

"Discount department store. What it used to be."

"What was it?"

"A store, Alice, a store. That sold large quantities of so-so merchandise at bargain prices."

"Oh. Was it the kind where you pay money?"

"Yes."

"I'd like to shop at a store like that. Did it have lots of things to buy?"

"Lots."

"I've never been to a place like that."

"I know. Let's see if we can break in. Right here."

Frank pulled up to a small door, probably an employee entrance, at the rear of the building. The store's front was covered with an armor plating of fiberboard and looked impenetrable, but this door had been nailed over with only a few boards.

A sign attached to one of the boards read ENTRANCE ABSOLUTELY FORBIDDEN—STAY OUT.

"That sign suffices to bar ninety percent of the population from breaking in," Frank said. "I wonder if the place has ever been looted."

"What do you think?"

"Let's see. Let me load this gun. You get the tire iron out from the back of the seat."

Frank fed cartridges into the clip of the semiautomatic, then jammed the clip back up into the handgrip. He cocked the gun and thumbed the safety on.

The planks came easily off the door, which led Frank to believe that the place had been looted in antiquity, perhaps as far back as the Troubles.

However, this was an out-of-the-way location. Maybe the store had been spared.

The door was locked, so he applied the hefty tire iron to the crack between the door and jamb near the doorknob. He pushed on the iron and leaned his weight against the door, and it sprang open easily, revealing a dark anteroom.

"Flashlight?"

Alice handed it to him. Before him lay a passage heading toward the front of the store with rooms letting off it. The first one looked like an office. And it was intact— desk, filling cabinets, and other appurtenances were all there. Frank took Alice's hand and entered cautiously, and they made their way down the passage.

After making a few turns and passing a few larger rooms, the passage debouched into the main area of the store.

The place was full of crates, boxes, and piles of goods. This was not a store, but a warehouse.

"Government warehouse," Frank said. "Look at this. Food, clothing, bedding . . . medicine, it looks like . . . Jesus . . ."

"Frank, what is it?"

"There could be stuff I need. Antibiotics."

"What're those?"

"Stuff that fights infection. Whatever I got might be an infection. Antibiotics could fix me up, if there're any here."

"Want me to help to look?"

"Sure, look around for the words 'penicillin' or 'tetracycline' or 'amoxicillin.' There are a couple of other words, too. Plenty of them, all different. I only know a few."

"Are you sure it could fix you up?"

"No, I'm no doctor. But they won't hurt me. I'm not allergic to anything."

"Will it help your foot?"

"Yeah, it'll guard against infection. Speaking of which, let's take a look at it."

"Over here, Frank. There's a bed."

It was a pile of mattresses, three of them, but it looked like heaven to Frank. He collapsed on top of it and stretched out.

"I should check the place out," he murmured. "I don't know if I can get up again."

"Give me the gun," Alice instructed. "I'll look around, you rest."

"No, no." Frank struggled upward, grunting. "Let's do it and then I'll rest."

They did a quick tour of the place. It was big, stuffed full of goods that would have fetched a high price in this impoverished country, had there been such a thing as money. There was furniture, appliances, clothing, shoes, household goods, toiletries and health aids. All the stock of a department store, plus more.

"This must be a cache of stuff for the higher-ups," Frank said. "Where they keep the remains of what wasn't looted long ago. Some of these goods must be years old. They must have gathered it all up from stores and warehouses around the country and brought it here."

Alice wanted to know, "What higher-ups? Administrators?"

"No. The real powers that be. Whoever runs Innerverse. The control center could be near here, and we've stumbled onto it."

"Do you think someone actually runs Innerverse?"

"Has to be. Somebody is calling the shots. And, as usual, they've relegated to themselves the lion's share of the national wealth. Or what remains of the wealth. And this is it. Wealth. Goods, consumable goods, millions of dollars' worth of them. And they're rare. Probably nothing like this being produced anymore. At least not in the Republic.''

''What's this, Frank?''

''A refrigerator.''

''It's so small.''

''It's for your apartment.''

''Really? The only ones I've seen are for cafeterias or warehouses.''

''That one's for home use. For people, not the government.''

It was a new concept for Alice. She nodded, taking it in for future consideration.

Frank looked at the back of one of the units. ''This is ancient. Uses freon. That was banned years ago.''

''I've heard of that,'' said Alice. ''I watched a program on it once. It was used long ago and it damaged the atmosphere.''

''That's what they said back in the last century. Wasn't quite true, it turned out.''

''No? You mean it was a lie?''

''Truth is funny, Alice. You can say things that are true in a certain way and they become a lie. Freon might have damaged the atmosphere—the ozone, was what it was all about. A certain kind of gas that protects the Earth from harmful kinds of sunlight. The ozone took some hits, but the long-term damage was negligible. At least, no one's ever cited any long term damage. Of course, freon's manufacture was eventually discontinued, because the fear was so great. So, maybe disaster was really averted. Hard to tell.''

Frank winced and sat down on an overstuffed chair.

''Are you okay?'' Alice stroked his forehead. ''You're hot, really hot.''

''I feel okay. I just need some rest. One good night's sleep is all I need. Let's go do that thing.''

Frank hauled himself up and they hiked back to the bedding department, on the way noting that some of the piles of cartons reached to the ceiling.

"This place is packed. Could be the main treasure trove, the central cache. But I don't understand, there's no security."

"Security?"

"Yeah, what's to prevent people from breaking into this place and hauling the loot away?"

Alice shrugged. "No one would do it."

"I keep forgetting. I'm wondering about the army, though. But then, they must be authorized to take stuff. They have the key to the place, probably. And it's parceled out according to rank, or merit, or a combination of both. Damn."

"What, Frank?"

Frank sprawled across the mattress with a great heaving sigh. "Jesus, that feels good. Come here, Alice, honey."

She crawled to him and hugged him.

"That's nice," he said. "That's nice. You're nice."

"I like this place, but I'm still afraid."

"Why did you say 'damn' before?"

"I realized that this is the army pay center. That's how they keep them on a leash. How they bribe them. The country's bankrupt. Can't meet its payroll. The army's being paid in kind, with goods that are decades old but still serviceable. But there's another angle somewhere. I remember what Jeters said. Something about Innerpause. Do you know what that is?"

"No, Frank."

"Innerpause. And he said 'Innerpause maintenance.' What the hell could that be? Those bastards did have Innerverse after all. But they have a different form of it. Innerpause. Maybe it gives an individual more leeway. I don't know. But those sons of bitches were wild, totally wild. I don't get it. Some people are totally controlled, can't move a muscle without prior authorization, and some people are almost feral. What the hell kind of place is this, Alice? None of it makes sense.''

''None of it makes sense,'' Alice echoed. ''None of it ever made sense to me. I hated it, always. Now I'm free, and you're free, and we're together. I like that. I want it always to be that way, Frank. I love you.''

A single tear dropped from her eye to his chest.

She raised her head. ''Frank, if this is an army place, shouldn't we leave? Frank?''

She heard his breathing and knew he was asleep.

Very soon she was asleep herself, in the darkness among all the wonderful, strange new things.

≫ Chapter Fourteen ≪

Out of a chaos of fear and loathing, Frank broke into consciousness with a start. He opened his eyes, and the darkness before him swam with monstrous shadows.

He yelled and sat bolt upright, waving his gun.

"Frank?"

Shapes undulated and coiled in the darkness.

Frank shouted, "Who's there?"

"Frank? Frank, you're dreaming. Wake up, dear."

"What?"

"You're dreaming."

"Jesus."

He rubbed his eyes and looked again. The shapes in the darkness receded.

He realized that he'd been having a fever dream. He hadn't had one since childhood, but recognized the symptoms. He also realized his headache was gone, supplanted by a weak, sick feeling and the telltale lightheaded dizziness of a high fever.

My God, what had he contracted?

Alice asked, "How do you feel?"

"Sick," he said. "Sick as a puppy."

Alice felt his cheek. "You're hotter than before. Frank, you need medicine."

"Yeah. Gotta look for it ... what's that?"

Alice put her hand to her mouth.

"You hear that?" he said.

140

She nodded.

The sound was difficult to place, but soon it became apparent that someone was moving somewhere off in the darkness.

Well, Frank thought, if it's the army boys again, looking for fun, I'll give it to them.

He'd start blasting the moment they poked their snouts into the place. He still had one clip's worth of cartridges. That ought to be enough to take some of them with him. He'd save the last two bullets for Alice and himself.

Another indeterminate sound. Toward the back of the building, where they'd come in.

He decided he probably couldn't bring himself to shoot Alice, no matter what. This was her world. He could do nothing to change it. If he hadn't come along she would have been better off than she was now. There was nothing he could do to save her.

More noise. It didn't sound like more than one person.

He leaned to whisper in her ear. "I'm going to take a look. Stay here. No, hide. Go off into those crates, lose yourself until I tell you to come out."

"Okay."

"If you hear shooting, stay low until it stops, and make sure it's me who tells you to come out. If you hear other voices, hide and don't come out until you're sure no one's around."

"Frank, come back to me."

"I'll come back, I promise."

"Take the flashlight."

"Flashlights and guns don't mix. You keep it."

With effort, he got up and staggered toward the rear entrance. The shadows still moved and threatened, but he ignored them. Someone was poking around out near the rear door, or in one of the offices.

He stopped at the end of the hallway that came out from the back of the building, and peered down it.

Nothing. He listened for a moment but didn't hear a sound. Cautiously, he advanced into the darkness, wondering if the wind had blown the door open or he had heard something outside and mistaken it for a sound inside.

Walking down the hall, his eyes picking more detail out of the murk, he saw that the back door was still closed, and he was relieved. Maybe he could push a filing cabinet up against it.

The thought occurred to him that he and Alice should be leaving soon. After all, this was a functioning government facility. Warehouse workers could show up for work this morning. He had been so exhausted last night that he almost hadn't cared, wanting only to collapse.

Wondering what time it was, he wished mightily for his watch; he hadn't seen it since the night he'd crashed.

He moved through pitch darkness, but his eyes had long adjusted to it. He stood still for a moment and listened. He heard nothing.

Must have been a rat or something, he thought.

But he'd better give it more time. If there was someone monkeying around, he would give himself away eventually. Frank kept absolutely still, leaning against the concrete block of the hallway, gun at the ready. He waited.

At least five minutes went by in silence.

"Frank?"

It was Alice, walking through the warehouse toward the entrance to the passage. Frank still waited.

· Light from a flashlight beam leaked into the passage and Frank's heart skipped a beat when he saw, in the swimming shadows toward the rear, two eyes luminescent.

Frank dropped to a crouch and aimed the pistol.

"Freeze!"

The small eyes blinked. They looked strangely unhuman.

Mrrrrrrwr.

"What the hell—"

"Frank?"

Frank broke out into laughter.

"Frank, what's so—? Oh, it's a kitty!"

"Jesus," Frank said breathing relief in great gulps. He put away the gun.

A small gray cat, looking nervous but not very afraid, was regarding him from atop a filing cabinet.

"Ohhh, it's pretty."

The cat recoiled a little from Alice's touch, but soon began to tolerate her stroking.

"It's just barely not a kitten, Frank. Isn't it cute? Do you like cats?"

"Sure. How are you, kitty cat?"

Mrrrrrwr.

"Nice to meet you. Alice, we'd better leave now."

"Can we take the kitty?"

"Why not. Take the kitty by all means. But let's get out of here. The warehouse workers might be here any minute."

"Do you think it belongs to them? The cat, I mean."

"Maybe, but cats are independent. Zombies aren't fit cat owners. Take him. Or her."

"I think it's a her."

"Her. Let's go."

"Let me check that bandage," Alice said.

He sat and she knelt and unwrapped the bloodsoaked rags. The toe-stumps ended in dark scabs. He felt nothing, no ache, no phantom pain from ghost toes. If only he felt half as good as his mutilated foot.

Alice found a janitor's closet and fetched back a pail of water mixed with strong disinfectant. Frank soaked his foot in it for a few minutes. When he brought it out again the stumps looked almost surgically neat.

"We need some fresh bandages," Alice said.

"Forget it. I saw cartons marked 'SHOES' and a couple that could have socks. Let's find me some shoes and heist some socks, and let's go."

Dawn was just breaking as they left. Frank felt not one whit better for the night's sleep. A deep fatigue was settling in his bones, and an ominous, sick, weak feeling grew by the minute. He had no appetite, and begged off breakfast despite Alice's insisting that he eat.

His head felt stuffed full of cotton, and there was a curious numbness to his lips. That he had sustained a serious head injury was certain; he simply did not know the extent of it. He looked at himself in the rear view mirror. His face was ashen and circles as dark as brows hung beneath his eyes. He looked like death warmed over.

But, having no other choice, he aimed the truck south and depressed the accelerator. The engine sounded worse today, rickety and loose. The pistons fairly clanged inside the cylinders and the valves sounded like a drunken marimba player. But the thing still worked, still chugged along.

He drove toward the lightening southern sky. This time of year the arc of the sun's path was still low, rising in the southeast, setting southwest. The sky was clear today, which gave him some gratification.

The road continued its sun-seeking way, never hinting that it would ever take a swing perpendicular. All side roads were blocked or overgrown.

"We'll have to walk it," Frank said, stroking the cat, who was investigating his lap.

"Frank, you're practically crippled. Come here, Kitty, don't bother him."

"I still have feet. What's left of 'em, anyway. I can walk. Just have to find a good walking stick, and I'll be fine."

But they kept driving, kept hoping for a way west.

"Why did those men do those horrible things to us?" Alice shook her head. "There was no reason. We never did anything to them."

"They did it because they were rotten. Nasty, mean, and rotten. Evil."

"That's it? Because they were evil?"

"That's it."

"But why? Why were they like that?"

"I don't know, Alice. I don't know."

"Why is there so much pain in the world? It's not right."

"It's not. But there's not much we can do about it. Innerverse was an attempt to do something. But ... well, you tell me. Did it?"

"No. It eliminated some bad things, but the rest it made worse."

Frank nodded. "The price is too high."

They drove and drove until Frank had the irrepressible feeling that they might have crossed the old border of Virginia by now. But he had no way of knowing. The map was useless, and still the countryside was bereft of signs. He longed to see the most garish, obtrusive billboard, the ugliest plastic fast food monument, anything that showed that commerce was alive in the land and that people and goods traveled, got around. He longed to be back in the land of the living, itched for anything that bespoke humans at their noisy worst, no matter how crass the activity. He would have given more toes to go to a professional wrestling match. He craved rich milk chocolate and things fried in fat; he wanted to see motorcycles parked at dingy roadside bars blasting raucous music. He wanted a hot dog loaded with chili and cheese. He wanted to go to an amusement park and eat cotton candy, come back home ... *home* ... and sit and watch hours of mindless TV and old movies.

This living-dead business was no fun at all.

Frank slammed on the brakes and Alice and the cat nearly slid off the seat.

"What is it?" she asked, grabbing the cat. "Ouch, don't scratch me, Kitty!"

"Road, back there."

A road to the right, to the west! He wheeled the ancient truck around in a U-turn, and gunned it back up the road. The tires screeched as he swung sharply left onto an amazingly well-kept two-lane asphalt road.

"Glory be," Frank breathed.

"Is this the right road home?"

"Home," Frank intoned. "Home ... yeah, honey, we're going home. Away from this crazy place."

She looked at him, beaming, happy. It made him glad. Sunlight formed a mystic yellow halo around her head, and to him she looked saintlike, pure, and transcendent. He forced his vision back to the good road and drove for a mile, then two, then three.

"So far, so good."

"How much farther?" she asked.

"No, you say, 'Are we there yet?' "

"Are we there yet?"

"Not yet, dear, not yet. But we're getting closer."

"Tell me about your farm," Alice said.

"Well, there's a hundred acres. Mostly we grow ..."

"We?"

"My dad. It's my dad's farm, but when I'm on leave I help out as much as I can. He has farm hands to help him most of the time. We grow corn, mostly. And we have hogs. We used to have some dairy cattle but they got too much for him. And there's a patch of vegetables for the table. Not much, as working farms go, but it fed a family."

"It sounds very nice."

"It is. Hard work, but rewarding."

"You think your dad will like me?"

"Of course."

"Does he like cats?"

"Sure. Likes dogs a little better, but he always doted on pets. I think he'll love you and the cat. Don't worry. By the way, do we have a name for this critter yet?"

"I dunno. I can't think of one."

"How about Zombie?"

"Okay. Zombie, the cat."

"Right. Nobody to tell you what to do on a farm. You're on your own."

"I'll love that."

"Not that it isn't rough, sometimes. Things can happen,

crops can fail. Bugs, drought. Hard to make a living. Always was, so I'm told.''

"I wouldn't mind."

"Hard to starve on a farm, though. There's always something to scrounge up. Not like the city you live in. By God, I think that in time everyone there is going to waste away from that bad food."

"Food's lousy," Alice said with a sneer. "I hate it. Hate the cafeterias, the rotten potatoes, the smelly, mildewed vegetables. Frank, I never want to see that place again."

"You won't. You'll like farm food. Dad's a hell of a cook, though he still thinks of it as woman's work. He can make a great beef stew. One of his best dishes. I don't know what he puts in it, but it is about the best . . ."

Frank saw the armored vehicle in the rear view and tramped on the accelerator. Where it had come from, he didn't know. It had probably lain in wait along a side road. Frank had no doubt it was waiting for him.

It was painted in camouflage colors and had big black tires. A gun turret topped it and a smaller gun barrel poked out from a bulbous housing in front—probably a machine gun. It looked like some sort of fast light reconnaissance vehicle. Maybe a small troop carrier. That gun on the turret could be a small cannon or recoilless projectile-thrower.

The truck's engine strained to get some speed. A long uphill grade lay ahead, and Frank had doubts the old heap could make it to the top, much less outrace a reconnaissance vehicle.

He weaved back and forth as they climbed. Not that it would do much good.

A clattering came from behind. Nothing hit. Frank looked back to see the machine-gun barrel spitting fire. It must have been a burst over their heads, a command to stop.

Frank mashed his mangled right foot to the floor and smashed the dashboard with his fist.

"Come on, you old piece of junk, get moving!"

He slammed the gear shift back into second, the engine whined and the truck picked up some speed.

Why the warning? he wondered. Did new orders come through, to capture instead of kill? Or did they want him for sport again, this time for long, slow torture, more skilled, more deliberate? And Alice too, he supposed. Fun.

He wasn't going to give up. Let them use the cannon. He would never surrender to that scum. Never.

An ear-splitting crack split the air behind them, and a gout of asphalt went up with a dull thud about a tenth of a mile up the grade.

That was it. One shot, and it would be over. Alice and him, dead.

He still would not give up.

≫ Chapter Fifteen ≪

The truck continued chugging up the grade through sharp twists and turns, the armored carrier disappearing and reappearing in the rear view window. Frank tramped the gas pedal and kept the transmission screaming in low gear, but the damned thing simply could not or would not get its speed over thirty miles per hour. The armored pursuit vehicle was gaining all the time, though, thankfully, it was no speed demon either. Heavy with armor plating, it purred up the grade steadily and implacably. Another mile and it would be tailgating.

It all depended on how high this mountain was. Frank could see no crest yet. With any luck the road would continue switching its way back and forth up the mountain, and that would provide enough cover until the truck reached the summit. Then, it would be a downhill race.

Up ahead, the road was choked with fallen tree branches. Frank swerved among them and did not lose much momentum. But the next turn was littered with a stream of gravel and loose dirt, debris left from a flash flood, and the old pickup's tires spun uselessly. The speedometer's needle dropped.

Frank mashed the pedal, stamped on the clutch and threw the gear shift into first. The engine wailed and spun the back wheels. The tires began to smoke until they suddenly bit into clean road again with a screech and a lurch.

Another burst of automatic fire came at them. A slug

pinged off the pavement just outside Frank's window, whistling off at a wild angle.

Frank grabbed Alice and hauled her down to the seat, then pushed her roughly to the floor. "Get down and stay down. They're not trying very hard to miss."

Alarmed, Zombie jumped up to the edge of the back of the seat and wailed. Frank grabbed her and threw her at Alice.

Not a moment too soon. Another rattle of the forward gun pod sent something smacking into the back window at the exact spot where Zombie had been. The windshield grew a thousand spiderwebs. He slumped in the seat and tried to keep his head in front of the metal of the window frame.

Then slugs hit everywhere, whanging off the pavement, riddling the rear window, pinging off the truck's cab and body.

"Jesus!"

The back window cascaded into crushed ice. Peering over steering wheel, Frank saw nothing through a windshield afflicted with proliferating fractures. It grew completely opaque, then began to shatter, wicked slivers flying from it, falling into the cab. Frank wondered how much more they could take, how many hits the truck could absorb before it coughed and gave up the ghost.

He couldn't believe he hadn't been hit. As he tugged the wheel from one side to the other, desperately trying to maneuver evasively, it suddenly occurred to him that an offensive measure might be in order. But what?

Rounding a tight bend that soared three hundred feet over a deep vale, they were temporarily immune from fire, and Frank slammed the transmission back into first. He roared up the road a short way, saw a widened section of shoulder, and made a sweeping U-turn, but not without running up on the cut bank on the other side of the road and nearly upsetting.

The truck thumped back down to the roadbed, and he floored it back down the road, heading for the turn. He would have to time it exactly, judging just right how far behind the armored carrier followed. A second's misjudgment, and he would be over the cliff.

"Alice, hang onto something!"

She clutched his knees.

The carrier came out from behind the bend at just the right time and Frank hit it dead on in third gear at about forty miles an hour, ploughing into the carrier's side and shoving it toward the precipice over more gravel and powdery dirt. The carrier's big tires spun helplessly. Frank slammed the gearshift into first again. The truck had enough momentum to push its heavy adversary to the brink of the cliff. The carrier's right rear tire went off the road and the front end reared up. Out of steam momentarily, Frank jerked into reverse, pulled back, and crashed forward again, hitting the vehicle's undercarriage. Frank could see the drive shaft turning uselessly.

The armored car upended and tumbled over the cliff. Frank had to stand on the brakes to prevent the pickup from following. He watched the big thing crash through trees and brush. It hung up for a second, caught in a bramble, the fell through and continued its wild tumble down the mountainside. Eventually, it disappeared from view. The sound of its crashing continued for a long time. Then, abruptly, no more sound issued from the gully below.

Frank turned his head. Another carrier was inching its way up the grade, about a quarter mile away.

"Shit!"

Backing wildly, slamming into the hillside, Frank turned and continued uphill.

Alice climbed up to the seat.

"Keep down, honey. Don't raise your head."

"Are they gone?"

"Yes, but there's another one."

"Give me the gun, Frank, I want to shoot at them."

"Wouldn't do any good, Alice. We're going to make it, baby. Just stay down for me, okay?"

"Okay, but I want to do something. I want to kill those bastards."

"We just killed half of them, now we'll try for the other half. Look in that glove compartment. Thought I saw some matches."

Alice opened up the glove compartment and Frank reached in and rummaged. "I'm sure I saw some . . . where did I?—here they are!" He extracted a small cardboard box.

The crest was not far off. Frank stopped the truck, slipped the gearshift to neutral. "Alice, honey, put your foot on this pedal, where mine is."

"Here?"

"Yeah, like that. Press down, and keep doing it. That stops the truck from moving back. Harder . . . that's it. Keep it like that, and don't let go. Move over a little."

"Okay, Frank. Zombie, stop biting me!"

After making sure the truck wasn't drifting back, Frank sprang out of the cab, went back and unlashed the ten-gallon gas can from its niche in the truck bed. Hefting it, he ran down the road a piece, unscrewed the cap, and upset the can, laying it on its side with the opening downhill. A gush of gasoline flowed out.

He waited for the stream of fuel to fan out a little, then took out the box of matches. Stepping back, he lit one and threw it, turning immediately to run.

The match hit the stream but went out. He lit another one, got closer, and threw it.

The spilled gas went up with a whoosh, and by the time he got back into the cab and began going uphill again, the gas can exploded, sending up a mushroom cloud of orange flame behind them.

"Not going to do much, but it should slow them down a little," Frank said hopefully. "Let us get up this grade."

A black plume of smoke rose from the fire. Frank kept watching the rear view as he wound second gear out to a scream, then shifted, the truck chugging ever upward. The summit grew nearer, nearer. When it was finally reached,

Frank threw the transmission into third, sped over the short level crest and thence downhill.

Keeping one eye on the rear view, Frank watched the mountaintop recede. As he rounded the first downward turn, the armored carrier still hadn't appeared at the summit, and hope bounded in his heart. Now the trick was to take these turns at maximum speed without crashing through the rusted guardrail and careening down the mountain.

He took the first turn cautiously at twenty miles an hour, downshifting into it and accelerating out. The grade wasn't steep yet as the road meandered down the slope under a sheltering canopy of trees. The guard rail was spotty, existing only in sections. Most of the right side of the road ended scarily in midair. The face of the cliff underneath was not perpendicular; trees grew from it, but the angle ensured that once you started down, you would go all the way to the river below.

That was a river down there, Frank noted, a ribbon of sunlight wandering through a green valley. It was beautiful enough to be worthy of a stop and look-see under any other circumstances.

Frank took the next turn boldly at forty-five, then braked into a sharper turn farther down the grade. The back end swerved a little over a wash of fine gravel, but Frank countersteered and averted a spin.

Alice was looking back again. "I don't see them."

"I'm worried about the bridge," Frank said.

"What bridge?"

"The bridge that goes over that river. It may be down. Probably is. This might be it, honey. We'll have to ditch the truck and run. Maybe swim."

"Is this the border?"

"No idea where we are, but that's the western bank of whatever this river is. We'll have to swim it. Can you swim?"

"No."

"You'll learn on the job," Frank said grimly.

"How is it done? Don't people sink when they get into the water?"

"No, you float. You have to remember that. People naturally float. All you have to do is float and move your arms. You pull yourself through the water with your arms."

"Okay," Alice said, nodding, seeming to understand. "Can cats swim?"

Frank winced inwardly. This was going to be impossible. Their chances of escaping were rapidly diminishing to near zero.

But maybe the road didn't go across the river. Maybe it hugged the bank on this side. He hoped it did. He had no confidence whatever that a major bridge leading west would still be open or even exist at all.

Machine guns rattled again, and Frank heard the tumbling, whistling buzz of a slug zipping by his ear.

"Alice, down!"

Alice ducked her head.

"Damn it," he said almost casually. "Didn't slow them up nearly enough."

"Frank, let me shoot at them."

"One inch armor plating, honey. Save the bullets for later. You'll get your chance to shoot."

"I hate them so much."

"So do I."

"Why don't they let us go? Why do they have to hurt us?"

Frank shook his head and leaned on the accelerator. Abandoning caution, he screeched through the next turn and tramped the accelerator.

Another burst of fire sounded, and this time bullets ricocheted off the truck bed and tail. One slug did not ricochet. It pierced the cab mere inches over Frank's head, caromed off the metal strip around the upper edge of the windshield and rattled alarmingly around inside the cab. Astonishingly, it hit no one and did no damage.

The next turn was a monstrous hairpin. Frank aimed for the inner curve and downshifted.

And there, lying on the road, was a wide wash of debris from the flooding: dirt, gravel, granulated clay, wood chips, a concoction with all the ingredients for disaster to happen.

And it did. The truck slid straight through the turn to the other side of the road. Frank countersteered wildly but it all happened in a second, and almost before he could react the little pickup was over the edge of the cliff, careening down the slope through a forest of laurel and sumac.

It wasn't a sheer cliff, and Frank dodged tree after tree. A slide of rocks and gravel formed a path down through the trees, and he tried desperately to keep on it and to keep the truck upright. But it was a losing battle. The truck hit a boulder, turned sideways, and flipped. Before it did, Frank had Alice and Zombie wrapped up in his arms and down on the floor.

The world tumbled around them, crashing and banging, branches snapping and shattering along with the babbling sound of rubble flowing down the side of the mountain.

It went on forever, the tumbling and turning and crashing, and the landslide sounds, and the rocks and dirt flying and the rest of the glass shattering and swirling in a million icy bits around them like a snow flurry, until at last they hit water. The cab began to flood immediately.

Dragging Alice, Frank wriggled out the window. The river was high, dangerously high for a boat, let alone for swimming. They surfaced and the current pulled them downstream, away from the sinking truck. Zombie clung to Alice's neck and Alice clung to Frank, who had trouble freeing his arms to swim. But he managed to get free and paddle with one hand. He looked downstream and saw white water and was afraid.

The first rapid wasn't much, but the next threatened with a huge whirlpool that nearly sucked them in. Man, woman, and cat, they bobbed their way through foaming whiteness and went immediately into another water slide, a long chute that ended in a froth of water and rocks and logs and tree branches.

Then he lost them. He was alone, tumbling through the rush of the river, being ducked and coming up for air, flailing his arms helplessly.

He cried for her, but he couldn't see anything but blue sky and overhanging trees and angry water.

Blackness enveloped him, and then there was nothing, nothing at all for a very long time.

≫ Chapter Sixteen ≪

He was awake a long while before he realized he was awake and not dreaming. Then the fact settled in, and the world was the world, and he was awake and in it. The scene around him was a reprise of his arrival in the Republic: a white room, a hospital room. He was in a bed and at the head of it stood machines that sometimes beeped and hummed, and from them trailed tubes that connected to his body. More tubes than the last time, more wires, too.

There were other differences. This room wasn't drab and featureless. He saw wood trim around the window and molding along the angle between wall and floor, and the walls weren't stark white but a pleasant eggshell white that was almost beige in the shadows. A table, flanked by chairs, stood in front of the sunlit window and on it was a lamp with an attractive shade, and beside the lamp there was a vase filled with yellow flowers.

He almost liked this room. Especially the way the sunlight made the coral-pink curtains glow.

The room's features and appointments presented themselves to him gradually as he lay there, as if introducing themselves to him one by one.

On the wall opposite the bed there was a painting, impressionistic washes of blue depicting a harbor with boats. It looked familiar, somehow.

There was a small crack in the ceiling, he noticed, about

half a foot long, right over the bed. This was not a new building, most likely. But well-maintained, he was sure.

Where was he? He had a vague recollection of people in the room. He must have been semiconscious at the time. He could not remember who the people were, but he remembered voices.

Suddenly, his thinking reordered itself.

"Alice!"

There was no answer.

He called her name again but again he heard nothing. He tried again, then again. No answer. No Alice.

The effort exhausted him, and he fell asleep.

Again, he awoke. The window was dark. The lamp on the table was lighted. The vase with the flowers were gone, but the machines were still there. He could see only their tops around his head. With some pain, he craned his neck and examined their various screens and tiny red indicator lights. He saw squiggles and blinks, but they told him nothing.

Where was he? Who was taking care of him?

He hadn't a clue, unless he was home. Unless he and Alice had floated to the western bank of that river and had been picked up by a border patrol.

That must be it!

Gladness swelled in his heart. That was the only explanation he could think of. Yes, it must be true. He looked the room over. Nothing like this was on the Republic side of the border. That lamp, the curtains, the molding, everything. It was too *normal,* too ordinary.

Too human.

Yes. He was home.

But what of Alice? Where was she?

She must have drowned. And the cat, too. Zombie, the cat. Gone. Both of them.

He cried, and then he fell asleep again.

*   *   *

The sun was coming through the window once more, rendering the coral-pink curtains into iridescent flamingo. A breeze stirred them gently. He could smell the outdoors. It was a spring smell, an earthy smell. A green smell. How could that be? But he knew it was green out there. He could smell it.

He was by now tired of looking at the room. He was tired of that painting. He wished someone would change it.

But they don't ordinarily change paintings in hospital rooms, do they? No.

Oh, wait, what was this? Something new. More flowers, on the bedside table. More yellow flowers. The ones in the vase must have wilted.

How long had he been here? Must be some time.

He was restless and bored, and his head itched. He took his right arm out from underneath the sheets and stared at it.

It was as if he hadn't noticed his arm before. Where had it come from? Why hadn't he used his arms before this? He felt his head and found it was covered in bandages.

"My fucking head," he said. "Always banging it."

He was tired, so he slept again.

Someone in a long white laboratory coat was standing in front of his bed. He studied the face. It was a face neither young nor old. The man was about forty, tall, with prematurely gray hair. The hair was longish and somewhat unkempt, somewhat offsetting the effect of his neatly tied four-in-hand and starched collar. The eyes were a soft gray. The wide mouth was drawn up into a faint smile. It was a friendly face, an open face.

But there was something about it Frank did not like. He couldn't put his finger on it.

"You're up!" the man said cheerfully. "Finally. You've been ducking in and out of a coma for a week. Glad to see you're coming around."

"Where am I?" Frank croaked. His mouth was like cotton.

"Here, let me get you some water."

The man held a plastic squeeze bottle up to Frank's lips. Frank took a sip of cold water. It felt wonderful.

"Where am I?" Frank asked again.

"We call it the Academy. This is our infirmary."

"How long have I been here?"

The man held up a clipboard. "Oh, about two weeks. You were in bad shape. You managed to get yourself not one, but two subdural hematomas. The first one was abscessed. You probably would have died if you'd tried to make it across the border."

"So, I'm still in the Republic."

"You're still in the Republic, I'm afraid. But we're taking good care of you. You have Mediverse, and it's doing a good job so far."

"Oh, God."

"Don't fret. It's a medical subsystem of Innerverse, and it can do things no surgeons can do. It's new, but it seems to be working on you. Those hematomas are dissolving and the damage in those areas of the brain is being repaired on a molecular level, neuron by neuron. Quite miraculous, really. You're going to have a complete recovery, Mr. Sutter."

"You know who I am."

"And what you are, but we knew that from the start. You're a spy. An undercover operative, sent into this country to conduct covert activities. Is that right?"

"What country are you talking about? This is the United States of America."

"Well, it was. And it will be again someday. There won't be any borders, and things will be as they once were. With one difference."

"Innerverse."

"Right. Innerverse. There's really no other way, you know. Without Innerverse, the human race will perish. Maybe not today or tomorrow, but eventually. That was with the old way, the way of so-called autonomous man and his over-precious freedom. But with Innerverse we can look forward to a future bright with promise.''

"And slavery."

The man laughed. It was a perfunctory snort of derision combined with a note of condescension.

"Who are you?"

"Sorry. I'm Dr. Herbert J. Streiner. I'm a physician and a biotechnologist specializing in applied medical nanotechnology. I'm also the Director of the Academy."

"Where is this place?"

"In Virginia. Central Virginia. Even before the Republic it was rural, out in the middle of nowhere, though it's very pretty. This was the site of a small government research laboratory and it has since become a number of things. Namely, a university, and administrative center, and a training facility."

"This is the control center, isn't it?"

"This institution first developed and implemented Innerverse, and now administers it. Yes, we run Innerverse, and Innerverse runs the Republic. You've guessed it. Good job, and you've done a good job spying and keeping one step ahead of us, but why not rest for now? Don't get worked up about anything just yet. You need about a week more flat on your back. Once you're completely out of danger, we'll get you up and into a chair, and then you can progress to full activity in stages. Bet you'd like to get up now, though, wouldn't you?"

"I feel okay."

"Good. That's what we want to hear. We'll get some solid food into you this evening. No more tube stuff. How does that sound?"

"Fine. Tell me something. Did you shoot me up with Innerverse again?"

Streiner looked apologetic. "I'm afraid so. It was necessary. We were wondering about you. You seemed to be exhibiting symptoms of immunity, but that wasn't the case. Were you aware that you'd been given your side's version of Innerverse?''

"What?" Frank's mouth hung open.

"I should say, your side's countermeasure. We found nanotech effectuators all through you, but yours seem to be defensive ones, designed specifically to counteract Innerverse. This was quite a revelation to us. We had no idea that any nanotechnology advances had been made on your side at all. Your people have done a good job keeping it secret. And a damn good job of keeping our spies in the dark, too."

"You have spies in the Central States?"

"Of course we have spies. Fair is fair. But none of them got wind of this." Streiner looked at him askance. "You mean, they didn't tell you?"

"No, I wasn't told."

Streiner was surprised. "They gave you this stuff and didn't tell you about it? Curious, I must say. And a little irresponsible. You've been an unwitting guinea pig."

That explains a lot, Frank thought.

"So, you're it," Frank said. "You're the leader. The boss of this whole country. Right?"

Streiner shrugged. "Antiquated notion. Boss, leader. Innerverse will one day make the concept obsolete. There won't be any leaders. There will be the community and the community's welfare, and the technological means to secure it. But, to answer your question, Frank, I'm only the director of the Academy's research team. There is an administrative team. If anyone has the job of running this country, it's theirs. They train all bureaucratic personnel, they give the orders, they make the country go."

"Are all the administrators here?"

"Yes. Everyone who has a hand in managing the ongoing enterprise, the ongoing experiment of the Republic, resides here at the Academy. You'd be surprised how small our numbers are. With modern computer systems, and the advances we've made since the birth of the Republic, we could run a country three times this size with ease.''

"Must be easy when every goddamned citizen in the country is a zombie.''

Streiner laughed again. "You're talking like the army boys.''

"Who the hell do you think you're kidding?'' Frank tried to shout but only croaked again. "Your *army* ... that gang of jackals has the run of the place. What's all this crap about peace and community when you depend on those jerks to keep everybody in line?''

"That's not true. It is true that we still need the army to contain certain segments of the population. The Controls, the Immunes, and those poor unfortunates who are beyond Innerverse's capacity to help, such as the mentally handicapped and the insane.''

"Why do you have the Controls?''

"Every experiment needs controls. The Founders—my father was one of them, but he's died since—the Founders didn't inoculate everyone. There had to be a control population for any number of experimental scientific reasons, and also because we needed an unaffected population as a backup if something went radically wrong with the experiment. But we had to keep the Controls here in the Republic, had to stop their emigrating out. So, the army was decontrolled with Innerpause. It renders Innerverse temporarily ineffective, but the subject must be reinoculated periodically. That's how we control the army boys.''

Frank grunted. "Boys.''

Streiner's shoulders slumped. "I know they're rough. Some of them are ... well, frankly, some of them are criminal. And it was criminal what was done to you. Your foot. But you see, that only shows up how necessary Innerverse is. With Innerverse, the sergeant who did that to you would not have been able to hurt you. He would have been incapable of harming another human being. Innerverse sees to that by pouncing at the first sign of aggressive emotions, smothering them before they can incite action. That's how Innerverse works. But he was not under its control when he did that to you. He had Innerpause. Do you understand?"

"He was a monster. A rapist. A—"

A pained expression crossed Streiner's face as he held up a hand. "I know, I know. And he's undergoing behavioral therapy. He won't be given Innerpause again. He's too big a risk. We've had problems with the army all along. They've presented us with any number of dilemmas over the years. But ..." Streiner sighed deeply. "They are necessary. Indispensable, in fact, until the day when the entire world has a new, perfected, and thoroughly tested version of Innerverse. Then there will be no armies and no wars, and no poverty, no crime. There will be nothing but human happiness and peace, forever. Don't you think it will have been worth it?"

"No. It's slavery."

Streiner nodded. "I realize that's how you feel. And I don't blame you really. In the coming weeks we're going to try to change your attitude. You don't know a lot about us. We want you to get to know us. But for now, rest, recuperate, get well, Frank. That's what we want."

"You tried to kill me several times."

Streiner shook his head sadly. "No. My orders were to find you and bring you back alive. Sometimes we can't seem to control the army boys at all ..." He laughed. "I still call them boys, because that's what their emotional level seems to be, sometimes. At about the level of a fourteen-year-old, maybe. Anyway, sometimes we simply can't control them at all, and when we tell them to bring someone in, we can't always be sure that they'll be alive. But that's the way it's always been, historically, hasn't it? How many times have police brought in a dead body instead of a live prisoner?"

"This isn't the real world," Frank said. "Don't invoke history. You're out of it completely."

Streiner gave him a strange, crooked smile. "You're absolutely right. Few people have realized this. With Innerverse, history in effect stops. So does the class struggle, and the war between the sexes, and all the rest of the so-called dialectical forces of historical development. You're perceptive, Frank. Intelligent. I think that you will finally come to an understanding of us, of what we're trying to do."

"I doubt it. Answer me another question. What happened to Alice?"

Streiner shrugged. "Who's Alice?"

Frank closed his eyes. "Never mind. I'm sleepy. I'm always sleepy."

"You'll get stronger day by day. Rest up, Frank. Get well soon."

When he opened his eyes again, Dr. Streiner was gone.

≥ Chapter Seventeen ≤

He awoke to find green eyes staring at him.

Mrrrrrrwr!

"Zombie," he said, smiling.

"And me, Frank."

Alice's face came into view.

He reached an arm around her neck and drew her to him.

"Alice, darling. My God, am I glad to see you. They didn't tell me...."

"You should have said you called her 'Alice' instead of her cognomen," came Streiner's voice.

Frank raised his head a little. The gray-haired scientist was standing on the opposite side of the bed from Alice, smiling.

"How are you feeling, Frank?" he asked.

"Fine, now. Now that I have my Alice back. And Zombie."

"We were worried about you," Alice said. "You almost drowned."

"What happened, Alice? I blacked out."

"I just floated, like you said. Zombie held on to me. It hurt a little, with her claws and all, but it was okay, I didn't mind. We floated down the river until the soldiers fished us out of the water. Then they went back up the river to get you. You weren't breathing, but they worked on you. Two of them did, and they brought you around.

Then they took you away and I didn't see you for a week. They brought me and Zombie here, and today they let me see you for the first time.''

"You're okay, then?'' he asked.

"I'm fine, I didn't get hurt. Not at all. And Zombie's fine, too.''

"I can see.'' Frank stroked the gray cat sitting on his chest.

Mrrrrrwr.

"Sorry about the misunderstanding,'' Streiner said. "I should have realized you were talking about your companion.''

Zombie brought her cold nose up against Frank's.

"I don't know who else I could have been talking about,'' Frank said. "Or were you thinking of just spiriting her back to the city and telling me she drowned?''

"Never crossed my mind,'' Streiner said. "We want to keep Alice for observation. She seems depressed.''

Frank shot Streiner a look. "No kidding.''

"Clinically, I mean. It might have something to do with her malfunctioning Innerverse. That happens.''

"You're going to reinoculate her?''

"Of course, but not with the old version.''

"I see. The new stuff, the stuff she's not immune to.''

"Not what you're thinking. We really don't know about immunity. There are several schools of thought. One says that there is no real immunity, just malfunction. Computer malfunction. The human body should have no intrinsic capacity to resist nanotechnology. However, there are some researchers who think immunity is possible. We just don't know. Really, we were thinking of giving Alice Innercircle.''

"What the hell's that?''

"What I and all Academicians have. It's a version of Innerverse that allows much leeway.''

"Anybody else have it?''

"No.''

"Strictly for the nomenklatura.''

"I know the word, Frank. We're not an elite. Not a ruling class. We're engineers setting up the machinery. Once that job's done, we're history."

"You'll wither away?"

"I get all the sly allusions, Frank. Clever, but not at all apt."

"Why Innercircle for Alice?"

"She doesn't have it yet. She has Innerverse 2, but if we decide she's right for Innercircle, we'll cancel 2 and give her that. She's very bright. Her work record is spotless and her ratings are consistently high. We think we can make a supervisor out of her. Who knows, maybe an Academician. She's bright enough. Far from spiriting her away, or liquidating her ... there's a term for you ... we're gong to make her upwardly socially mobile, so to speak."

"How do you feel about that, Alice?" Frank asked.

"I want to go home with you."

"There you are, Dr. Streiner," Frank said.

"That won't be possible, Alice. No one can emigrate from the Republic."

"Except your spies," Frank put in.

"No one. People with the gift of Innerverse simply can't live in a society with dog-eat-dog competition. They wouldn't last two weeks. They'd be eaten alive."

"I still want to go with him," Alice told Streiner. "I don't want to live here anymore."

"Why, Alice? What makes you think the grass is greener in the Central States?"

"They have freedom."

Streiner shook his head. "They have more constraints than you realize, and when you parse it all out, you really have more freedom here. Freedom from want, freedom from getting trampled underneath the rushing feet of avarice, freedom from having your sex be a liability. Lots of things, Alice. What about the economic security?"

Frank said, "Those crumbling high-rise cell blocks and the rotten food are security?"

"Frank, we need to have a talk. A long one. You'll have to be oriented inside our frame of reference, our coordinate system, before you'll be able to understand us. When you're up and around, and I think your schedule calls for that today, in fact . . . when you're up and about we want you to come to our nightly dinner. The entire faculty eats together every night in the refectory. Sort of a family thing, you know. Before that, though, I want to give you the Cook's tour of the place. You'll need to be in your wheelchair, and that will be in a few days. How does that sound? By the way, are you getting some solid food?"

"Still liquids only last night."

"Well, okay, that's at the discretion of Dr. Farber, the neurologist. She has your case. Look, I'll be running along. Alice, you can stay as long as you like. Okay?"

"Thank you."

"Bye now."

Streiner waved as he walked out, lab coat trailing.

"Thought he'd never leave," Frank said.

Mrrrrrrwr, Zombie commented.

"Frank, what are we going to do?"

"Well, I'm going to get well first. And then we're going to get out of this monkey house. Haven't figured out exactly how."

"Did they give you Innerverse again?"

"Same thing you have, I guess. Innerverse 2."

Alice cast her eyes down. "I know, I can feel it. It's like a nightmare coming back. I'd almost forgotten what it was like. Frank, it's awful."

"Honey, don't fret. We're getting out of here. Just give me time to think. Meanwhile, don't let them make a bureaucrat out of you."

"They've assigned me to training courses."

"Go to them, don't make waves."

"If I don't, Innerverse will make me."

"True. But don't fight it, for now. Test it, see how strong it is. If it's too strong to fight directly, there's al-

ways the chance your body will resist this strain like it
did the old one.''

"I've tried fighting," Alice said. "No good. This one
is strong, Frank. Very strong.''

Frank nodded ruefully. "I figured. I've got to test it
myself, though.''

"Be careful. I felt so awful I thought I was going to
die in another minute.''

"Bastards. The community welfare.''

"What?''

"Something Streiner said. Anyway, did you get a look
at this place? Are you free to roam?''

"Oh, sure. They didn't lock me up or anything. But
you can't leave the grounds. It's beautiful, really. Trees,
grass, nice buildings. Like a park, only nicer.''

"I'm eager to take a look-see myself, if they ever let
me get up.''

"Do you think you can walk?''

"Let's try. Get these sheets off me.''

"What about these wires and tubes?''

"Yank 'em out.''

"Won't that hurt?''

"After the toe business, nothing hurts.''

They were interrupted by the arrival of lunch. A young
male orderly pushed a tiered cart into the room.

"Solid food for you today," he piped. "Doctor's orders.
Can you feed yourself?''

"Sure.''

"I will, if he can't," Alice said, taking the cat off the
bed.

Alice set up Frank's cantilevered bedside table and
placed his tray on it.

"How's the food here?" Frank asked.

"It's wonderful.''

"This certainly looks unobjectionable.''

On the tray was a plate holding meatloaf, mashed potatoes, gravy, and creamed peas. Flanking the entree were
a dessert cup full of what looked like rice pudding and,

on the other side, hard rolls with a pat of yellow butter-
stuff. Frank took a fork and cut through the meat, speared
it. He smelled it before popping it into his mouth. He
chewed experimentally.

"Not bad," he said. "Tastes like real meat."

"That's not even half as good as I get," Alice said.
"Last night they served steak in the refectory."

"Steak? Real steak?"

"I think it was. I've never eaten real steak. I've had
patties that were supposed to be meat, but I don't think
it was."

"You mean that farm stuff was maybe the first real
animal flesh you ever had?"

"Maybe."

"Well, this is real ground meat. They have it doctored
up more than I like, but it's pretty good."

He began to eat in earnest. Alice buttered a roll for him.

"My God," Frank said. "Don't tell me. Real butter?"

"Try it."

He did, nodding. "I'd say so."

"Tastes great, whatever it is. I've tried it."

"Nothing like fresh-churned country butter," Frank
said. "Sweet cream butter."

"I've seen pictures of farmers churning butter. Do you
do it by hand?"

"Not if you can avoid it. My dad used an electric mixer.
Whatever the method, you can't beat the real thing."

"But it's not supposed to be good for you."

"It clogs the arteries. I like it."

The cat bounded up to the bed. "*Mrrrrrrwr!*"

Alice laughed. "Zombie wants some."

"You feeding this cat?"

"They do in the lab, they told me."

"Here you go, Zomb," Frank said, proffering a tiny
morsel of meat on the end of his fork. Zombie sniffed,
approved, and took the food in a bite.

"Keep her away from that lab," he said. "They might
try to make her as good as her name."

After lunch two orderlies came in to lift Frank out of bed and seat him in a chair by the window, dressing him in a terrycloth robe first. He sat comfortably, looking out the window, which gave on a wide aspect of trimmed lawn bordered by hedges. He watched fleecy clouds move majestically across the sky. He watched birds peck at the lawn. He listened to insects buzzing about. The earth seemed very good out there. The sunlight was golden and good and he longed to be back home. He wanted to drive the tractor and plow up a couple of acres, and then go back to the house and fix all the things that needed fixing. Then he would lie in a hayfield and let the rest of the golden day happen around him.

But he wasn't home, he was here. And here he would stay unless he found a lever with which to pry himself out of Innerverse's vise.

He wondered what they would ultimately do with him. Maybe they didn't shoot spies, just absorbed them. That was probably the case. Why waste the bullets when you can render any enemy harmless by other means? He marveled at the value system that could balk at shooting a spy yet suffer a renegade army to prey upon the populace.

And what happened to Immunes and other misfits who got a knock on the door late at night? What would really happen to Alice? Was Streiner telling the truth or was he lying to string Sutter along? If so, for what purpose? Maybe they wanted something from him. Information. But if they had a vast spy network operating in the Central States, they would need no information from him.

Maybe they wanted corroboration of info they already had. He wondered about interrogation. He was again in Innerverse's thrall, so that meant, theoretically at least, that they could simply order him to divulge everything he knew, and he would have to obey under pain of Innerverse's lash. This possibility made him fearful. It was torture plain and simple, but he did not know how long he could stand up under it. Could they give him something to increase the pain? Maybe. They had all sorts of versions of Innerverse. Perhaps they had one that specialized in torture.

But if that were true, why hadn't they interrogated him already? Because they couldn't, because they wouldn't, or because they didn't need to?

He had no answers. So he sat and looked at clouds and flowers and hedges and lawns and thought about home.

≫ Chapter Eighteen ≪

The next afternoon they wheeled him up and down the hall, and he spent the afternoon in the solarium looking at picture magazines.

He walked for the first time the next day, going to the bathroom by himself. That afternoon he was wheeled out through the doors and spent time in a pleasant courtyard, basking in the sun and not doing much else but thinking of ways to escape.

The next few days were increments of increased activity, and inside a week he was walking the grounds around the infirmary. The building was neo-Georgian and the other buildings of the campus were the same. This, he concluded, must have been a college campus at one time. University of Virginia? No, not big enough. Some four-year college or small university. The original research facility must have been on the campus.

He walked down a long concourse lined with white birch and saw that it stretched along a row of buildings to the edge of the campus. He followed it all the way to a sidewalk running along a street where he could see the ruins of a town. A college ghost town, silent and deserted. He decided to leave the campus and explore, but he had not even crossed the street before the nausea began.

It was intense enough to double him up. Dry heaves racked him and did not abate until he had recrossed the street and was back on campus.

He sat on a stone bench and belched for five minutes. "Well, so much for that."

At least he knew where he stood. He marveled at the power of a thing that could detect the barest hint of disobedience, even the casual thought of it. Had he really been determined to escape right then? Would he have continued walking and left Alice behind? No, not really. But Innerverse 2 had detected something in him, interpreting it as rebellion. Whatever that chemical index had been, it had not been strong emotion, not aggression, not anger or hate. How could Innerverse know what he was thinking? Or did the body also in a certain sense think along with the mind? That must be the answer. The "mind" was not a purely mental phenomenon. Every thought in the brain must be accompanied by a physical response somewhere in the body. Every thought triggered an emotion or was itself an emotion of some sort. All one needed to do was to learn to recognize emotions by their telltale chemical sign, and one could in effect read the mind, by reading the mind body.

He walked back to the infirmary, satisfied that he understood something, that he had cracked at least part of the puzzle. But much more enigma remained.

And how does one fight it?

He recalled what Streiner had said about easily canceling one version of Innerverse before replacing it with another. Frank's task was clear. Find out more about this cancellation process and either steal the means for it or talk someone into giving it to him. Perhaps one of Streiner's colleagues might be persuaded, might be won over? Alice had been a beacon in the outer darkness. Surely his finding another in the inner sanctum was not entirely impossible.

He met many of Dr. Streiner's colleagues the next day, when Streiner himself conducted him on a tour of the Academy.

"This is only part of the lab complex," Streiner said as he led Frank down a long hallway, past door after door.

The place looked like any laboratory conducting research in the biological sciences. Frank saw cages full of rats, monkeys and other animals. (Monkeys imported? No, simply bred in captivity like the rats.) There were rooms full of computer equipment. There were offices, meeting rooms, storerooms, and other facilities that Frank couldn't quite place. In just about every room, researchers in white lab coats busied themselves among all the paraphernalia.

"This is the heart of it, though," Streiner went on. "Nanotechnology research. There are other labs that do more mundane stuff—agriculture, medicine, and whatnot. Ultimately, all technology will one day have a nanotechnological base. We'll be able to do everything with it. Grow food, cure diseases, manufacture goods. We're still in the early stages of development, for all that we've been at it for thirty or more years. A hundred years from now, who knows what shape these techniques will take? Who knows what new applications will come along?"

"It must be something to have a whole country to experiment on," Frank commented.

"True. But it's not entirely unprecedented. There have been large-scale social experiments before. I can think of some obvious examples, and some not-so-obvious ones. In here, Frank."

Streiner led Frank through an anteroom full of desks and computer stations to a large corner office. The door was open.

Inside, an attractive woman with straw-yellow hair was seated behind an expansive polished desk heaped with computer printouts and other paper. She had brilliant blue eyes, and when she came around the desk to shake Frank's hand, Frank saw with curiosity that their blue was so intense they almost burned.

"Frank, I'd like you to meet Dr. Sellers. Mary Sellers."

"Dr. Sellers, happy to meet you."

"Has Herb been giving you the tour of our little world?"

"Yes, your noble experiment."

Streiner said, "Wasn't it Prohibition that was called a 'noble experiment?' "

"Proved to be a foolish one."

"True. And like all experiments, Innerverse could fail. We're scientists, Frank. Our worldview incorporates the possibility of failure. All theories, all hypotheses must be tested. If proved wrong, they're thrown out. A simple process, really. A rational process."

"You call this country rational?"

"What do you say, Mary?" Streiner asked. "Are we crazy?"

"We don't think so, Frank," Dr. Sellers said. "In fact, we think we're the first rational civilization to come along. We've thrown away ideology, belief, and dogma, along with every kind of unfounded assumption."

"Absolutely," Streiner said. "Gone are democracy, capitalism, socialism, Marxism, and sectarian belief, all really transforms of one another."

"From a scientific point of view," Dr. Sellers said, "they're all sets of unfalsifiable propositions, all equally useless."

Frank looked at Sellers. "I assume religion is gone, too."

"Completely," Streiner answered. "No remnants exist within the Republic, no catacombs, no underground movements. All sectarian belief has been wiped out for good. Religion was needed once, as a social glue to bind societies together. But it's not needed now, and the negative aspects, the sectarian strife, the hatreds and prejudices, were never needed. All gone now—Catholicism, Judaism, Shintoism, Buddhism, and the rest. All in the dustbin of history, finally."

Sellers crossed her arms, nodding. "And good riddance, I say."

Frank asked, "How about among the Controls?"

Streiner smiled. "The Controls. As time goes on and the experiment proves to be more and more of a success, the Controls matter less and less. Sure, there are still masses being said and candles being lighted somewhere in the Republic, and prayer shawls being donned in ad hoc synagogues and all that. I suppose what I said before was overstatement, but I was speaking about what happens within the confines of Innerverse society. Most of the Controls are in their sunset years now. Most of them will be gone within a decade. In two decades, few, if any, will be left.''

''And you'll have the pure form of your utopia,'' Frank said.

''We hope so, we hope so,'' Sellers said.

Frank was curious about her. He thought, but couldn't be at all sure, that the same note of confidence and complete conviction that sounded in Streiner was not echoed in her. Her eyes . . . was it fancy on his part? . . . her eyes seemed to question, seemed to probe. She looked at Frank as if in him she saw something new on the scene, some fresh possibility crossing her horizon. Possibility of what? He did not know. Something was hidden behind that brilliant blue gaze. He filed this datum for future reference.

''Very nice to meet you,'' Frank told her.

''Same here. I hope you're coming to dinner tonight.''

''I'm looking forward to it.''

''In fact,'' said Streiner, ''let's go to the refectory next, shall we?''

The refectory was a large dining hall, but it was not a cafeteria. It looked like a typical upscale restaurant, potted plants and all, the tables set with silver and white linen. The far end of the room was lined with French windows letting out to a terrace and a garden beyond.

After a tour of the kitchen, they walked out a back door and down a tree-lined path to a small building with a playground, equipped with swings and jungle gyms, to one side of it.

''Children,'' Frank said.

''Yes, our children. But we don't live in families, Frank. The children live in their dormitory, over there. We have no families, as such. I myself have a son and daughter in this school.''

Streiner returned Frank's odd look with a smile. "I know who they are, Frank, and they know me. In fact, they call me 'Dad.' Don't think these are test-tube babies or something, raised as automatons. I can see you're thinking along those lines. No, they're my kids, and I take full responsibility for them. They are simply raised by the state, not me or my wife.''

Frank noted the first mention of sexuality and the implied monogamy. He wondered about living arrangements.

"How many children in the last fifty years or so before the Republic were raised in daycare centers?''

"But they went home at night.''

"And so do these kids. Their dorm is their home, they decorate it themselves, and they live quite happily, Frank, I assure you. Ask them. As for their education, they get the best here.''

"Do other kids get the best where they are?''

"Frank, remember that this is temporary. When the Republic gets going on its own, when things have established themselves and have stabilized into an unalterable pattern of organization, this will vanish. Sure, we're an elite, Frank. And these kids are our kids, pampered and nurtured. We love them. We want the best for them. They are the future . . . come on in and say hello to the staff, Frank—''

"That's not what I asked you, Dr. Streiner,'' Frank said as he walked through the open door.

"Sorry, what?''

Inside was a large space divided up into different activity areas. It looked like any large daycare or nursery school. The children ranged in ages from two through about seven or eight.

"We have our schools organized a little differently than what's usual. This daycare nursery-school motif is continued for kids up to and including ten-year-olds. After that they enter the Athenaeum, and we'll see that next. The

Athenaeum is grade school and high school compressed into five years. By the time a kid is fifteen, he's ready for the university.''

The thirty or so kids looked healthy, happy, and busy. They looked no different from any kid Frank had ever seen. Smiling, bright, and enthusiastic, they didn't act like zombies. The only thing odd was that they all wore lab coats, though dyed in bright colors. Some sported candy stripes or polka dots.

"Do they have Innerverse or Innercircle?" Frank wanted to know.

"Another version entirely," Streiner said. "We've nicknamed it 'Poohverse' or 'Innerpooh.' A few wags say 'Innerbrat.' It's gentle, very low key. Kids don't need as much guidance as adults, strange to say, Kids are malleable, tractable. A little nudge in the right direction and they'll go. Child behavior disorders are taken care of with the adult version, but we've seen little of that. Now, in the nursery school here, they get an educational approach that combines the best of many theories of education, from behaviorist to Montessori. The cream of the educational experimentation of the last century. And it works, it works.''

Frank inspected the usual artwork and posters and science projects.

"This is our head of the teaching staff, Jane Allbright," Streiner said, introducing a small, brown-haired woman in her thirties. Frank shook her tiny hand.

"And this is the staff, Jerry, Bruce, Kathy . . . and . . . Karen? Karen. And Melissa.''

Dressed in garishly dyed lab coats, they all greeted Frank with cheery smiles.

"You have a nice facility here," Frank said.

"We like it, and so do the kids," Jane said. "Though sometimes they wear us out.''

They all chuckled ruefully in agreement.

"I can imagine," Frank said. "Well, nice to meet you all.''

"Bye!" piped one child, a red-haired cutie, waving at him.

He waved back as he left.

The Athenaeum was next. Inside and out it looked like any private boarding school, except that there were no traditional classrooms. Everything was done by computers, with teachers monitoring. Each child had his own personal computer. Some of the kids looked bored and some day-dreamed, but no more so than any schoolkid in any era.

"Let's visit the dorms next," Streiner said.

"Dorms" didn't quite say it. The residence buildings were divided into apartments, some small, others quite spacious. Assignments according to rank, Frank surmised.

"This is mine," Streiner said, opening a door. "Come on in. Like a drink?"

"Are we talking alcohol?"

"Indeed we are, anything you like. Vodka, whiskey, you name it."

"Whiskey on the rocks would be fine."

The place was decorated in faultless, if eclectic, good taste. Some of the furniture looked like museum pieces, and no doubt once had been just that. The white computer CRT screen on the desk in the corner was an anachronistic note.

"Duncan Phyfe," Streiner said, standing at a small bar and pouring.

"I beg your pardon?"

"You were looking at that Sheraton-style sofa, there. It was designed by an American furniture and cabinetmaker by the name of Duncan Phyfe. P-h-y-f-e. He died about 1850 or thereabouts. His furniture goes well with most of the period architecture on campus."

"Very nice indeed."

Streiner handed Frank a glass full of ice and whiskey. "Sour mash," he said. "Hope you like it."

Frank sampled it. "Real sippin' whiskey. Not everything here is early American."

"There actually aren't a lot of colonial pieces."

"Well, middle, whatever. Now, this is Chinese?"

"Yes, a lacquered screen, Chi'ing dynasty, eighteenth century."

"Beautiful."

"Yes. I love it. The place is a hodgepodge, really. No attempt at consistency or completeness. There's furniture from about a dozen periods and makers. Late colonial, Federal, Victorian, Chippendale, Sheraton, Hepplewhite, and a few European and Oriental things thrown in. As I said, just things that I happened to like, and it's not all historical. See this? Mies van der Rohe, Barcelona chair. Modern, though you could put that in quotes. I guess in a sense it's an antique, too."

Frank sat in the Barcelona chair. "Uncomfortable as hell."

Streiner relaxed on the sofa. "Modern design isn't about comfort," he said with a chuckle. "Drink up, Frank."

Frank sipped his whiskey.

"You said something before we went into the nursery school," Streiner said. " 'That's not what I asked you,' you said. What did you want to ask?"

"About kids in the rest of the country. Do you love them, too?"

"Of course. They're our kids, too."

"I never saw any of your schools except this one, but if the conditions I did see and experience carry over into your schools, things must be pretty grim."

"I'll admit they are ordinary. But as I said, this little island of privilege will not last indefinitely. Once we've fully tested the new version of Innerverse, it will be swept away into history."

"And then all the schools will be grim and useless."

"There won't be any elite schools, that's true."

"That's your only objective, equality?"

"One of them."

"But who will run the country? How will you train young minds to do the work that must be done? How will you train the doctors, the lawyers, the productive citizens?''

"Frank, your thinking is limited by certain assumptions. If things work out, education will be an outmoded concept.''

"How could that possible be?''

"As for training doctors, Mediverse will eliminate the need for any and all medical macrotechnology. There will be no hospitals, no beds, no medicines, no pills, no nurses, and no doctors, either, finally. Nanomachines will maintain and monitor human health and will do so with precision and with minimum expenditure of energy. 'Medicine' as a discipline will take its place beside bloodletting, alchemy, and other curiosities of science. And at the end of that road of development, Frank, is a goal so fantastic that you'll say it's a pipe dream.''

"What is it?''

"Immortality. It's foreseeable, if current trends maintain themselves. Did you know that Mediverse can cure most forms of cancer? Not all, yet, but most. We've made great strides. We've also made some inroads into Alzheimer's and multiple sclerosis. Heart disease was a breeze. There's no reason anyone should ever again have a heart attack due to atherosclerosis, ever again. And who knows what will happen in the future. It's within our grasp to eliminate every single disease and debilitative condition to afflict humankind. Isn't that as bright a future as you can imagine?''

"It'll be wonderful. But how will you train your nanotechnologists?''

"We'll train them here.''

"On this swept-away island?''

"We'll be in business for generations, yet, Frank. I'm speaking of great sweeps of future history here. Indulge me.''

"Yes, I think you will be in business for some time to come. Will your son become Director of Research someday?''

"He won't inherit it, if that's what you mean. No birthrights, no inheritable titles in this aristocracy. If he's qualified, if he has the talent, and if he can convince the community that he merits the job, it's his. But not unless all those conditions are met first. The same goes for my daughter, for that matter. Don't think there are any gender prerequisites for the job."

"Interesting. A meritocracy capping off an autocracy. By the way, how did you get the job?"

"My father, Herbert J. Streiner, Sr., was the first Director of Research at the Academy. Yes, I did inherit the job, in a sense. But the buck stops, so to speak, with me. You think we're rulers, Frank, but we're not. We're not despots. We're scientists conducting an experiment. We have as our objective the ancient aim of science, to understand the universe. In this case, the human universe. Ourselves. Man is the ultimate mystery, Frank. The only truly important one. Who cares whether the universe is finite or infinite, or expanding or contracting, who cares what elements are to be found on the farthest star or galaxy? The universe is finite, all right, and it's right up here." Streiner pointed to his head. "The skull is its event horizon. And its elements are the ordinary ones linked into amino acids that are in turn configured into proteins. The protein universe is the only one that counts."

"But who'll run the show, Dr. Streiner? Who'll run the family business when all your sons and daughters are zombies?"

"I wish you wouldn't use that word, Frank. It's not appropriate."

"Answer the question."

"Innerverse will run things."

"What?" Frank was incredulous.

"We have hundreds of ongoing research projects on this campus, Frank, and we have a very active artificial intelligence project going. You'd be amazed what we've come up with. Look at this." Streiner raised his voice. "Adam?"

"Yes, sir?"

The voice came out of the air, it seemed at first. But as it spoke further Frank located the source: any of a half dozen small speakers set into and distributed about the ceiling.

"Adam, I'd like you to meet Frank, our guest."

"Hello, Frank. I'm Adam. I'm a computer system dedicated to maintaining this dormitory complex. My duties are to monitor all heating and cooling equipment and regulate them, to maintain appropriate interior temperatures, to see to regular inspection and maintenance of all electrical circuits—"

"That's all, Adam. Thank you."

"You're welcome, Dr. Streiner."

Streiner was smiling. "Do you have anything like that in the Central States?"

"Don't know," Frank said. "Haven't followed research into artificial intelligence."

"Adam is only a subsystem, and a limited one. We have full-fledged machine intelligences helping us in the labs. And once we get Adam's technology down to nano size, we will have a fully sentient Innerverse capable of carrying on indefinitely into the future as a self-creating, self-correcting, self-expanding entity. An internal overseer who will guide mankind to its ultimate destiny."

"Which is?"

Streiner took a drink. "Why don't we talk about that over dinner? And we'll talk about you, too, Frank."

"Let's talk about me now," Frank said. "By the way, you mentioned a wife."

"Dr. Sellers is my wife," Streiner said.

"So you have marriage."

"Yes, or monogamous relationships, call them what you will. Lots of things from the old culture have carried over. There may be some anthropological reason for monogamy, and then again there may not be. We don't know. It doesn't matter, really. In the future there won't be any marriages, and there might not be any relationships per se."

"What were you saying about bright futures? Sounds pretty bleak to me."

"Not what you think. We're not going to eliminate sex. Just jealousy, exclusivity, and possessiveness."

"How about friendship?"

Streiner grinned. "We don't want to throw the baby out with the bathwater. We simply want to wash out some ancient, set-in stains. But we were talking about you."

"What about me? What are you going to do with me?"

"Do with you? Nothing. Though I think you'd make a good general."

"Eh?"

"How would you like to head up the army?"

"You're joking, surely."

"I'm not. You're a military man. Career?"

"Yes."

"You're a lieutenant? How about an instant promotion?"

"Why do you think I'd take the job of leading that pack of scavengers?"

"We've been lax about them, I know. Letting them run wild. Here's your chance to whip them into shape, to weed out the baddies. Make the army into a servant of the people, as they should be."

"Forget it, Streiner. Get yourself another tin Hitler for your stormtroopers."

Streiner finished his drink and looked at Frank levelly. He put his hand in the inner pocket of his sports coat. "Have you forgotten that you murdered several human beings over the past few days? You shot one point blank, through the chest, for no apparent reason. An innocent life, Frank."

He pulled out what looked like Frank's Glock semiautomatic and pointed it at Frank.

"And you took it. How can you judge?"

"I was wondering when you were going to show your teeth, Streiner."

"Not at all. Here."

He flipped the gun around and offered it butt first.

"What's this?" Frank took it and immediately pointed it back at Streiner.

"The culture of violence," Streiner said. "It'll never die unless it's killed. You'd shoot me now, if you could. But you can't."

Frank's finger tightened on the trigger. Simultaneously, a powerful wave of nausea hit him. He clutched his middle, bent over and belched loudly. "You bastard."

Streiner smiled. "Uncanny how it knows, isn't it?"

"Uncanny."

"You can't hide that chemical telltale. It's a huge one, by the way, the one that signals that a human being is about to commit a violent act. Any violent act. Flashing lights, sirens, fireworks. Unmistakeable. For Innerverse, anyway. Did you know there are visual cues as well? The face drains, the pupils constrict. We could control behavior from outside the body if we wanted to, purely by observation. Laser beams would read you like a book, note this and that index, and signal for action. But that would probably be clumsy. Innerverse is much more efficient taking its reading internally. Go ahead, Frank. Pull the trigger. Pull it. Takes only an ounce of effort."

Slumping, Frank dropped the gun. It thudded to the carpeting.

Still grinning, Streiner picked it up.

"You feel no remorse for killing that man?"

"I did what I had to do."

"As do we, Frank. When you graduate to Innercircle, as one day I think you will, you'll feel remorse for what you do." Streiner put the gun back into his pocket. "I'm starved. You are coming to dinner?"

"Wouldn't miss it for the world."

"Good. Let's go." Streiner looked at his watch. "The staff should be gathering for the banquet."

Frank belched and said, "Banquet?"

Streiner nodded, beaming. "You're the guest of honor."

⪢ Chapter Nineteen ⪡

The dining hall had been rearranged for a banquet. Satellite tables seating six to eight surrounded a head table near the French doors. Each place was set with elaborate silverware and a large fruit cup.

When Frank walked in all eyes were on him. He saw Alice seated at the head table and walked to her, gave her a kiss. Zombie was under the table, and when he sat she sniffed his shoes and rubbed herself against his shins.

He reached to pet her, looking under the table, and when he looked up again he saw that Dr. Sellers had sat down next to him, and on her right was Dr. Streiner.

"I think you're all aware of who our guests are this evening," Streiner spoke. "Not that we get many guests here, especially foreign guests. Anyway, in case you haven't run into them during the course of your various duties, I'd like to introduce Frank Sutter and his friend, Alice."

"And Zombie," Alice said, holding the cat up.

"*Mrrrrrwr!*"

Everyone laughed.

"You know my policy is eat first, talk later," Streiner said, "so let's eat."

Frank dug into the fruit cup. He hadn't had fresh fruit in . . . he didn't know how long. It was delicious.

After Italian wedding soup and shrimp in lemon-butter sauce with garlic, the entree was chicken, though not the

188

rubber variety traditional with banquets. Hardwood flame-broiled to juicy tenderness and topped with a delicate herb sauce, it was a triumph. Asparagus with Hollandaise and new potatoes in butter and parsley complemented.

Dessert was a rich vanilla pudding capped with a layer of hot fudge, whipped cream over all, cherry-topped. After eating, Frank felt a sense of satiety and of danger. What was this folderol, anyway, giving them a banquet, of all things? A subtle interrogation technique? He remembered reading about the clever traps sprung by the Third Reich on Allied flyers during the Second World War, smothering dollops of false camaraderie covering a cynical attempt to extract military information, leading questions posed in seeming casual conversation over dinner and drinks.

But what information could he give them that they didn't already know through their spy network? He wasn't sure about all the applications of Innerverse yet, but he saw no reason why they couldn't just come out and ask him anything they wanted to know, then sit back until the pain and nausea forced him to comply.

He wondered about that. Would such a method work? Could he hold out against it? And how long could he hold out?

On the other hand, they could just let the army torture him again. Would Streiner allow it? Perhaps the unctuous chumminess masked an underlying obduracy, a cold ruthlessness that would not balk at torture, no matter how much he pretended to find such things barbaric.

Was the banquet ploy a first attempt, the rough stuff to come later if it failed?

He didn't know. If Frank could have his druthers, he'd take this method. Just watch what you say, he told himself. Talk, gab, play along, give away the obvious, but tell them nothing about OSO, about his mission. Nothing, tell them nothing.

Another thing. What was Dr. Mary Sellers' knee doing pressed against his?

Aside from the obvious, that is.

Conversation during the eating was limited to shop talk between Streiner and members of his staff, the chief shoptalkers being Dr. Norman Hingham, the Assistant Director of Research, and Dr. Ann Shelikov, Team Leader of the Nanotechnology Project. Hingham was a personable young man in his early thirties, and Shelikov was a little older, short-haired and horse-faced. Frank tried to follow the conversation closely, but arrived at little understanding. The talk was mostly in jargon.

When the dessert dishes had been cleared away and coffee was being served by the kitchen staff (who all worked swiftly, silently, and with amazing efficiency, rattling not so much as a plate or spilling a crumb of food), Streiner leaned back and said, "Sometimes I wish tobacco weren't a thing of the past."

"It might be a thing of the future when we get Mediverse perfected," Hingham said.

"It might at that," Streiner said. "We could damage our bodies any way we want, and Mediverse would make repairs as we go along."

"Neat," Hingham said with a grin.

Streiner had his coffee poured. "But I doubt we'd want to take risks like that. Nor divert energy and money to raising nonessentials like smokable weed."

"Probably not," Hingham admitted, eager to back off.

"We will have other pleasures. More wholesome. Like health, for instance."

"Absolutely," said a woman staffer.

"Do you smoke, Frank?" Streiner asked.

"Occasionally," Frank said.

"Really. They're still smoking in the States?"

"Sure. Cigars are making a big comeback."

The staff seemed to find this intensely interesting.

"Tell me, Mr. Sutter . . ." Hingham began.

"Lieutenant Sutter," Frank said.

"Sorry. Lieutenant."

"Call me Frank."

"Frank, are the authorities in your country unaware of

the dangers of smoking, or are they capitulating to the tobacco-growing interests? I mean, the deleterious effects of smoking were first documented decades ago, in the last century, and mountains of data are available on the subject. Tobacco is clearly a public health hazard. Yet you say tobacco is still grown and sold?''

''Yes.''

Hingham looked at Frank. He shrugged. ''Can you possibly defend that kind of breach of public trust?''

Frank shrugged back. ''No. Should I?''

Hingham was baffled. ''You have no justification? You're not willing to . . . I mean, really, Lieutenant Sutter. That's plain irresponsible.''

''Of me, or the government?''

''Of the government, of course. I'm not suggesting that you as an individual— Well, frankly, it's puzzling. Very puzzling and upsetting.''

''I'm sorry it upsets you. Tobacco's a filthy habit. People like filthy habits. And that's all there is to it.''

''I'm afraid that's not all there is to it, Lieutenant.''

''Please call me Frank.''

''Frank has a point,'' Streiner said. ''The tendency of the human animal to defer paying the piper is notorious. And the baseline human is little better than an animal, unable to think beyond the range of the moment.''

''What's a baseline human?'' Frank wanted to know.

''A human being without Innerverse,'' Streiner said. '' 'Baseline' is our lingo. You could call such a creature 'autonomous man.' the human being possessed of what the theologians called 'free will.' ''

''Free willfulness,'' Ann Shelikov said.

Streiner pointed to her. ''That's more like it. Augustine described man as a creature neither good nor evil, but with a marked predilection for evil. We're in agreement with Augustine, and we go against the intellectual tides of the last century in differing with Rousseau. We don't see man as basically noble, corrupted only by the state. We're not Marxists in that we don't see human evil as a function of social class. As behavioral scientists we look at the behavior of very young children and see budding monsters, limited only by size and brainpower. We see greed, egocentrism, belligerence, cruelty, and an almost reflexive rebellious streak. All the ingredients for human depredations on other humans and nonhumans, and on the natural environment. The only thing preventing the individual from giving vent to every primitive impulse is a fragile construct called a conscience—the superego—which is continually at war with these primeval instincts. It's a wonder civilization ever existed at all. But of course it didn't, not really. Century after century, an endless succession of so-called civilizations committed atrocities on an ever-increasing scale.''

''But there's such a thing as morality,'' Frank said. ''All cultures have moral codes to regulate behavior.''

''In our view, civilizations—or cultures, if you will—and their so-called moral codes reduce to nothing more than a sets of rationalizations for aggrandizing and perpetuating themselves, through war, conquest, and other means. Sometimes these codes reflected the designs and self-interest of the ruling classes, and on occasion those of a single man, the king or dictator.''

''But surely within a society—'' Frank tried to interject.

''There the Marxists were right. 'Crime' is really defined by social class. When the higher classes acted antisocially, they used to have to add a modifier. 'White-collar' crime, for instance, as distinguished from crime plain and simple. But of course antisocial behavior is antisocial behavior, no matter who commits it. Crime is crime.''

''Why isn't everyone a criminal,'' Frank asked, ''if this veneer of conscience is so thin?''

''The standard forms of criminal behavior are not the only kinds of destructive behavior, Frank. There's also behavior in the mass, such as overconsumption, overpopulation, social injustice, and the rape of the environment. Self-destructive mass behavior. The question is, how do you control man in the mass? This is an ancient concern.

The history of civilization reduces to frustrated attempts to control human behavior, but an astonishing amount of the effort has gone into absurd restrictions on which orifices sexual organs can be put into, or what foods are fit to eat, or what chemicals can be used for recreation. Irrelevant matters, letting pass all the issues that do matter, like invading other people's territory, mass slaughter, and social inequities. Almost everybody agrees that traditional codes of behavior and morality are vague and contradictory. Sometimes they are impossible to adhere to, and very often they are fraught with double standards and hypocrisies."

"And Innerverse is your answer to the ancient problem of behavior control," Frank said.

"Exactly. The only technological approach ever conceived, aside from some scattered behaviorist efforts, like aversion therapy for habitual criminal offenders, which never amounted to anything. The behaviorists were in their element when they produced results with very young retarded children."

"I didn't have much psychology in college," Frank said. "I have only a vague idea what behaviorism is. Or was."

"Too dreary to go into," Streiner said. "Rats running mazes, pigeons pecking at circles. It was an absurd, crudely mechanistic psychology of human behavior, rooted in 19th century determinism. Incongruously, it was based on results of experiments in *animal* behavior. Crazy stuff. How it could have achieved any scientific credibility is utterly incomprehensible. The guy who dreamed it up wrote some popular books on his notions of utopia. The perfect society, according to this bird, would be engineered by behavior technologists giving out candy to people who behaved as required and *not* handing it out to those who didn't."

"Candy?"

"Almost literally. You read some behaviorist literature and you see that most of the human subjects they ever

experimented on were the very young or the retarded. As
close to pigeons as they could get. You see years of experiments based on rewarding kids with little chocolate can-
dies. No punishment. Actual punishment was rejected out
of hand by these people. The founder ... Skinner was his
name, by the way, Burrhus F. Skinner ... wanted to build
a utopia without punishment, without 'negative reinforcement.' The only 'reinforcement', as he called the candy-
giving, to be negative would be the *withholding* of the
candy. No administering of punishment. Of course the
candy was supposed to stand in for any reward—money,
food, sex, whatever. Whatever is valued or desired. Any
good, any pleasure. But you can see the problems with
this approach. The theory goes that you eliminate unwanted behavior be reinforcing desired behavior. But the
two are not always mutually exclusive. You could reward
diligent work in workers but have no way to prevent them
from falsifying their work records. You could reward all
sorts of socially desired behavior and have no way of
preventing people from going out at night and committing
atrocities. Another problem is that this is a system of
bribes. It's paying blackmail. Blackmailers are never satisfied and are ever greedy. And what happens when you run
out of candy? How can you do anything if you don't have
any candy to hand out in the first place, as is the case in
a poor culture? No, behaviorism and behaviorist utopias—
and Skinner was never taken seriously as a political
thinker—were laboratory daydreams.''

Dr. Shelikov spoke up. ''Innerverse is at odds with behaviorism from the start. Behaviorists went so far as to
deny any reality to the inner state of the behaving organism. Thoughts, emotions, feelings, memory, character, anything that went on inside the brain or inside the skin was
considered irrelevant. With Innerverse, the interior conditions of the organism is all the reality there is. Interior
states are the root of all behavior.''

''Exactly,'' Streiner said. ''Outside stimuli can vary

greatly, yet people still feel the same way, act the same way. This distinguishes the human from a flatworm.''

Frank said, ''Innerverse is also at odds with behaviorism in that it doles out punishment fairly liberally. Am I right?''

''I wouldn't say liberally,'' Streiner said. ''How many times have you actually felt the nausea reaction, Frank?''

Frank shrugged. ''Half a dozen, all told.''

''Do you consider that harshly punitive? How many of those instances was the result of your testing Innerverse to find your behavioral delimitations? Be honest.''

''Most of those instances,'' Frank admitted.

''You see. Now, most people only have to feel Innerverse once to learn. Then they don't do that behavior again. Why? Because they *know* Innerverse won't let them do it. Interior states again.''

''It's still punishment.''

''Yes, absolutely. But is it so bad? Is there actually any pain? Any physical pain?''

Frank had to allow that there actually wasn't.

''Any permanent damage? None. If we wanted to, we could tune Innerverse to produce incredible pain. Agony.''

''Threat noted,'' Frank said.

''It's not a threat. What good would it do us to have people doubling up in pain all over the place? None at all. You couldn't run a society like that. As I said, once is enough for most people. I won't prevaricate and say the nausea isn't unpleasant. It is, and you don't want it to happen again. It's not real nausea, by the way, Frank. It's all in the brain. That's where all discomfort is really felt, of course, but Innerverse doesn't upset the stomach. What it does, actually, is produce an instant version of clinical depression, just as instantly reversible. Calling it 'nausea' is only an approximation of what it feels like. It's more like the nausea that Sartre, the Existentialist, talked about. Free-floating spiritual anxiety. A quick look into the dark abyss of existence.''

"It felt like a bad case of indigestion to me," Frank said.

"Really? Most people describe it as an overpowering fear of some unknown, unseen malevolence."

"That, too," Frank had to concur.

Streiner took a sip of his coffee. "All the same, getting back to how this train of thought started, I still wish that we could come up with some harmless vice on the order of tobacco-smoking. But I suppose our principles simply won't admit it."

"Your principles seem to permit alcohol. Why not tobacco?"

"We've been trying to make a teetotaler out of our Director for years," Dr. Shelikov said. "He's incorrigible."

"In another time, another milieu, I might have been an alcoholic," Streiner admitted. "I like a bit of the grape. Innerverse helps me with my problem, though, and I've averted addiction thus far. But I continue to indulge myself, and I'll be the first to admit that I'm taking advantage of my privileged status, that I'm an elitist, that I'm a hypocrite. Alcohol is poison, it's true, no denying it, and it should be banned. And it will be. But with privilege come obligations and with those obligations go some perquisites. Alcohol is one of mine. Frank, if you have any questions for us . . ."

"I have many," Frank said.

"Shoot."

"One, where is all this going? What do you hope to accomplish?"

"We hope to accomplish the salvation of the human race," Streiner said. "We've been heading for destruction for a good century now, and we mean to get us off that road. To do that we have to scale down human civilization. We have to take egocentric man down a peg or two. He's not one step below the angels, as the medievals had him. He's an animal with a brain grown too big for his body. He's top-heavy. He has a brain that lusts after material comforts but doesn't know enough to think of long-term consequences. He has the brains to clear a forest to plant food but doesn't realize that soon there will be no more forest to clear. He has more than enough brains to build weapons of mass destruction but doesn't realize that his neighbor has the same capacity. Man is really not a rational animal. Correct behavior can occur to him, but he's usually under constraints and contingencies that he simply cannot control. Innerverse sees to it that he lives by the dictates of his conscience. For who created Innerverse? Man himself.''

"Yeah," Frank said, "but exactly what man? And how?"

"I think I told you my father invented Innerverse. Here, at this university. It was developed and tested at this research facility."

"How did it get from here into the population?"

"Frank, you need a history lesson. Several. We've enrolled you in classes at the university. For you it will be graduate school. Some basic orientation courses."

"God, not more flipping documentaries."

Everyone laughed. "We don't do documentaries here, Frank. All the courses are computer-taught by interactive software. You go at your own pace. The history of Innerverse is pretty straightforward. It was a plot."

"Plot," Frank said.

"Yes, quite frankly a conspiracy. Briefly stated, there was a point during the Troubles when it became apparent that something drastic had to be done or the whole country would come unraveled. When the plague hit, what technical types like to call a 'window of opportunity' presented itself. The government ordered mass inoculations, and my father offered the government a solution to what was in essence a problem in mass behavior. If you know your history, riots and city-burnings were widespread at the time. Behavior, destructive behavior. Through connections, through channels, my father presented his proposal: to inoculate the population with Innerverse, which had been developed as a behavior control method for the criminally insane. Along with plague vaccine and serums, a select segment of the population got Innerverse. Simple.''

"Simple,'' Frank said. "And the authorities at the time knew about it.''

"Absolutely. The President of the United States knew about it.''

"Amazing.''

"Not really. That was a desperate juncture of the country's history. After that, it was only a matter of time before the power center in the nation shifted from Washington to right here,'' Streiner said, tapping the table. "I suppose it is amazing when you think about it.''

"And you inoculated the army, too.''

"At first, yes. But that limited their effectiveness. For a time, we nearly lost control that way. But we developed Innerpause on a crash priority basis. Rather, my father and his colleagues at the time did.''

"I see.''

"You'll get all the details in the history course. Any other questions?''

"Will I have final exams to study for?''

Streiner laughed. "I'm glad you still have your sense of humor. No, you'll only be auditing your courses. Any objections, by the way, to our enrolling you?''

"None that I can think of. I am a spy, and you'll be feeding me information.''

"You're always working, aren't you? Typical military type.''

"We never sleep. I have one more question.''

"Fire away, Frank.''

"What are your designs on the rest of the world?''

Streiner's smile was furtive. "I'm afraid we have big designs. Naturally, we want to save the whole human race, not just part of it. One day we'll be ready to send Innerverse to the ends of the earth. Not yet. The experiment isn't completed yet.''

"How long?''

"We really don't have a timetable as yet. We must be sure that Innerverse produces no long-term genetic effects, no long-term damage. It will take years more to ascertain this. Some of us want to take it through another generation. I myself think we might be ready in another ten years."

"How will you do it?"

"Take over the world?" Streiner's grin turned impish. "That, Frank, I'm afraid is a state secret. We do have a few of those."

"You deal in secrecy wholesale, if you don't mind my saying it."

"I suppose we do, in a way. We think it best. The less the outside world knows about us, the better off we are."

"Do you think your army has the capability of enlarging your territory?"

"Good lord, no," Streiner said with a snort. "Do you really think we'll spread Innerverse by military conquest? That would be in flat contradiction to our principles."

"By sabotage? Slip it in the water supply?"

"There are any number of methods, Frank. All secretive, all untraceable. No defense against any of them."

"I don't know about that," Frank retorted. "You were caught unawares by our countermeasures."

"And very weak they were, I'm afraid. Rather primitive. I'd even say pathetically so."

"They worked."

"That's your soldier's bravado speaking, Frank. They worked, but they're not enough to hold off Innerverse very long. Of course we'll incorporate counter-countermeasures in any future offensive effort. Thanks for providing us with that."

"Only too happy."

"I'm going to call an adjournment," Streiner said. "I hope this dinner had been as pleasant for you, Frank, Alice, as it has been for us."

"It was wonderful. My compliments to the chef, or chefs."

"I will convey them."

"My thanks to you all," Frank said.

He got a round of applause.

He stooped and grabbed Zombie. "Let's go Alice."

Frank walked with Alice out of the room, his thigh still tingling from the insistent pressure of Mary Sellers' knee against it. She had kept it up all through the meal and the ensuing conversation.

≥ Chapter Twenty ≤

Frank had been assigned to a room in the bachelors' dormitory. Evening was settling down on the campus as Frank kissed Alice goodnight at the door to the single women's dorm.

"Like I'm back in college," Frank said with a chuckle.

"Can't we sleep together?"

"Of course not. It's not ordered, so it's forbidden."

"Frank, I can't stand it. I can't stand being this way again."

He took her by the arms. "Pull yourself together. Don't give up."

"I just want . . . I want to kill myself."

"Stop that! I mean it, and don't let me hear you talk that way again."

She cried on his shoulder.

He struggled to put conviction in his voice. "We will get out of this."

"I don't know," she said.

"Believe it. You have to believe it. We're going to go home."

"I want to go home with you."

"You will. Dry those big eyes."

She sniffed, fumbled in a pocket, took out some tissue and wiped her nose.

"You okay?"

"Okay."

"Kiss."

She kissed him and they parted.

Walking back through the lengthening shadows, he thought of the shrimp.

The shrimp. Here in Virginia, they were eating shrimp. Caught by . . . fishermen, presumably. Where? In the Gulf of Mexico? New England? Transported by whom? The army. A crack squadron of jet transports that flew special food in for the elite.

Elites of any time and place are the same. Living by the efforts of others, they reserve the best for themselves.

Or . . . raised on fish farms? They had tasted like Gulf shrimp, had the taste of seawater in them. But maybe they were freshwater shrimp. Could shrimp be raised in fish farms? He hadn't the foggiest. So, maybe no food-delivery jet. From his intelligence studies he knew that jets rarely flew over the Republic. There was no air force to speak of, no airlines, no commercial air freight traffic, no private aviation. Nothing.

Nothing. It was a republic of nothing, a vast zero from east coast to the western edge of the Appalachians, from the Canadian border to the tip of Florida

Presided over by a tall smarmy guy with unruly gray hair and a taste for the grape. Absolute ruler, despite his assertion that he was only Director of Research. The so-called administrative staff had been present at dinner, and it had been clear who was in charge. A hereditary ruler, as one day his son would be, if he could bear the heavy weight of the crown.

Sutter went to his room, his spartan, white-walled room. It really was no more austere then the average dorm room. A combination desk and computer terminal in the corner, bed under the window, nightstand, chest of drawers, closet, bath.

No lock on the door, per Republican habit. He sat at the computer terminal and tried to get into the general data storage, to get information. But access was blocked. They had not yet given him the proper codes and passwords. He started "school" the next day, eight A.M. sharp. Well, this would be interesting, and would kill some time while simultaneously fulfilling the intelligence-gathering part of his mission.

He flicked off the terminal, undressed, turned out the lights, and stretched across the bed naked. It was a warm spring night. Speaking of tobacco, he thought, I could use a smoke. He wasn't sleepy, and there was nothing to do. Some university. The damned place had a library but it was locked up. All information was electronic in form. He didn't care much for that, liked the feel of a book, the smell of one, the smoothness of the paper, the heft of a weighty tome. He hadn't ever been a voracious reader, but he liked to read. He was tired of the picture magazines, but then again, maybe he could find one with the latest in fish farm technology. He hadn't seen so much as one fin in the food market, much less significant quantities of fish. But no matter where the fish came from, farm or sea, there was no doubt as to who ate it all. The elite, of course. The upper and middle managers, leaving all the Alices of the world to scrounge among rotted leaves and tubers. He wondered why scurvy was not endemic. No citrus, either. Vitamin C capsules on the black market, probably. Was there a black market? No, Innerverse prevented that. Or did it?

Idle thoughts. He needed some hard data. Innerverse's origins were still not completely clear.

Political bombshell, about conspiracy in high places. What party had authorized the enslavement of half a nation? What monstrous pusillanimity had gone into such treachery? He wished he knew recent history better. Well, whatever party, they would pay dearly when the news got out. He had a hunch that the government's hand was in the thing. You don't mount a huge conspiracy like that without help in high places.

A knock came at the door, and, almost immediately, the door opened. He rose on one elbow, expecting to see Alice walk in, but it was not Alice.

Dr. Mary Sellers, in a jogging suit.

He reached for the bedclothes.

Seeing him, she halted. "Oh, sorry. Do you mind?"

"Come in, Dr. Sellers," he said, pulling the scratchy blanket over himself.

She came in and sat on the bed.

"I wanted to talk with you," she said.

"Of course. What about?"

"Lots of things. I'm intensely interested . . . we all are . . . about what life is like over there. In the Central States. I was wondering if you could tell me a few things."

"Such as?"

"The standard of living. I imagine it's fairly high."

"Comparatively, still, put up against most of the world. Not as good as maybe the Chinese have it. Took them centuries but they finally surpassed the West."

"They're half the world's population now," she said. "Not surprising."

"Takes more than just population. Look at India."

"Let's not," she said. "Look, let me get it out. I want to sleep with you. I don't usually throw myself at men, but I don't have much time."

"Nice suit," he said.

She smiled, rose, and began to undress. She took off the top and threw it on the nightstand. Then she dropped the pants, rolled them up and deposited them neatly in the same place. She was wearing nothing underneath. He kicked the blanket off the bed and stretched out again, and she sat down as before but a little closer to him. Her large breasts were pointy, the nipples dark pink in the dim light that spilled under the closed door. He reached out and stroked her breasts, then bent and took the left nipple in his mouth. She let out a little moan.

He turned his head up and asked, "How can you do this?"

"How?"

"Innerverse lets you commit adultery?"

"Innercircle lets you do almost anything except violence," she said, pushing his face to her breasts once again. While he nibbled, she groped for his stiffening penis and handled it, slowly, gently.

"How do you feel about your husband, if you don't mind my asking?"

"Let me show you," she said, and bent over his body. He watched her long blond hair fall to hide her face, her working lips and tongue.

When she could speak again, she said, "There is no marriage, he isn't my husband. If you want to know, I hate him. Everyone does."

"Everyone?"

"You have no idea how unhappy most of us are."

"You have the best of everything here."

"It's not material. How would you like to spend your life cooped up in a place like this, never seeing the outside world? All of your life and your activity centered around one man."

"You don't like your work?"

"Building his dream world? No. I love science, science is good. But what he's doing . . . what we're helping him do . . . it's a lie. It's all a lie. That stuff about waiting ten years. That's a lie, too. We're developing the means to spread Innerverse now, and the project is nearing completion."

"I see. Does anyone know you're here?"

"I'm supposed to be night-jogging. We don't have much time."

"Okay."

He lay back and she took him into his mouth again, and when she was ready and he was ready she straddled him and impaled herself, then began to move on him.

She satisfied herself, and him, for a long while. Her breathing became heavy, but she did not make much sound, silently doing her work.

She stopped just short of his climax, and he relaxed.

She got off and stood. "Would you do something for me?"

He rose and said, "Sure."

"Come here," she said and led him to the desk. She bent over the writing area of the desk, relaxed her back and let her haunches rise. He stared at her perfectly-shaped buttocks, at the shadowy declivity between them.

"I want you to take my other hole. I like it that way. Do you mind?"

He did the thing, and climaxed inside her. He stayed inside while she busied herself with her fingers, until her body quivered and spasmed. She gasped.

Slumping, loose and spent, she remained bent over the desk. He stroked the globular buttocks, the backs of her smooth thighs, her glossy delicate back, then helped her straighten up.

Leaning back against his chest, his arms around her, she said, "Do you think that was perverted?"

"I enjoyed it, I have to say. Did you?"

"I like it. It's nasty, and that's why I like it. He disapproves of it, and that makes me like it more."

"You really hate him."

"Oh, it's not hate . . . it's loathing, I guess. Loathing for the empty life we lead, our so-called dedication to humanity. He's a good person, I guess. Really. He's brilliant, truly brilliant."

"What he's doing is good?"

"I don't know any more. He thinks we can rule the world. I think it's impossible. And it's not right. No, I guess the goal is all right. His intentions are good. What he wants is good. An end to war, to hatred, to violence. That's good, isn't it?"

"Sure."

"I mean, isn't it? I've always thought so. But this way, this way is . . . it'll never work. The thing's not fully tested, he says, but he secretly believes we can go ahead with full implementation. It's wrong. There'll be a catastrophe."

"Why?"

"Innerverse 2 is full of bugs. He knows that, but thinks

we can debug it on the fly. He says you people are closing in on the secrets.''

They lay down on the bed.

"Listen," he said, "can you tell me if you know the fate of the operatives who came before me?"

"None of them showed up here. I'm sorry, but I don't know what became of them."

"I'll assume they became absorbed. Maybe they didn't have the countermeasures."

"You don't know?"

He shook his head. "But that's not important right now. Tell me something else. Are you willing to help me escape?"

"I wish I could," she said. "But I can't get at the wiper."

"Wiper?"

"The stuff that wipes Innerverse from the body. It's called Reformat."

"Reformat. And it's kept under lock and key?"

"And alarms. The security's really tight. I have access to it, but I have to justify any use."

"After the fact, or before?"

"Both. Streiner signs the authorization form and checks the report after."

"Is there some way you could . . . well, let's see. Set some aside the next time you use it?"

"There'd be a discrepancy on the supply report."

"I see. But all you have to do is free me. I'll take care of Streiner."

"But . . ." She looked at him. "You'll kill him?"

"If he tries to kill me. I will simply leave. But you have to free Alice, too."

"I'd do it, but . . ." She shook her head. "I just don't know if I can pull it off. I'm afraid of him."

"Of course. Half his power. He's strong. But if he has Innerverse . . . or Innercircle, he can't prevent me from leaving."

"He could call the army."

"Right. Well, I can handle them. I just need some Reformat in order to be able to do it."

"Take me with you. I want to leave this place."

"I will if Alice comes, too."

She looked at him. "I suppose it's too soon ... I've thrown myself at you ... foolish of me. But ..."

He stroked her platinum hair. "I'll take you, if it is within my power. But I'm going to need help. I'll also need complete specifications on Innerverse, to develop countermeasures."

"You won't need anything if I can pull off something I've been working on for years."

"Which is?"

"Innerverse can be spread with a harmless bacterium, easily communicable. The Innerverse replicating machines hide inside the organism and break out when it enters the body. It's only been tried once—on a limited scale. When your country's army invaded. It worked."

"So the stuff could be spread around the world ..."

"In record time, and no one would know it. However, there is nothing, absolutely nothing to prevent other nanomechanisms from being secreted inside the organism."

He eyes narrowed. "Reformat?"

"Yes. In which case—"

"Everybody who gets the organism and who has Innerverse is set free."

"That's it. In theory it's simple."

"What's complicating it?"

"Hiding the sabotage from Streiner. He looks at everything, all my research. I've been doing it in secret, keeping track of things mostly by memory. I don't dare notate anything. But it's all there. You simply have to make the logical jump in the data. Substitute one set of molecules for the other, and you have, instead of a weapon, a counterweapon. Against Innerverse itself."

"Does he suspect?"

"I don't think so. He would have said something by now."

"When can you make this stuff?"

"No date's been set for production. But you could let loose some of the stuff by just breaking a petri dish."

"How would the weapon ... the Innerverse-spreader ... be deployed?"

"A missile, a bomb, anything that could release a cloud of bacteria. It's an airborne bacterium, like some forms of plague. But completely harmless."

"I wonder ..." he began.

"But we don't need a bomb. You could just drive through the city throwing culture dishes out the window. It'll spread like wildfire."

"Why haven't you done it?"

"One, because I haven't been able to make a batch of Reformat-laden bacteria. And two, if I did and infected everybody here, it wouldn't do any good. We're isolated. Streiner would simply order everyone reinoculated."

"If he found out about it."

"He'd find out. Someone would tell him. Out of habit, if nothing else."

"Obedience becomes a habit, doesn't it?"

"It does. Anyway, he'd know when everybody up and left this lousy boring place."

"Could we enlist allies?"

"Don't count on it. Everyone is terrified of Streiner. Terrified of ..."

"What?"

"It's a dread. What happens after Innerverse is gone? You see, it's our world, it's all we know, all we've ever known. We're thoroughly sick of it, disgusted with it, but terrified of the world without it. I honestly don't know if I could survive in a world without Innerverse."

"Of course you could. Innerverse is ... an anomaly. It will pass."

"Not if Streiner has anything to do with it. I have to go. I'm overdue now. He'll begin to wonder where I am."

Hurriedly, she began to dress. He lay back, the urge for a smoke very great now.

"I still don't understand one thing," he said. "You seem able to do almost anything with Innercircle."

"Not true," she said. "Not true at all."

"What happens when you disobey? What's happening now to you doing this? What's the penalty?"

She turned her head. "Guilt."

"Guilt?"

"Yes. You see, Innercircle was first, not the other way around. Innercircle was the first Innerverse. It was developed to simulate feelings of guilt in people who seem to have no inborn sense of right and wrong. Habitual criminals. That was the focus of the original research project."

"Chemical guilt, chemical conscience?"

"Nanotechnologically-induced guilt. Call it, artificial conscience."

"But how can you quantify such a thing?"

She shrugged. "Every human emotion has a chemical counterpart. Unless you believe in the soul and consider such things purely spiritual. But research in brain chemistry early in this century came up with a molecule that induces feelings of remorse, of sadness and regret over wrongdoing. Guilt."

"And that's what you feel when you disobey?"

"Yes. It works. And it's cumulative. I've been under stress doing this secret research. The feeling is building in me. Some nights it's overwhelming. You may think it would be better than the nausea, but it's not. It's worse, it builds over time. It's an oppressive, crushing weight, to fight him, to fight Innercircle. But I keep fighting."

"I'll help. Let me get into the database, increase my understanding, and I'll think of something."

"I have to go. Strange, we haven't even kissed."

"No, we didn't."

He rose and kissed her, and she clung to him and forced her tongue into his mouth with an almost frantic desperation.

She wrapped him in her arms. "I'm afraid I won't have

the strength to come see you again. I want to. Tomorrow night. May I?''

"Of course."

"I want you to do whatever you want with me. Take me any way you want. I'll do anything."

"I'll see you tomorrow night. Same time?"

She nodded. She pecked his cheek and went out the door and left him alone in the darkness in the bare, spartan room.

≽ Chapter Twenty-one ≼

Speaking of guilt, Frank thought.

He felt more than a pang of regret for his dalliance with Dr. Sellers, and hoped Alice would not have to find out about it. It would upset her greatly, he knew. Not that he had any choice in the matter. An ally here was necessary for escape, and if he had to perform sexual favors for vital information and help, he would do his duty. There came to him an ancillary prick of conscience for his liking this duty a great deal. Sellers's desire proved almost insatiable over the next few nights. She taught him a trick or two, and he was surprised.

But the more he thought about it, the more he considered his feeling guilty a great silliness. Maybe Innerverse 2 had its guilt-bestowing component as well?

"Classes" began, and he got down to the work of studying the engineering specifications for Innerverse. They weren't secret. It was all there on the screen. Of course, he had monumental problems understanding most of it. He had studied organic chemistry as an undergraduate, but this was no undergraduate course. These "molecules" were huge complex mechanisms. Some were computers, some were machines with moving parts. Some were both. The three-dimensional specifications for just one nanocomputer took up immense amounts of data storage and soaked up random-access memory to process and display. But the school's computers handled it. He suspected the system's main processing units were very old supercomputers. But he did not have direct access to them or to the area they were housed in.

He rolled through long strings of atoms configured in complex ways. It was all too much. He'd never make a dent in understanding any of this stuff. His task was to steal this information, get it out of the country.

How? He'd have to please Mary Sellers more. She must help him, or he'd get nowhere with nothing.

But there were monumental problems in the way.

"The guilt's getting to me, I think," she said a few nights later.

"How?"

"I said it's hard to describe. Don't you know what guilt feels like?"

"Sure."

"Same thing. It makes you feel worthless, flawed."

"Are you sure it's not partly physiological?"

"Not if you mean outside the brain. I know how the thing works, and it's guilt, pure and simple. You can't shake it. Funny . . ."

"What?"

"It makes the sex all the better. I . . . I don't know how to explain it. The lousier I feel, the more I think I'm betraying everything I hold dear, the more I enjoy these sessions with you. It's crazy. But Herbert keeps this crazy world going. It was his dad's creation, and now he's lord of it."

He said, "Don't give in to the guilt. Don't think you're betraying anything. You know how nuts he is, how crazy this whole place is. How utterly wrong and immoral and insane."

She turned on her side. "I *know*. I'm utterly convinced of that. What you just said. I've been convinced for years. But it makes no difference with Innercircle. Innercircle picks up the cues, knows I'm doing something naughty, and turns up guilt up another notch. It doesn't know about morality. It's only a machine."

"Sometimes it seems almost human," he said.

"I guess it's attained the status of a low-order artificial intelligence. Though don't ask me whether it's self-aware. I'm not even sure I care whether it is or not."

"It's only an infernal machine, as far as I'm concerned," he said. "A machine that controls, instead of being controlled. Out of control, is what it is."

"Do me again, will you?"

"Front or back?"

"Front, this time, darling. I'd like to run away with you, leave this place for good. I'd like to go home with you. You have no idea how miserable my life's been. No idea. I'd kill to go with you ... My God, I don't think I've ever actually come out and said that before. The guilt went up another notch."

"Are you okay?"

"I'm fine. Do me, hard, as hard as you want."

He rolled over onto her and entered her forcefully. She gasped, but moved her hips to facilitate his entering.

Her breath came hot in his ear. "Did I tell you that I sometimes take a knife to bed with me?"

"Oh?"

"When I go to bed with him. I stole it from the kitchen, a big one. I keep it under the bed. And I fantasize about plunging it into his heart. When he falls asleep. I just take it ... out ... and ..." Her breath caught.

"Am I hurting you?"

"No . . . no. Not at all. It feels so good, Frank. I love . . ."

"You don't have to say it."

"God, I think I'm going crazy. Fuck me, darling. Fuck me."

He began moving again and continued for some time. Then he stopped and held himself deep inside her.

"But you couldn't do that, could you? Kill him."

"I don't know. I don't really know, but it just seems sometimes that I could, that I will, it's only a few feet from where it is under the bed to his heart. Just a matter of a few feet, a few seconds . . . then . . . it hits me, the guilt. And I can't do it.''

"It hits so suddenly?''

"One time I tried, I reached for it, and I tried . . . but I must have passed out. Something happened. I don't know what, I just passed out.''

"It's got to be more than guilt, Mary.''

"I know the mechanism. I know how it works, and it's the reaction that's intended. It can paralyze you.''

He began again, moving himself inside and through her for a long while, his strokes mounting in intensity, a fine sweat covering him, until she climaxed under him, her legs, a tender vise, squeezing him spasmodically.

She groaned and they both lay still.

"So, he's safe,'' he said. "I guess that goes for everyone here, he's safe from everyone.''

She took a while to answer.

"Yes, he's unreachable. I don't know how to reach him and I'm his wife. If I'd found a way I would have done it long ago. I hate him so much, so bloody much. And I love you, Frank, I love you.''

He felt another twinge for using her this way. A while later he rolled off her and she sighed.

"I made some noise that time,'' she said. "I guess I come like gangbusters, don't I? Hope no one heard.''

"Do you think anyone else knows?''

"I don't know. Probably.''

"Will he find out?''

"He has before, Frank.''

"So he knows?''

"Sure, I think. He won't do anything. I've had many affairs.''

"I see. But I'm a special case. A foreign spy.''

"You're the nicest foreign spy that ever made love to me. Am I the noisiest woman you've had?''

"Actually, no.''

"Have there been many?'

"No.''

"That's what you'd say in any case. I don't mind, though. I'm not the jealous type. I rather like the fact that people sleep around. That people don't obey rules. Anything that throws a monkey wrench into his plans."

"But he has no stake in monogamy, particularly. Does he?"

"Don't take what he says as gospel," she warned. "He lies. He regards me as a possession. The best of the lot. He thinks every other woman here is unattractive. 'Dogs' he calls them."

"From what I've seen, he's not far wrong."

"Maybe. But I'm his territory, he's staked me out, and he wouldn't give me up. He preaches progressivism in sexuality but he's lying, lying every single word. He's berated me for every single affair. He does absolutely nothing, but he belittles me without mercy. And he won't stop. He'll do it for months, every night, taking me apart fault by fault, flaw by flaw, dissecting my character, or my lack of it."

"Character," he said.

"What?"

"Funny concept for him to worry about. According to him, it really doesn't exist."

"No, not to him. I tell him this, but it doesn't seem to matter. I've let him down. Him. The project. The world, it all depends on me and what penises I take into what orifice. The rotten son of a bitch. He's the problem."

"He's never had an affair?"

"He prides himself on his purity. We make love three times a year, maybe. And he's not interested in other women. I wish he were. I really wish he were, and that he'd let me go. I've asked him to release me, begged him over and over."

Frank's days were busy. He spent them in the equivalent of a monk's carrel, staring into a data screen. Around him, his fellow students, zombies all, did the same thing, learning their administrative lessons. Exactly what these consisted of wasn't clear to Frank. He could never bring himself to stare over someone's shoulder. Streiner had said the Academy was a training center, and it was. Here the top managers of the country learned how to conduct the affairs of the country and what policies to implement. They did not have much say in the creation of those policies, this being the bailiwick of the administrative academicians, in conjunction with the Planning Center, a sort of permanent economic task-force of economists.

Streiner came strolling through the classroom one day.

"Learning much, Frank?"

"Much, thanks. It's amazing how efficiently you run the whole country from here. You've accomplished an age-old dream in reducing the size of government down to the essentials."

"The secret is flowcharting, Frank. Flowcharting."

"I can see," Frank said, tapping the maze of interconnected rectangles, circles and trapezoids on the screen. "It's all here. An oiled bureaucratic machine."

"We take as our watchword one from the last century, 'downsizing.' "

"Downsizing?"

"Yes. We want to reduce the scale of everything. Reduce, cut back, limit. Population, waste, resource usage— all are tending down in this country."

"And production."

"Yes, and production. But reduced population will take care of that, don't you think?"

"Maybe, if you don't cut things too close."

"Oh, I know we have shortfalls. All command economies have shortfalls. It's the nature of the beast. But what's the alternative? A burgeoning cancer of an economy that must grow and devour in order to thrive? The planet can't put up with that much longer, Frank. Surely you can see that."

Frank shrugged. "So people have been saying for a long time."

"Time's running short. We have to learn to make do

with less, a lot less. It won't be so bad, Frank. We can even learn to like it. We can learn to like clean air and endless forests and clear water. Those things are easy to like.''

''I like forests. Like 'em fine, but I like to eat, too.''

''Eating and forests are mutually exclusive? Not so, Frank. Look, we're not Luddites. Surely you've seen our energy farms and our intensive agriculture stations. That's not primitive technology, Frank. It's the latest stuff. We don't need big corporate farms to grow food, we don't need millions of acres of land. Here . . .''

Streiner tapped some keys. ''Let me show you the Food Technology Library . . . here. Look at these facilities. See this plant, here? It can put out five hundred tons of cultured soy protein a day. It's a prototype plant, none are operational yet, but give it time. We'll be able to feed the world with just the food-producing resources of a state the size of Tennessee.''

''We have Tennessee,'' Frank reminded him.

''Yes, you do. Sorry. And look at this aluminum plant, here. It runs on practically no energy at all and raw material dug out of the old landfills.''

''All very ingenious. But it won't work.''

''Why do you say that?''

''I saw it, Dr. Streiner.''

''You saw what?''

''I saw your perfect society firsthand. Experienced it. Ate the food, squatted in those high-rise hovels you call residence blocks. Everything's falling apart. They're no goods in the stores, and you have constant energy shortages. You must have raw material shortages, too. You won't have the gasoline to power the machines to dig up those landfills.''

''We'll have people, Frank.''

''You have no capital.''

''I repeat, we have people.''

''You can't do anything without capital . . . seed corn. You know what seed corn is, don't you?''

"Yes. But as long as you have human capital, you have the basis of wealth. Labor is the basis of wealth, Frank. Labor applied to land."

"No it isn't. Labor is the basis of subsistence. Capital is wealth."

Streiner smiled. "This threatens to turn into a dorm room bull session, Frank. As I think I told you, we're not Marxists, so I won't defend some straw man you want to take whacks at. It's good that you believe in something, though, and I respect your beliefs. You've made some good points, and we'll do our best to address them in carrying on our work. I'll leave you now, Frank. Have a good and productive day, all right?"

"One more thing, Dr. Streiner."

"What's that, Frank?"

"Why am I here? Why are you making a schoolboy out of me?"

"Why, I thought that was obvious. We want to win you over to our side. Look, we think we're right. We think we're doing the right thing, the necessary thing, in making this revolution of ours. The Innerverse Revolution. But for it to succeed on a world scale we'll need to convince some people."

"I though you didn't need to convince people. You can just command them."

"It's always better when you win their hearts and minds, Frank. It's always better."

Frank turned and stared at the screen. "No doubt."

"You'll come around, Frank. I know you will. Mary thinks so, too."

Frank looked over his shoulder as Dr., Streiner left the room.

The man in the carrel next to his right was staring at him. He had no doubt overheard and wondered who this stranger was who rated so much attention from the headmaster.

Frank's mood was sour. "What are you looking at?" Frank growled.

The man quickly turned back to his screen. "Sorry, citizen."

Nausea spiked in him. Why? Because he had wanted to punch Streiner's face in for him. He felt like getting up and doing it right now.

Give me that knife, Dr. Sellers, he thought. Let *me* sleep with the son of a bitch.

He doubled up in gastric agony. A long while passed before he could straighten up again.

Jesus Christ, you can forget about it, but it's still there inside you, waiting for you to think bad thoughts.

He thought more. What if he dosed himself with narcotics? He'd turn into a marshmallow, but maybe drugs would damp the pain enough for him to get in one rebellious, wildly aggressive act. One shot . . . Jesus, he wished for his gun. Just one shot, and the s.o.b. would be dead.

But what would that accomplish?

Innerverse would still be alive, its molecular tentacles still around the country's throat.

But shooting Streiner would be a start.

Okay, how to do this. One, get a weapon. Two, get some drugs. Let's try it.

Or he'd be a schoolboy forever. He'd never flunk out. They wouldn't let him.

≫ Chapter Twenty-two ≪

He saw Alice evenings after dinner, and they would walk the campus together. Neither had much to say. They shared no "courses" and had data carrels in different buildings, so they had no school chat to share.

He could tell that she sensed something. Women, Frank had always thought, had a sixth sense about the Other Woman, not that he'd been in this situation many times before. But all men, at one time or another, are brought up short by the temporary anomaly of having two foci for their romantic attentions.

Though sensitive, Alice was not one to harbor suspicions, and she gave voice to none. Instead, she seemed to feel that somehow Frank did not like her anymore, had forgotten about her.

"Silly you," Frank said, "thinking that. I think about you all the time."

"Do you?"

"Of course. Thinking of you keeps me going. We'll get out of this, and we'll be together."

"And happy. I want so to be happy. I've never been."

"No wonder. This place isn't made for human happiness. Human perfection, maybe. Duty, right thinking. Though I'd put quotes around all of that."

They walked through greening spring evenings dark with long tree shadows. The campus was quiet, hushed, the ivy-covered buildings crossed with latticeworks of office light. These surroundings would have passed for any small college campus anywhere, anytime within the last two centuries.

"So neat, so ordered," Frank said, "but so deadly."

"Deadly boring."

"That, too."

"Well, here we are."

The Singe Women Students' dorm was lit up for the evening. Frank kissed Alice good night in front of the double glass doors. The security officer at her desk in the lobby looked out at them, puzzled at this public display of affection.

"See you tomorrow," he said.

"Frank, I'm worried."

"About what?"

She shook her head, saying, "I don't know. Something's going to happen."

"Something is always about to happen, anytime. Don't worry, precious. I'm working on a way out."

"Okay, Frank. I love you."

"I love you."

"Good night."

He walked back to his dorm, where he would meet Dr. Sellers in about one hour. Guilt was building in him, too, and he was almost convinced that Innerverse had something to do with it.

He paused at the front door and listened, he didn't know for what. He looked around. He heard nothing, but he sensed something . . . or thought he did. Something different, but he couldn't put his finger on it.

Faint . . . voices? He listened more.

No, nothing. He looked up the side of the building to his second-story window, wishing for a ground floor room. Ivy clung to the walls well up to the third story. How traditional, ivy-covered walls. He wondered how much of it was a single plant, and how long that plant had lived, draping this red brick dormitory like a green blanket. He went in, mounted the stairs and opened the door to his room.

"Frank."

It was Mary Sellers training the Glock on him.

"Mary. What—?"

"Here," she said, offering him the gun butt first.

"What's this?"

"He had it. In his sock drawer, just sitting there."

"Yes, I know he had it. But it's not going to do me any good."

"Kiss me."

"Huh? Well—"

He kissed her, and she sent her tongue probing forcefully into his mouth. He was taken aback this time, for some reason. Her aggressive sexuality now seemed to have ulterior motives.

He eased her away. "What's going on, Mary?"

"That's a kiss of betrayal, but you're not the one being betrayed. You're infected."

"With what?"

She grinned at him. "I did it. I made a batch of bunny plague today, loaded with wiper. Reformat."

"Bunny plague?"

"I call it that. It was tested in rabbits. In about an hour you'll get the sniffles, and in about three or four more hours, you'll be free of Innerverse Two."

"You're sure the wiper works on Two?"

"I designed it specifically for Two, but it wipes all versions."

"Just one kiss?"

"You want more?" She leaned toward him.

"I mean, that's all it takes? Just the infection?"

"That's all. I dosed myself with it, of course. I prepared just a few thousand organisms. But that's all that's needed."

"What do we do now?"

"Wait. Let's lie down."

"I'd better get going," he said, striding to the window. He looked out. Something must be brewing out there.

"Why? No one knows. Come lie down, Frank. It'll be just a few hours."

"You'd better go back," he said. "You'll be missed."

"I'm staying with you, Frank. I've made my decision. No going back now."

"But Streiner will get wise."

"He won't know what's going on unless he's been checking my work more closely than I think."

"Could he know?"

She shrugged. "It's possible. I've given him enough grounds for suspicion in the past."

Frank stayed at the window, his gaze sweeping the campus. He tuned his hearing to the outside for sounds of approach.

"What's the matter," Mary asked as she stepped out of her jogging pants. "Don't you trust me either?"

"Mary, I only have your word for it."

"I know," she said glumly. "I don't blame you. Why believe me? Why believe any of us, the people who have the keys to this madhouse? We're mad, too. Utterly mad. Frank, please believe me. I need someone to trust me, to take my word at face value. To know I'm telling the truth." She came to him.

"Please, Frank."

"I believe you. Mary, you should get away from the window."

She went to her knees and pressed her face to his groin, throwing her arms around his hips.

"Thank you." She took a deep breath. "Well, if you're going to just stand there ..."

She tugged down his pants.

He continued to watch the evening go down over the campus, eyeing the shadows, looking for unusually purposeful movement. He did not move from his station as he felt her tongue lave him in secret places, felt her mouth draw him in and tighten.

He heard voices again.

"What's that?"

She freed her mouth to say, "What's what?"

"I hear voices. Maybe shouting."

"Could be the trainees."

"Trainees?"

"Batch of them leaving tonight. There's usually a going-away party."

"Oh."

"It's usually my duty to say a few words in goodbye. I dropped in before I came over here. They're still boarding the bus, probably. All you're hearing is loud goodbyes."

Now that he listened closer, the noises did sound innocuous. Perhaps that's what he'd heard before.

She continued her ministrations and presently his knees quivered as his prostate strained to empty.

She rose and kissed him, her lips and tongue peppery with semen. He held her close.

"Thank you," he said. "I'm deep in your debt."

"For a blow job, Frank?" she said with a laugh. "Anytime."

"Not for that, for releasing me. It must have taken tremendous willpower to resist Innercircle."

"Oh, the guilt is spiking," she said. "But when I'm having sex I can handle it. I see now that sex was the means to overcome Innercircle. Never realized that before."

"Maybe it was love?"

"Yes, Frank. Yes. It was love."

"Or hate."

"Love's inverse? I don't know."

"Shit." Frank hiked up his trousers.

"Frank, what is it?"

"Get back," he said, forcing her away. He flattened himself against the wall and peered out.

"Soldier boys?" she said.

"Two of them coming up the walk, in white suits and masks."

"Damn," Mary Sellers said, biting her lip. "He knows about the bacillus. Those are biological hazard suits."

Frank slipped the clip out of the gun and checked it. "Four rounds."

"But you can't use that yet."

"Not yet. Wait till they get in."

"Then what?"

Frank watched the two armed men until they entered the building. He waited a few seconds more, then lifted the unscreened window all the way. He began to climb out.

"Wait, I'm coming with you," Mary said, struggling into her clothes.

"No."

"I'm coming, Frank. You'll need me to get out of this place."

"I'm climbing down the ivy."

"Go ahead, I'll follow. Don't you think I've sneaked out of dorm rooms before?"

Hanging from the window sill, Frank grabbed a swatch of ivy and tested it. It seemed to support his weight, so he let go the sill.

Climbing down wasn't as hard as he'd figured, but he didn't at all like the vulnerability. More soldiers could come along at any second. When he hit ground he looked up to see Mary clambering down monkeylike, barefoot, her limber body no stranger to athletic activity. Well, she did jog every night that she wasn't being adulterous.

She jumped to the grass. "Ouch," she said, and favored one foot. "Damn it, I couldn't find my shoes."

"I've got to get Alice," he said.

"Right," she said. "You lead."

They struck out into the night running, keeping to the shadows, hugging the sides of buildings. More sounds of shouted orders came to their ears, along with the slap of hard boot-leather against pavement. It was hard to guess how many soldiers were about, but from the sound of things it was half a platoon at least.

They ducked behind the rhododendrons in front of the library and watched through the leaves as four soldiers double-timed by.

"I'm disoriented," he said. "Which way?"

Mary pointed across the quad. "There."

His directional sense set aright, he led the way, sprinting across the grass of the quadrangle to the entrance of the Women's Dorm.

He burst through the door and waved the gun at the woman at the front desk.

"Away from the desk," he commanded. "What room is Alice in?"

"Who?"

"The woman they call Alice. I don't know her cognomen or whatever the hell it is."

The woman looked frightened. "She's not here."

"Where is she?"

"They came and took her. The army."

"Where did they take her?" He aimed at her.

"I don't know. Don't shoot me."

"What room?"

"Twenty-eight."

Mary came in, and he handed her the gun.

"Make sure she doesn't call in," he said, and then dashed upstairs.

Room Twenty-eight was empty, but he saw a small bowl full of water on the floor by the window, and a cardboard box full of sand in the bathroom. A cat lived here. This was Alice's room.

He closed the door and went downstairs to find Mary not exactly holding her prisoner at gunpoint, but the woman had not moved.

"Dr. Sellers, I don't understand . . ." she was wailing. "When I saw you kiss that man. . . ."

"Never mind, go back to your duties," Mary said.

"Yes, ma'am."

They ran out into the unquiet night.

"Where could they have taken her?"

"Your guess is as good as mine, Frank," she said.

"Where's the army base?"

"A few miles away. But I doubt if Herb would send her there. If he's found out about the bacillus, which it looks like he has, she might think she's infected . . ."

"So Alice is still on campus."

"Probably. But what are you going to do? You can't save her, Frank. If we can make it to the motor pool. . . ."

"Mary, I can't leave her."

"I guess I can't expect you to," she said. "Listen. I know a back way to the old library. It's closed up, no one goes in there. We can hide there, buy time to think of something."

"Okay."

The back entrance to the library was at the bottom of concrete stairwell, and the door, unlocked as most doors were in the country, led into an old basement of pipes and boilers and storage rooms full of musty books, all festooned with dust and cobwebs.

"I actually use this place," Mary said. "Everyone thinks the database has everything. Not a week goes by when I don't have to fetch some old book or journal out of here."

Time had not done much to the first floor of the library. The place looked disused, but could have been opened for business the next morning after a little dusting and tidying up. Shelving was intact, if sagging, and the old books sat timelessly upon them. It was a well-stocked college library with the usual departments and divisions.

"The only way to stop the infection is to kill us," Frank said.

Mary Sellers nodded. "Right. But he wouldn't."

"No? I don't doubt he would for a second."

"The infection passes in a few days. All he has to do is hold us here."

Frank shrugged. "Killing us would be cheap insurance."

"He can insure to the hilt, if he wants to. It's hard to stop an epidemic from spreading."

"But to spread it, we need to get out of here."

"As I said, it's an airborne bacillus. When you start sneezing, it'll be released."

"How far can it travel?"

"Hard to say. It's not an especially lightweight organism, and it's loaded down with the wiper molecules. But it will spread. Our leaving is insurance for us."

He looked at her. "Hard to believe you have Innerverse at all," he said.

"You still don't trust me, do you?"

"But you don't seem to be suffering any . . ."

Then he noticed it. In the darkness her eyes were gray but they still radiated. He saw now that it was indeed suffering, great suffering, set off with a gleam of fear and pain.

"I think I believe you," he said, holding her face with both hands. "You really are taking a beating for this. But it's all inside your head."

A single tear fell from her right eye, its trail glistening. "Yes. That's where the pain is. It's so horrible, it's been so . . . awful. . . ."

He held her close, stroking her back.

"We'll get out of this, I promise you," he said.

How many times had he said it? He was beginning to doubt it himself.

≥ Chapter Twenty-three ≤

"They've got Alice," Frank said. "What's your guess as to where they're keeping her?"

"The lab, probably," she said. "Herb will want to examine her."

"Then I have to go to the lab."

"You'll be caught."

"If they reinoculate me with Innerverse, will the Reformat kill it again?"

"Yes, but Reformat stays effective for only twenty-four hours. Then it breaks itself up."

"I'd better act quickly. Are you coming?"

"Don't you think you'd better wait a few hours? Otherwise, that gun will still be useless."

"It hasn't done me much good up till now."

"Look, trust me. Wait. Things may be a lot different in a few hours."

"Why?"

"Give the bunny plague a chance to work."

"But . . . When Streiner finds out Alice isn't infected, do you think he'll let her go?"

"He'll probably hold her hostage. He's figured out by now that I've infected you. And he'll want to keep you here."

"Maybe . . ."

"What, Frank?"

"Maybe we should leave, get this thing spread. Find a town and start . . . I don't know, breathing on strangers."

"Kissing is an effective way."

"I'm willing to do my part, but I won't do the men."

"Leave them to me."

"After the stuff starts to work, maybe the situation will change radically."

"But that's a roundabout way to do it." Mary had a strange look in her eye.

"What's wrong?"

"Hm? Oh, nothing. It's just that this guilt load is doing strange things to my head. I can't describe exactly what."

"You haven't a thing to feel guilty for. Quite the opposite, in fact."

"I know, I know. I can appreciate that intellectually, Frank. You have to understand that my mind knows exactly what the situation is, but the glands and the enzymes are thinking something entirely different."

"Glands and enzymes think?"

"In a way, they make thinking possible. Unless you believe in the soul, thinking isn't possible unless the body is functioning normally. What's abnormal is that Innerverse . . . or Innercircle in my case—is manipulating my body to produce strong feelings that contradict what my mind is saying. I try to resist but it's almost impossible. The body rules the mind, some of the time. It's like trying to ignore that you're drunk."

"What are you feeling?"

Mary leaned against the wall and stared off into the darkness. "Failure, of having betrayed everything I ever worked for. All that research into nanotechnology. It will be gone, forever."

"No, it won't. It won't be lost, it will be put to good uses."

"Most of it was in behavior control."

"They'll find ways to use it for good purposes."

"Is behavior control inherently wrong, Frank? Did I spend my life working for evil?"

"You had no choice in the matter, Mary. Innerverse isn't about choice. It's about power. The power of human beings to control other human beings, to dominate, to rule. It's brute force in chemical form. Can't you see that?"

Mary looked at the floor. "I suppose so. I see it, but the feeling won't go away. A feeling of loss . . . worthlessness."

He grabbed her and shook her. "That's Innerverse, not you! Shake it off, Mary! You're not guilty of anything. You're a hero!"

She burst into tears and crushed herself against him. It was a while before her sobbing abated. Meanwhile, he tuned his ears outdoors again, and listened as boots hit stone, closer and closer.

"Let's go, Mary," he said.

By the time they reached the top of the basement stairs, someone was fumbling with keys at the front doors.

At the bottom of the basement stairs, Frank stopped and peered into the doorway to the boiler room with the exit door. "Would they know the basement door is kept unlocked?"

"I don't know," she said. "I first forced it open long ago. I don't think anyone ever found out."

No one was covering the back exit. They came up out of the stairwell and ran out into the night again, across another meticulously trimmed lawn. Vaulting a low hedgerow, they came to a wide stone walkway.

"Where's the motor pool?"

Mary gestured and ran right, and he followed her between two buildings, across another lawn, and through a copse of white birch and silver maple. At the edge of this wooded patch stood a long low building with long horizontal slits of windows.

"This is the garage," Mary said.

Frank went up to one of the windows and peeked.

He instantly ducked down.

"About six of them in there," he whispered.

"We'll never steal a car," she said. "It's hopeless,

Frank. I didn't do this right. I just didn't play it right. I should have—"

"He would have found out about anything you did," Frank said. "Stop berating yourself and get your voice down."

"There must have been a way, must have been. I should have killed him—" She pressed her face into her hands.

"You couldn't have killed him. Quiet, now. Come on, let's get closer to the lab."

"We should give up," she said.

"I'm not going to, not yet."

"There's nothing left. Frank, he'll kill Alice. He'll do something to her."

"Can he kill?"

"He can do anything he wants to," she said.

"Does he have Innerverse himself?"

"I don't know. I've always wondered. Sometimes I think so, sometimes not."

"Be a good thing if we knew for sure. But let's get there. We might do some negotiating."

"What do we negotiate with, Frank?"

He looked at her. "Let's find a bargaining chip."

"Fine. But I'm wondering one thing."

Frank stopped at the corner of the building and looked back at her.

"What's that?"

"I can't figure how you're doing what you're doing right now."

"What?"

"Running. Disobeying. Acting rebellious. It can't be Reformat, it takes time to break out of the bacillus and deploy. You must be immune.

"Maybe. I hope."

"Or that countermeasure your superiors inoculated you with is stronger than Herb figured. But we wiped you when you got here, so I don't really know what's going on."

"Don't try to figure it out. Let's go. Which way to the lab?"

They were about fifty yards from the building when they surprised a single white-shrouded soldier walking nonchalantly out from behind the old physical sciences building, as if on a constitutional.

He halted and did a double take. "Hey ..." he said vaguely.

Frank raised the gun and shot him once through the shoulder. The man went down. Frank walked to him and picked up the submachine gun.

"God, it hurts." The soldier clutched his bloodied shoulder in agony.

He looked very young to Frank. Maybe eighteen.

"Could have been worse, kid," Frank told him, running off. "Arm wound's worth a million bucks."

They began to run, hearing shouts that the shot had prompted, and on hearing the close approach of troops, ducked into some pines between the science building and the old fine arts complex.

A burst of automatic fire sent slugs thwacking through the branches above them.

"I think we've been spotted," Frank said calmly.

They ran for the corner and as Frank rounded it, he sent a few rounds behind him almost absent-mindedly.

He was running again, he realized. He'd been running for days, weeks—how long had it been?—being chased, always running, but with nowhere to run to, no place to hide.

He was beginning to get good and mad.

Bullets whizzed by his ear as he rounded a corner and found that he was following Mary out into the open, and there on the walkway sat the same sort of armored vehicle that had chased him and Alice up the mountain. One lonely soldier stood guard. Again surprise and a dark night made for limited reaction time, and again Frank fired immediately. The guard took a bullet in the stomach and fell.

A fusillade of shots pinned them down behind the vehicle, slugs pinging off metal wildly. Frank fired with both guns over the vehicle's fender, ducked down, let the answering fire strike sparks off the pavement all around, then popped up for another rejoinder.

"You okay?"

Mary nodded. "We'll never make it."

"Take this," he said, handing her the machine gun. "Just point it and pull the trigger. Get up here like this. When I say go, start shooting at them. I'm going to try to get through the hatch at the top. Empty the clip. When I get the thing moving, we'll head for that alley, then you climb up."

"Right," she said, taking the gun.

Frank waited for a lull in the firing, then yelled, "Go!"

Mary jumped up and began firing the gun wildly, the barrel riding up on her, spraying bullets in a wide angle toward the concourse between the fine arts and science buildings.

Frank clambered up to the gun turret and dove into the open hatch. He fell straight down through the hole and nearly broke his neck when he hit the deck.

He sat in the driver's seat, noting with satisfaction that it was an automatic transmission and that the controls looked straightforward enough. He threw the gearshift into low and depressed the accelerator, and when the vehicle didn't move, noticed the brake handle. He pushed that forward, and the vehicle lurched.

Vision was supplied by a wide video screen in front of him. It was disconcerting at first to drive by an image and not the real thing, but he soon got used to it. He pointed the vehicle at the alley on the other side of the walkway and drove until he felt that it was safe for Mary to climb aboard.

He didn't have to yell for her. She came clambering down the ladder.

"We could leave now, drive away," she said.

"I have to get Alice."

"Right."

He drove over lawn and sidewalk, crashed through a few hedgerows, mowed down an acre of forsythia, and trampled a beech tree, but he got to the other side of the campus with no one to bar his way.

The lab building was unguarded. The second floor, where most of the laboratories were, was lit up.

He stopped the vehicle, put on the parking brake, and got up to examine the vehicle's big gun. It was a recoilless rifle. He found the ordnance box, picked out a rocket shell, opened the breech of the gun, and loaded.

"See how that's done?"

Mary nodded.

"When I fire, reload."

"Yes, sir."

The aiming was done at the fire control station, next to the driver's seat. He soon had the aiming mechanism figured out.

First, though, he fired off a few bursts from the forward machine gun. The shots took out glass all along the second floor.

"Think he's up there?"

"He's up there," Mary said.

Frank went up the ladder, poked his head out of the hatch. He looked around. No troops in sight.

"Hello there!"

Frank turned his head. It was Streiner, leaning out of a shattered window.

"Nice shooting, Frank. But we have Alice up here. If you and Mary don't give up, the army boys will go to work on her."

"Where's all the fancy talk now, Dr. Streiner? For once you're acting like the thug you are."

"The thug you forced me to be, Frank. Come on out of there."

"If you touch so much as one hair of that woman, I will level this building, and then I'll start on the campus."

"Frank, give it up. Mary is a sick woman. She needs

help. Her Innerverse has obviously malfunctioned. You're not doing her any good either.''

''You have ten seconds, Dr. Streiner. You're going to lose all that nice equipment. To say nothing of all the data.''

''Frank, don't do that. We can talk. Come up here and we'll parley. You have my assurance that you won't be harmed in any way.''

''I'm not about to trust you, Doctor. Five seconds. Mary! get ready to reload.''

Frank jumped back into the troop carrier and went to the fire control station. Then he saw her.

Alice was waving to him from the window.

''Shit.''

Streiner appeared behind her, smiling.

''We're sunk. Damn it.''

He felt Mary's consoling hand on his shoulder.

≫ Chapter Twenty-four ≪

"Hope you don't mind spending a few days here, Mary," Dr. Streiner said, ushering her into the tiny room. There was a cot in a corner and nothing else besides a door to a small powder room.

"Oh, I don't mind," Dr. Sellers said.

"Nothing will happen to her," Streiner told Frank, who was leaning against the door jamb with a gun barrel poking into his back.

"She'll just stay here until the infection passes. Isolation." Streiner turned to Sellers. "And then we'll repair your regulator. I think we'll have to put you on Innerverse, my dear. For a while. Until your behavioral anomalies correct themselves."

"One or Two?"

"One."

"Don't trust your own technology, Herb?"

"Obviously there are problems with Two, dear. Bugs."

"Lots of bugs, Herb. You'll probably have to scrap the whole project and begin again."

Streiner shrugged. "If necessary."

She looked at him with utter contempt. "Did you ever in your life have a genuine emotion?"

"A genuine, warm, sloppy, dangerous human emotion? I'm glad to say that that aspect of my behavior has been thoroughly repressed. I'm an old Freudian, in a way. To be repressed just might define what makes us human. What

238

would you prefer, some raging troglodyte? Maybe you would. The way you throw yourself at men speaks for some deeply atavistic impulse in you, dear. I think you'd enjoy having some brute knock you over the head and drag you back to his cave.''

''Brutality would be preferable to the life in death that I've led with you.''

''Really, Mary. You're obsessed with death. To wit. . . .''

He reached inside his lab coat, withdrew a large kitchen knife and threw it on the cot.

''There it is, your murder weapon. My murder weapon. I want you to think about killing me, fantasize it, and get it out of your system. It's something that has obviously obsessed you for years. I want you to feel the maximum guilt for it. Maybe that will be cathartic.''

''The only catharsis I want is your death, you monster.''

Streiner shook his head. He pointed to Frank. ''You go with this man on a murderous rampage, and I'm the monster.''

''Fuck you.''

''Reduced to sputtering obscenities. Honestly, Mary, this worries me. I don't understand how I did not perceive this in you when I chose you to be my wife.''

''I'm not your wife, I'm your slave. Your whore.''

''That's a role you play admirably. But you won't get any more parts like that, my dear. I think besides Innerverse, you need some good old-fashioned aversion therapy. I might have to use Chastisement on you.''

Mary Sellers paled visibly.

''He'll get it,'' Streiner said, pointing at Frank again. ''And his woman.''

Mary looked at Frank. ''It's torture, Frank. I'm sorry.''

''Chastisement is not torture, it is simply punishment.'' Streiner said to Frank, ''Remember when I said that Innerverse could be configured to deliver far more than the nausea reaction? It's true. We could make life a living hell for anyone. I've long thought that we'd need some kind of backup, something to use in cases of absolute incorrigibility. Chastisement is that backup.''

Frank said, "Do you really think that more naked force will prop up your little empire?"

"Yes. A little naked force goes a long way. I realize the jig is up, partially. Mary's done her best to bring us all down. Before she infected you, Frank, she went around campus and vamped every male Academician she could lay her hands on. And a few women, as I hear, Mary. That right? And you didn't stop there. You infected that last busload of trainees. And now they'll go back to the cities and spread the bunny plague, and in a few days, a week at the outside, no one in the cities will have Innerverse.''

An unfiled unexplained datum came to Frank's mind. The woman at the dormitory saying, "When I saw you kissing that man. . . ." She had not been referring to Frank, and in fact it was Alice that she had seen Frank kissing. Now he understood.

"That's right, Herbert. You've lost. The Experiment is over."

"Not quite yet. Although you have made me rethink Innercircle and its implications. Far too much leeway, far too much behavioral slack. If you'd had Innerverse this wouldn't have happened. That's my fault, and I take full responsibility. I'm still thinking about Chastisement for you, Mary. It's not settled. I want to spare you, but you'll have the deciding vote. If I see some genuine contrition, some true remorse for what you did . . ,"

"Genuine contrition? How on earth could you expect anything . . . anything . . . gen—" Mary sneezed. She sneezed five times in quick succession.

Streiner looked at his watch. "Right on schedule. Reformat should very quickly rid you of Innercircle, and you'll be free. You'll be able to exercise your free will, if the theologians are right. Maybe you'll achieve genuine contrition that way, when you realize that you've almost sabotaged mankind's last hope for peace and stability.

That's a big thing to feel guilty about, Mary. It's a sin, if anything is. Better get some rest, Mary, dear. See you later.

"Come with me, Frank," Streiner said after he had shut the door and locked it with keys on a big key ring. He walked off jingling them absently.

The gun barrel poked him in the back and he followed Streiner down the hall.

Frank, Streiner, and the soldier guarding Frank went down an elevator to the first floor, and Streiner led them to the right and through big doors into an amphitheater-style lecture hall.

What looked like the entire Academy was assembled. Armed, white-shrouded soldiers lined the walls.

Alice was handcuffed to a chair in the pit.

Streiner walked down the stairs to the pit and stood behind the demonstration table that stood before the large green chalkboard on the front wall. He put the keys on the crowded table.

The demonstration table was laid out with all the apparatus for a mass inoculation: dozens, maybe hundreds, of syringes, vials of serum, jars of cotton balls, bandages, bottles of disinfectant, and so forth.

"Put him in the chair," he said, indicating the empty chair next to Alice's.

The soldier kept poking Frank painfully in the back on the way down. Irked, Frank swung around and hit the man in the stomach and watched him double up and fall.

Instantly, four of his comrades were on Frank, and they hauled him down the stairs and cuffed him to the chair.

"*Behave!*" Streiner shouted at Frank. "Behave as you ought, for once, damn you!"

Frank smiled at him. "Your first emotion, Doctor. First one I've seen. Congratulations. But it's not surprising that it's a desire to *control* that really drives you."

"Yes." Streiner tugged at his neat white collar. "If anything drives me, it's the desire to do science right, to make experiments work. That's something quite beyond your ken, I'm afraid. You only want to kill people and to be able to enjoy it.

"My fellow colleagues," Streiner went on. "I've called you here tonight because we face a crisis unprecedented in our experience, a crisis that threatens the Experiment as a whole. Some of you know first hand what's happened, what our colleague Mary Sellers has done."

Someone sneezed.

This brought a wry curl to Streiner's lips. "And I see the consequences are quick to follow. That means we must act fast. We have before us the task of reinoculating the entire population after the effects of the bunny plague pass. I want to assure you that there is no cause for undue alarm. Mary didn't think things through very well. She's caused us a good deal of bother, but if we keep our heads and act quickly, we can save the Experiment. Of course we'll need the full cooperation of our military, and we'll have to make sure—"

"Dr. Streiner, please?"

"Uh ... what is it, Dr. Hingham? We haven't much time."

"Is it true that we're to be inoculated with Innerverse, not Innercircle?"

Streiner looked uncomfortable. "Yes."

Hingham was shocked. "But why?"

"Innercircle has proved to have some bugs that we simply haven't seen before. I can't take the chance of something like Mary's insanity cropping up again. At least not now, in this crisis. For the immediate future, you'll all have to submit to the standard regulator."

A murmur of discontent went through the assembly.

"This is outrageous!" Hingham said. "We'll not be turned into common zombies!"

"I don't want to hear that term used again, Hingham," Streiner said ominously. "You're acting like a common soldier boy."

"But, Dr. Streiner, we've lived our lives with Innercircle. It's part of us. Now that's it's gone ..."

"It's gone already? Dr. Hingham, I'm counting on our theories of human nature to carry us through this crisis. If we've been right, the habit of obedience has been deeply reinforced in the population. A brief interruption of the reinforcement schedule won't upset years of training. The regulated populace will simply carry on over these next few days. The habit of disobedience just isn't present."

"I think you're wrong, Doctor," another voice spoke.

"Dr. Shelikov? What makes you say that?"

Dr. Shelikov rose. "You're so blind, Dr. Streiner. You're supposed to be a brilliant scientist but you might as well be a zombie, for all that the world impinges on your consciousness. Everybody in this room knows what I'm talking about. We are sick to death of it."

Streiner was puzzled. "Sick to death of what?"

Someone shouted, "Of you!"

Streiner was taken aback. "What's that?"

"You're the only threat!" someone else yelled angrily.

"Yes, you and your megalomania," Shelikov said with mounting venom. "You haven't the foggiest notion of what we all think of you, of what we've thought but been unable to express all these years. You're a self-righteous, pompous prig incapable of admitting a mistake. You talk a good scientific line but you're nothing but a martinet, a tin dictator. You think you're something on the order of Einstein, but in reality you're the most deluded man in the world."

Streiner looked around wildly. "You must be insane, too. Is everybody crazy in here? Guards, seize her!"

Then, with no warning, there was a sound that stopped everything. There fell a ghastly, unnerving silence. Streiner's mouth hung open.

A sneeze. It had come from one of the hazard-suited soldiers.

Another sneeze followed. Then, a soldier near the front tore off his plastic mask and sneezed five times in quick order.

"My God," Streiner finally said in agony. "What did she do?"

Shelikov said, "Do you really think she was the only one, Dr. Streiner? Didn't it ever occur to you that she might have had help?"

Streiner looked stricken. "No."

"I helped her, Doctor. I designed an improved bacillus. These standard bio-hazard suits are no protection at all. The army is free, Doctor. Your personal stormtrooper brigade is totally uncontrolled."

Streiner shouted at the top of his lungs, "*Jesus Christ, woman, do you know what you've done?*"

"Yes. It's over, Dr. Streiner. But it's been over for years. Everyone here but you knows that the Experiment has been a total failure. It's been more than obvious, but you had no inkling. What it all comes down to, really, Doctor, is that you're a lousy scientist."

Streiner pulled out Frank's gun. "Get up here."

"Don't be absurd." Shelikov's look was one of icy contempt.

"I'm ordering you to get up here. Administer the Chastisement to these subjects. This is a golden opportunity to test it. Frank, this is going to be rough on you, but it won't be physical at all. No nausea, Frank, just a nightmare that you won't wake up from. It might drive you permanently insane, and if it does, we'll know to ameliorate its effects a bit. First, we'll learn from you, and then we'll try it on your other strumpet. Dr. Shelikov, I gave you an order!"

Shelikov crossed her arms adamantly. "I refuse to take part in any more unethical experiments!"

Streiner aimed at her. "Get down here this instant or I'll shoot you! I can do it! Don't think I can't."

"I know you can, Doctor," Shelikov said. "Only I have kept your dirty little secret all these years. I know that you don't have Innercircle. Or Innerverse, or any other regulator!"

The assembled Academy rose to its feet, howling with outrage.

"You're the only free man in this country!" Shelikov shouted on. "And you want to be the only free man in the world. God of creation, controller of all behavior for the entire human race. Can you even begin to grasp the enormity of it, Doctor? The depth of your megalomania?"

"That's a lie! I'm not insane. I'm the only sane one of you bastards. And I will shoot you, Shelikov, you fat, ugly cow, if you don't come down here and obey orders!"

The white-coated Academicians roared their disapproval.

One man got up and approached Streiner. "Doctor, put down that weapon!"

Another of Streiner's colleagues, a woman, got up and rushed her boss. She was quickly followed by others.

"Get back. Get back, I tell you!"

Streiner backed up against the chalkboard. "Guards, do something!"

The soldier nearest him tore off his mask. "We want no part of this! You have to work this out among yourselves. If it's over, it's over. Let us know what you want to do. All right, men, let's blow this chickenshit outfit." He and his comrades began to stalk out of the lecture hall.

"Wait, don't leave me! I order you to stay and maintain order. I order you! I control you! I control all of you. Get back! ... Get back! ... No!" He squeezed the trigger, but the gun just clicked. It was empty.

Shelikov was the first to get to him. She went right for his eyes and they both went down. She rolled off him, and she and the assembled scientists began methodically to kick Dr. Streiner to death.

Streiner yowled like a tortured animal.

A soldier unlocked Frank's handcuffs and then Alice's. Frank grabbed Streiner's keys, took Alice by the arm and they both ran up the stairs and out of the lecture hall, Streiner's hideous screams at their back.

Frank led the way upstairs to the room where Mary Sellers was a prisoner. Frank unlocked the door and rushed in.

Mary Sellers's body lay on the bloodsoaked cot, her jugular vein slit neatly. Blood had soaked the bedclothes and had dripped to the floor, forming a large, bright red pool.

He would never know whether Reformat hadn't worked in time or ersatz guilt had finally commanded its ultimate act of contrition. Perhaps, he came to believe later, what had done the deed was simply a deep and intractable despair, borne of long years spent in darkness, alone and helpless and afraid.

≽ Epilogue ≼

"Haven't fished a farm pond in years," Colonel Lehman said as he cast his line out again. "Nothing like a well-stocked pond."

"I don't know how well-stocked it is. Dad was ill this spring. Didn't get to restocking, I don't think."

"I'm glad you got back in time to help him with the harvest," Lehman said. "We had a good growing season."

It was a radiantly sunny day in central Illinois. There was no haze, and towns as far as ten miles away stood sharp up on the horizon like miniatures in a model railroad layout. Grain silos looked like spaceships poised to blast off. The land was as flat as the Earth could be, looked as flat as the plains Indians once believed it to be. The sky was a blue bowl with an enormous sweep of curvature, and boasted not a cloud.

"I can't get over how normal everything seems, compared to the Republic," Frank said. "I'd forgotten what normal was. That place was . . ."

"A nightmare," Lehman said, nodding. "And when you got through with it, it got worse."

"Haven't heard the latest. Are there still riots?"

"Oh, I think they've settled down in most of the cities. Damndest thing, after years of repression, after years of peace, all the muck bubbled up. Murder, mayhem, rape, pillage and loot."

"All the good stuff."

"And we have to bail 'em out, as per friggin' usual. Getting old, that. Going to cost billions. And we aren't the richest country anymore, either. That's what gravels me."

"We still have the most productive farmland."

"That we do, at least we've kept that, with all we've lost. Basis of wealth, land."

"And the labor applied to it."

Lehman eyed him askance. "What you been reading lately?"

"Not much, too much work around here. I'm not complaining. Nice to be a civilian again."

"And not a guinea pig," Lehman said.

"I ought to sue you birds," Frank said. "Injecting me with that junk and not telling me."

"Secrecy is always regrettable but usually necessary, at least in military matters. And it can backfire. Are you really resentful, Frank? If they'd found out about our having any nanotechnology at all, they would have come up with counter-countermeasures by the dozen. We never would have caught up with them."

"I'm not resentful at all. Job had to be done. I'm wondering how I would have acted if I had expected to be immune."

"We had no way of testing the countermeasure against Innerverse. It was a shot in the dark, and four attempts at putting an immune agent behind the lines had failed. We had to tell you to avoid getting caught at all costs, knowing that you probably would. But I knew you were resourceful enough to get back when you realized you were immune. That was a big gamble, and we gambled with your life, Frank. That I realize. Not the first time. We wanted to get you back with Innerverse still neutralized inside you, so we could study it further and ultimately devise a means to wipe it out, as Mary Sellers did. She saved us a lot of bother, poor woman."

"She did. I'll never forget her."

"Don't forget, you have Alice."

Smiling, Frank turned toward the house. "Dad's teaching her to cook."

"Few women want to be farm wives these days," Lehman said. "You're lucky, Frank. She doesn't know and therefore can't despise any of the so-called clichés."

"What's wrong with clichés? She's never had anything remotely like the farm in her life. Freedom, independence, peace without oppression. And good food. Speaking of Alice, here she comes."

Alice was walking across the mown hayfield toward them, wearing a blue-checked dress, her hair as yellow as the corn silk in the next field. Zombie walked at her feet.

"Frank!"

Frank laid down his rod and stood.

"Frank, I made beef stew! Myself!"

"Great!" Frank yelled. "We'll be up in a jiffy!"

"Beef stew?" Lehman said skeptically. "Why, I thought we were going to have fish ... Hey, I got something!"

Lehman yanked on the rod and started winding in. It took a while to reel the catch in and raise it out of the water. The catch was an old high-topped shoe, leaking water from the sole.

"Talk about normalcy and clichés," Lehman said, laughing. "Why, that's out of some old movie."

"I was worried you'd snagged the body," Frank said with a grin.

He ran to meet his wife.

AVONOVA PRESENTS
AWARD-WINNING NOVELS
FROM MASTERS OF SCIENCE FICTION

A DEEPER SEA
by Alexander Jablokov   71709-3/ $4.99 US/ $5.99 Can

BEGGARS IN SPAIN
by Nancy Kress   71877-4/ $5.99 US/ $7.99 Can

FLYING TO VALHALLA
by Charles Pellegrino   71881-2/ $4.99 US/ $5.99 Can

ETERNAL LIGHT
by Paul J. McAuley   76623-X/ $4.99 US/ $5.99 Can

DAUGHTER OF ELYSIUM
by Joan Slonczewski   77027-X/ $5.99 US/ $6.99 Can

NIMBUS
by Alexander Jablokov   71710-7/ $4.99 US/ $5.99 Can

THE HACKER AND THE ANTS
by Rudy Rucker   71844-8/ $4.99 US/ $6.99 Can

GENETIC SOLDIER
by George Turner   72189-9/ $5.50 US/ $7.50 Can